# SEVERANCE
# OF
# MINDS

# SEVERANCE OF MINDS

*The Ancient Spells Trilogy 2*

*This book contains varying degrees of the following: bodily injury, descriptions of war, consensual sexual content, grief, and death. Please read safely and responsibly.*

SEVERANCE OF MINDS

Copyright © 2024 by Jodie Angell

Cover art and design: Artscandare

ISBN: 978-1-0686881-2-6

# ABOUT THE AUTHOR

Jodie Angell is from the rainy valleys of South Wales, whose love (after coffee, of course) has always been fantasy, romance, and a touch of darkness. She lives with her fiancé, but regularly visits her parents and their scrumptious Frenchie, Harvey.

She loves to read, crochet, play cosy games, and keep her plants alive. When she's doing none of those things, she'll be deep in writing or planning her next fictional world.

*For Mum—without you, my passion for stories and writing would not exist.*

THE BARREN
TERRITORIES

DELLHOLLOW

The
Badlands

ZHAH

SOUTHERN
PENINSULA

SOUTHKEEP

The Realm
of
Arogath

# Prologue

*O*vercome with the desperate need to flee, to cling onto something that would relieve me of my pain, I flicked through the pages of the book I'd taken from the temple.

*What was I hoping to find?*

*Nothing would hinder me on my path for revenge. I would make her pay for the innocent blood she had on her hands.*

*Adrenaline coursed through my veins as I halted on the pages that referred to portals.*

*A compelling sensation filled my body, as if my Mage nature knew I would find the very thing I needed. What darkness would it reveal to me?*

I plucked a translation dictionary from my shelf and laid it next to the leather-bound book, referring to it each time I came across a new incantation. The bag of crystals dug into my hip. I pulled them from the pocket and tossed them aside.

"You lied to me, Juliette. They protect no one."

I turned the pages over every time a spell translated into something that would be of no use. There were curses of necromancy and blood magic, but I needed something strong enough to kill Makdou. She had the Crimson Kiss. I needed something of equal strength for when I would fight her, one on one.

My gaze landed on something that looked like another portal spell at the end of the chapter. The compelling sensation within me intensified. The portal at Southkeep connected the world of the living to the world of the dead and took a group of Dark Mages to create and open it. I would have to open this one alone.

According to the translation, it would lead to a different dimension somewhere outside of our universe, where our time didn't exist. It was a straight connection to a facility for training of warriors. If a Mage could conjure the portal and cross through it, then they would be welcomed into the facility, acknowledged as a powerful Mage who sought refinement.

Refinement. I wasn't sure if it was what I was seeking. But if I could access a part within me that would strengthen my magical abilities, turn my anger and hatred into something useful, then I would be able to return to Arogath and defeat Makdou. The facility for training could help me *defeat Makdou without becoming the very thing I despised—a Dark Mage. What other choices did I have?*

*I repeated the chant in my head, until I could pronounce each word without difficulty. I needed to be quick.*

*With my hands spread out before me, I read the spell in full and visualised a portal with a purple centre, one that would lead to another world.*

*My mind was clear, absent of hindering uncertainties.*

*The fury pulsed through my body, allowing the portal to form in front of me, glowing a magnificent purple and buzzing with the sound of electricity. I stared at it wide-eyed, the loud buzz filling the Citadel. It wouldn't be long before my friends became aware. I wanted them to see me leave—I'd abandon them as they'd done to me.*

*Within moments, hurried footsteps made their way towards the room. The door burst open, and the High Elves stood in the doorway.*

*"What the hell?" Kiirion gaped.*

*"A portal." Theodas frowned and held his hands up in front of him. "Evalyn, don't."*

*"It's too late," I shouted over the loud crackling sounds of the magic coursing through the swelling gateway.*

*"It's not too late, my queen," he pleaded. "Let us help you."*

*"You cannot help me." The compelling sensation urged me closer to the entrance like a magnet. "You have proven that."*

*I took my first step towards the portal. The High Elves lunged forward to block me from entering. I* launched a fiery bolt of light from my hand, sending the Elves crashing into the glass wall behind them, shattering it as they collided.

"Evalyn!" Felix yelled, appearing at the scene. His eyes still drooped from the exhaustion and torture endured during his time spent at Southkeep, but it made me despise him more. He was weak. They were all weak.

Eric, now cured of the plague and evil magic, stepped towards me with his arms open. I hesitated for a moment, contemplating his embrace.

"Let me help you, the way you have helped me," he begged, his voice shaky.

"I did more than help you, I saved you!" I produced more red balls of light in my palms, ready to throw them towards anyone who stepped in my way. "What have you done to repay me? Nothing. You are all responsible for the death of my son."

"Wait!" Valneris lunged forward to grab my arm. I threw the balls of light at him, sending him into the bookshelves on the opposite side of the room.

"Goodbye." I stepped into the portal and darkness consumed me, leaving the traitors in the chamber, far, far away.

I drifted through the dark nothingness that fell between dimensions. Now free of pain, I allowed myself to relish it. Knowing how much I'd wanted to die, how I couldn't bear to live in a world without the very being who had lived within me, I let myself hover through the empty vastness around me.

I floated through the endless void for a long time. Maybe days, months, or maybe even a few seconds. Soon, a small, white light appeared somewhere in front of me. I stretched my hands and focused to bring it nearer. The light grew and swelled, marking the exit of the portal.

Concentrating all my power and ability, I pulled the exit close enough for me to fit through. As soon as my fingertips connected with the surface of the portal, sensation returned. And with that, the burning pain in my chest resurfaced.

Eager to find what I was looking for, I climbed through the portal exit, landing on the cold, concrete flooring of an open temple. A thin layer of sand covering the floor found its way between my fingernails as I scrambled my way across.

Rising, I scanned the temple. I was alone in a room held in place by four pillars and walls made of sandstone. I listened for any noise at all. A voice, or even a movement. No sounds reached my ears, so I edged towards the archway across the room.

I followed the narrow corridor that continued around different bends with multiple other corridors sprouting from it. Staying in the main passageway, I stared at the doorway at the end. My heart pounded and a magnetic sensation within lured me closer.

I opened it, then entered, enticed by the compelling sensation.

The room was lit by an array of candles of all sizes. Their warm glow lit the detailed and delicate battle tapestries that hung on the walls. A man dressed in a black, embroidered cloak sat in a sculpted chair in the centre of the room.

"Ah, Evalyn," the man muttered in a voice so calm, so gentle, it was almost eerie. "I have waited a long time to see you."

*I stared at him, unable to recognise his face. Had I travelled all this way for one man? My voice creaked out in a whisper, "Who are you?"*

# Chapter One

"You've been expecting me?" My voice raised several octaves.

The seated man paused writing and looked up from his work. His face was touched by age—creased forehead and dull, weathered skin, bald head. A goatee sprouted from his chin. Something about him demanded respect—perhaps the way he held his shoulders straight.

Who was this man? More importantly—*where* was I?

"Oh yes, Evalyn." His gold and jewel-encrusted chair was in a room made of simple stone walls without carvings or statues. He held a quill, the tip hovering an inch above a parchment page of a leather-bound book clutched in his other hand. "Your arrival has been written in the sheets of time since the dawn of the Noble Ones."

I eyed him and processed his words. His voice, calm and casual, echoed against the high sandstone walls. Daylight streamed in through the dusty windows and illuminated his olive skin.

My son had been prophesied…and murdered for it. If one foretold fate had failed, could another?

His embroidered robe, not as ornate as the sapphire-encrusted robe Makdou, the deceiving Dark Mage wore, created a wave of nausea in my stomach.

"How do you know of the Noble Ones?" I wandered to the wooden table, then glanced at a small charcoal block positioned amongst some candles.

A lavender flower burned in the centre of the charcoal, swirling its sweet-scented smoke into the air. Above the block, the smoke halted, then flattened as if held in place by something invisible. Within seconds, the smoke disappeared.

I furrowed my brows, trying to understand exactly *where* the smoke had gone. The lavender continued to burn.

"The book promised a facility for training warriors. Is this the place? Or has the book betrayed me too?" I cleared my throat and narrowed my gaze at him.

"So many questions… Why?" He created a steeple with his fingers. "To answer your first, I am Reuben, the master of this Temple. Why do you frown so?"

"I will stop frowning when I find out all I need to know."

"All in good time, Evalyn. In your world, you were exposed to Elysium, the realm of the dead. For someone who has seen several dimensions, it would be logical to assume you are now in an alternative timeline."

I scooped up a red gem from beside the smouldering lavender and turned it over in my palm. "A place where my time—Arogath's time—doesn't exist?"

The man put his quill and book aside and relaxed in his chair. He spoke of inter-dimensional travel as if I'd arrived with the knowledge of it.

"Tell me, is this the place I've searched for?" My tone was sharp.

Reuben rose to cross the room, his robes gliding along the concrete floor. He lit a new block of charcoal, placed a fresh sprig in the centre, then blew the lavender, sending a cloud of sweet-scented cloud swirling above.

He lifted a scroll from its glass cabinet next to an archaic bookcase lined with rolled parchment, and leather-bound books. The scroll's edges were worn and bent as though it'd been handled many times.

"I believe you already know it is." He stroked the scroll's smooth parchment.

"You ought to get to the point." I crossed my arms, my fingertips resting on my scales.

The trees outside the window shook in the breeze and cast long, jagged shadows across the concrete floor.

"At Southkeep, you entered Elysium," he said. "A place you were never meant to go. Prophecies rarely fail to come true. There is a possibility you changed your timeline completely by accident, although I cannot say for certain."

"Does this mean my son died because I entered Elysium?" I flicked a strand of hair out of my face. Coldness hit me, sweeping over every inch of my body.

"I cannot answer that, nor can I predict events or presume the reasons for their occurrence." He handed me the parchment, with runes inked across it.

Makdou had stolen my necklace to complete the Crimson Kiss spell. Maybe the runes meant something else altogether.

"What do these runes mean?" I placed my fingers on the symbols. "These here—they are on the necklace Felix gave to me."

"This one on the left is the four elements wind, earth, fire, and water—their individual runic symbols merged to show unity. The middle symbol is the marriage of the individual runes for crown and blood. Ah, this last one—the most important— balance," he said.

I raised my eyebrows. "Are you sure? They sound like—"

"Your life?" He smiled. "The elements, like your friends. The next one represents your crown and claim to the throne of Arogath and finally, your duty to maintain peace between the triads. I read the scroll every day, so I know what happened to you— what Makdou did. It is unfortunate she is more powerful than you are," he said. "Although, there are some things in this scroll you will not be aware of."

I turned the scroll around and studied it. Normal parchment. "What could possibly be in here that I wouldn't know? After all, it *is* my life."

"Felix's ancient ancestors came from this realm," he said.

"What?" I gaped at him. "That's not possible. He's spoken of his family before, and he mentioned no such thing."

He smiled. "This happened many centuries ago, of course. There is a legend amongst our people that tells the story of a Great Mother Tree—a tree with extraordinary healing abilities. Such a treasure needed to be concealed from our enemies. Felix's ancestors played a pivotal role. After all, they were Mages."

"Surely not." A nervous laugh escaped my lips. "He would know if he had Mage blood in his veins."

"Would he?" He cocked his head. "Once they hid the Great Mother Tree, his ancestors fled this realm and lived as Humans in your world. Although, I have wondered if this is why Felix sensed you would need his necklace."

I shook my head. "I don't know what to say— this isn't what I expected."

"We can discuss it more later, but we need to focus on what you need to know right now. Refinement is why you are here, and refinement is what you will receive," he said.

"Tell me the name of this place, and I will look

at this…*my* timeline." I kept my gaze fixed on the smooth surface of the ivory parchment.

"Indeed. We call it the Temple of Peace."

I untied the string, then unravelled the scroll as far as my arms could stretch, revealing drawings of the events I'd lived through. The day I left the Eyrie. The fires at Westwilde and Rushdale Forest. My first night of passion with Felix. Heat rose in my cheeks.

"Come." With an air of grace and fluidity, Rueben drifted towards a stone archway, then down the steps on the other side—his robe trailing behind.

After placing the scroll and its string on the glass shelf, I followed him.

"As you mature, meet new people, and encounter new challenges, more is added to the scroll. After the Mages left, the sentient magical energy had no host to channel itself through, so it took to writing the scroll until they returned." He led me out into the open air where several small buildings jutted out into a courtyard.

The smell of molten iron drifted from the blacksmith's to the left and the woody scent of damp straw from the animal shelters hung in the air. Chickens clucked as two servants shooed them into their coops. Dung marked the cobbled floor towards the stables. Trees grew in the centre, and people gathered on the benches underneath the branches. A strange purple fruit hung amongst the green leaves.

I pushed onto my tiptoes, cupped a fruit in my hand, then brought it to my nose. Its sweet, rich aroma tingled my nostrils. Intertwined flowering vines scaled the walls of the temple.

"Why is there a scroll of my timeline?" I skipped to keep up with the man as he came to a stop in front of the brick wall.

He placed his hands on top of the moss-covered surface and gazed at the snow-blanketed mountains on the horizon.

"I'm not from this realm, wherever *here* is." I peered over the wall and gasped at the long drop. This new world—somewhere I didn't know—was familiar, situated on a cliffside like the Eyrie in Arogath.

He focused on a single eagle gliding across the sky. "Although the prophecy did not come true, you are meant for something, and this kingdom can sense it. We are here to help you. Please trust us."

The eagle's feathers darkened into shades of purple as it shrank into the skyline.

"This planet is connected to yours in more ways than I can explain," he said.

His words offered no logic. I abandoned my home, on the whim of a book, to find I'm connected to another. I hoped this new world would give me a solution. A new life. A new land. A new hope.

Resting against the stones, I surveyed the contoured mountains covered in snow, the glistening river flowing below us, and the clear sky. Cool, fresh air filled my lungs.

"It's incredible, isn't it?" He turned to face me, then clasped his hands. "Welcome to Swynvale."

—◦—

The melodic notes of a harp filled my ears as I approached a room down one of the Temple's many corridors. Soldiers practised close-range combat on sackcloth dummies. Older warriors fought in duels with either long bamboo sticks or blades. The sticks thudded against each other as the soldiers parried their opponent's attack.

Curious, I leaned on the doorframe and observed the moves akin to a dance.

Swords etched with curling calligraphy shone under the light from the torches affixed to the stone walls. Fights were followed with cheers and pats on the back after each duel ended. It seemed those who resided in the Temple ensured the realm's protection. I had no such protection in Arogath.

A man fell to the floor with a loud thud, and I jolted. The harpist stopped playing. Blood oozed from a wound on the soldier's arm where a blade nicked the skin above his elbow.

The wounded man's opponent slit the gash open with the tip of his blade. "Aye, it'll be good for you. Best get used to blood being spilled."

I clasped my stomach, wondering if my own belly had been sliced open with a blade. In desperate need of fresh air, I fled to the courtyard, then rested my hands against the wall and glanced to the sky. Each breath was ragged, and my eyes brimmed with tears. I swatted them away, but my vision remained blurred, and my chest tight.

I needed to learn how to use this anger against

Makdou and do what my friends failed to do—put a stop to her for good. They'd let me down.

I'd returned from Elysium, lying in a pool of my own blood and no baby in sight. Sofia must've cut him out of me and taken him away before I regained consciousness. I fled Arogath, having never laid eyes on him, without saying goodbye. Where was his body now?

Not so long ago, I had danced around the banquet hall with Felix. Our son had been with us then—a part of me.

"Evalyn," Reuben called from behind me, voice smooth like silk. "Come on, you can't stay out here. Come inside and join the others."

"Give me a minute," I breathed deeply, although my chest constricted each intake of air.

A heaviness ached behind my ribs, right where my heart pounded. Closing my eyes, I focused my attention on the rustle of nearby trees, the call of a bird, and the floral scent of flowers in full bloom.

I flattened my shaking fingers against my thighs and opened my eyes. "Okay. I'm ready."

He led me to the training room, and the soldiers bowed to him. One soldier was dressed in polished armour, his dark hair pulled into a tight bun on top of his head. He reminded me of Kiirion.

They faced each other, then shook hands. With a bow of their heads, they sparred, each movement quick and sharp as they weaved their way around the other, blocking hits at an incredible speed. The other soldiers watched from the sidelines, dodging out of the way as the fighters came too close.

How quickly would the war between the Triads

in Arogath have ended if we'd trained soldiers to this level of skill? When Reuben pushed his opponent to the floor, he bowed, offered him a hand, then plucked him from the ground.

"This is Seth," Reuben said. "One of our finest soldiers."

"He gives me far more credit than I deserve." Seth smiled with an affectionate twinkle in his eyes. His friends gave him a pat on the shoulder before they retired from the training room. "If it wasn't for his shelter, protection, and training, I'd be as ill-skilled as a Human babe straight from the belly."

His words seized my heart, and a tightness formed in my chest that would not loosen. I pressed my lips together, hiding their trembling, for images of my unborn child flashed in my mind. Memories I couldn't suppress, pain that resurfaced in surprising waves.

"You have brought me great honour." Reuben bowed to his companion.

"Go easy on him." Seth laughed. "He's getting old, and frail." He dashed from the training room before Reuben could respond.

"I apologise for Seth's brash behaviour." Reuben faced me to take my hand. He stood like an oak tree, calm and strong, ancient, and wise. His demeanour allowed me peace despite my inner turmoil. "If you are to stay here, then your training will begin."

"My son's murder broke my heart. My friends' betrayal broke my spirit—they couldn't stop Makdou. That's why I came here." A numbness spread through my being as I uttered the words aloud. The truth. I placed my hand over my chest in a feeble attempt to soothe the ever-present ache.

"Do not fear your anger—your emotions—as they will make you stronger. Swynvale has a habit of doing that." He let go of my hand, then strolled back and forth across the stone floor. "This realm is peaceful and has a mind of its own. It looks after its own and makes them feel the way they should—safe and free."

His last two words fell heavy, carrying a weight of importance and something I desired for myself and my people. The sooner I could learn what I needed to in Swynvale, the sooner I could fulfil my duty to my kingdom.

"It works much like your Elementals," he said. "There is one difference—here, there are no magical beings to do the work of this realm. The very realm itself will aid you in time of need. It protects the balance of life."

He waved his hand and a ball of light appeared, projecting a view of an ocean forming into a great beast, engulfing and destroying the ships. "The natural magic killed the enemies on those vessels. Although, it will not kill all our enemies, as we are not prioritised over the other clans."

The scene changed to an army of Orcs who burned Human civilians in a field outside their homes. Thick clouds of smoke shot into the sky. Crops were set ablaze, and survivors ran through the corn fields, desperate to escape their fate.

"Orcs—they're everywhere."

"Of course." His brows drooped around his eyes. "They have colonised many realms, Evalyn."

"I'm aware of how brutal they can be." The image flickered in my mind's eye: the Dark Mages and the Ezen Riders stood atop the valley in Southkeep. The Orcs became a mere threat to be dealt with in comparison.

"We all have our enemies." He waved his hand again, and the ball of light evaporated. "And you are here to kill yours—Makdou."

"Then you understand."

He was right. Something was in the ground I stood on, in the air I breathed. I feared nothing.

"Show me what you can do." He strode into the centre of the room, then stopped. With time and age, he'd withered into an ancient husk, yet I sensed only strength.

I concentrated on my cupped hands. A ball of magnificent white light manifested in my palms, swirling and dancing. My white light appeared occasionally when it broke free from the shadows within me. It was more often red, made of fear and sheer determination to survive.

"Good." He frowned, and deep creases appeared around his eyes. He focused on the magic I held, and it turned red.

"How did you do that?" My concentration snapped, and the light disappeared.

"A manipulation spell." He flicked his hand with ease. "The spell reveals the sorrow and the pain you bear alone, every day."

"W-what are you?" My voice shook. Was he a Mage? Or something else?

"A person made of flesh and blood, like you." Reuben conjured a light of his own, which transformed into a dial with multiple symbols displayed on its ethereal surface. "But I am Human, and you are Mage."

"The magic." I became transfixed by the shimmering blue light surrounding the dial as it turned in slow movements. "How?"

"I am one with the realm," he replied. A few seconds afterwards, his spell dissipated.

"You said this world doesn't have magical beings to do its work, but you are one."

He smiled. Was he right about this world? The magic pulsed through the realm and the green of nearby trees became vibrant. The scales on my upper arms tingled with power that surged through the air. Aware of everything I knew and had experienced in my own kingdom, I should be accustomed to the bizarre ways of magic. Something of my father was within me after all. Something Human.

"Join the others." Reuben gestured to the door leading into the courtyard. "Eat, rest. I will show you more tomorrow."

"Aren't you going to eat with us?"

"I must pray." His lips curved into a half-smile, then he ambled towards a narrow archway on the left wall of the training room.

He pulled back the ornate tapestry curtain and revealed a vaulted room illuminated with flickering candles. Sour orange and sweet cinnamon wafted into the training area. Reuben stepped inside, and the heavy curtain fell back into place behind him.

I headed to the grand hall via the walled courtyard. A purple-tinged twilight fell over the

Temple. Moths darted towards the flickering candlelight in the windows.

The soldiers from the training room congregated at a table near a door left ajar at the back of the hall. The opening allowed a snippet of the mist-covered mountain to come into sight and the soft breeze to swirl in.

I lingered in the doorway until Seth waved me over. A pleasant smile spread across his mouth. Bowls of meat stew were positioned next to a selection of dates and raisins baked into pies. The sickly-sweet smell of the large, purple fruit enticed me, yet I couldn't work up the nerve to taste such an unusual food.

I reclined into the seat opposite Seth and observed the people sitting around the table—Humans with slender noses and freckled faces, some with blemishes and acne marks. I sank further into my chair, made vulnerable by my contrasting appearance.

"You'll get used to Reuben's riddles soon enough." Seth grunted around a mouthful of meat stew. "Don't worry too much about it. You'll understand him someday."

The glare of a woman opposite me caught my attention. In brooding silence, she narrowed her gaze on me. I smiled, but the gesture was not returned.

With the ladle in hand, I poured the stew into my bowl.

"Does your hair always glow?" The woman pointed a dainty finger at the strands of hair draped over my shoulders.

At first, I frowned, drawing a blank. But when I glanced down, my hair shone a warm and radiant red. "No. It's new."

"It's the realm." Seth took a sip of water. He swallowed, wiped his mouth, then continued, "The magic flowing through Swynvale is making you stronger. You were meant to be here."

"You sound a lot like Reuben."

The men at the table laughed.

Surrounded by a room full of strangers, I reflected on my level of endurance, my ability to survive. We'd been unprepared for the Crimson Kiss. We were aware of its purpose yet relied on its absence over the last few centuries to see us through. We failed.

"The Orcs are brutal creatures. Have you not yet found a way to control them?" I asked.

"The feud between Orcs and Humans is as old as the universe," the bald man muttered. His skin was dark, his shoulders broad and toned. "They've colonised many areas of this planet. According to the tomes in our libraries, such colonisation has been documented through the centuries."

A silence fell over the table. Would we find a solution to the problem plaguing not just my kingdom, but this one too?

"Lighten up, Dmitri." Seth crammed the last of his meal into his mouth. Even feasting like a pig, he was handsome. A strand of his dark hair fell free from its bun.

I scanned the shadows of the mess hall. Soldiers with blank expressions slumped in their seats.

"They've had a rough time." Dmitri followed

my gaze to the table of lifeless warriors. He touched the scar on his face. "Blasted by a powerful spell conjured by an Orc. Some sort of Dark Magic they've used over the past few months."

"I'm familiar with that. Orcs and magic—a dangerous combination."

"Why have you come here?" The woman stared at me. "Why would you leave your own realm?"

"Er." Unable to fathom any other words, I clung to the story they all knew. "You know why I'm here. It's written in the scroll, remember?"

"You don't have to abide by what is predicted to come of you," she said, her voice cold. "You changed your fate, although by accident, and I'm sure it can be done again. Your friends—you left them."

"That's *enough*, Lilith," Reuben ordered as he appeared.

The soldiers around the table jolted, then straightened, now in the presence of their master.

She huffed, shunted her chair backwards, then fled the hall.

Reuben's stern gaze disappeared. Dmitri rose from his seat to bring Reuben a tray of meats and a bowl of stew. Seth glanced at me and smiled.

Lilith's hostility didn't make sense. Even if every part of my being compelled me to question her and demand an explanation for her ignorance, I couldn't. My soul was at peace with this new land. Its magic had fused with mine and locked itself into place.

I needed to let myself heal, regain my strength, then I'd be ready to fight back.

16

# Chapter Two

The bathing room was empty by the time I arrived. I'd grown fond of the grand bathing room of the Citadel and while I longed to deny it, I missed it. This wasn't anything like the Citadel and all its fineries.

Once I'd stripped, I relaxed into the tub and glanced at the wall. Candlelight illuminated the grooves in a battle painting hung beside a small window on a grey stone wall. My gaze followed the coarse brush strokes of soldiers who held banners and swords, marching towards victory. Couldn't there be a painting of a meadow or something peaceful? Anything but another battle.

Unlike the rest of the Temple paved with

concrete, brown mosaic covered the bathroom floor. My stone bath was separated from the others with dividers, and only a sliver of the wall-long painting could be seen from my position.

In the tub, I drew my knees to my chest.

I'd been fortunate enough to have hot water poured for me while soldiers had no choice but to share the same water for bathing. Felix and I had slipped into the bath together in what seemed a lifetime ago. The moment of happiness allowed our bodies to connect in more ways than one, our burdens washed—

"Evalyn?" A female servant peered around the divider. "Your presence has been requested."

Seth and the other soldiers, two of which I recognised as Dmitri and Lilith, had gathered in the Armoury once I arrived after getting into clothing.

The three of them fastened their chest plates, stuffed their hands into gauntlets, then draped fur cloaks over their shoulders. The sound of clanking metal echoed through the room as other soldiers dressed, then sheathed their swords into the scabbards hanging from their waists.

"The Orcs have invaded a nearby settlement," Seth said to Lilith.

"I'll come." I grabbed a spare chest plate from its stand, drawing it over my head.

Perhaps coming face to face with the Orcs would reinforce my need to stay focused on strengthening and improving my magic to destroy Makdou.

How far away was this settlement, and what was the extent of the damage caused by the Orcs?

Dmitri and Seth each rested a leg on a log as they

tugged on their boots. They exchanged glances.

Reuben remained straight-faced. He'd swapped his robes for steel armour, and two long thin blades were strapped to his back. "Take this as a fair warning. The Orcs of our world are brutal. Be prepared for anything."

"I'll handle it." I snorted.

He dipped his head in acknowledgement.

Seth guided me into a small windowless room. Shelves lined the walls, displaying axes, blades, maces, and bows. "You'll need more than your magic." He pressed his lips into a thin line. "Reuben is right. These Orcs are ruthless."

He handed me a blade, and I stumbled. They were heavier than the Arogathean swords back home. I stretched a hand, running my fingers along the string of a bow propped against the wall. Unsure of how to use a bow, I decided against it and grabbed a long sword instead. I picked up a soft leather satchel, placed my blades inside, then hoisted the strap on to my shoulder.

"You'll need more armour too. A chest plate alone won't do." Seth broke our eye contact, passing me gauntlets and greaves from the shelf. "Here you go. I've been meaning to offer my condolences to you, Evalyn, although there is never the right time. I am sorry for your loss."

"I wonder what life would be like now if my friends had stopped Makdou from reaching me. I wanted to be protected, saved. Felix…he couldn't save me." I stared at the worn floorboards as tears stung my eyes. A lump formed in my throat, immovable. "A knight of the Eyrie. He failed his duty."

"I don't blame you…for blaming him," he whispered. "Grief does cruel things to people."

We left the Armoury behind the prayer room, meeting the soldiers in the courtyard between the long wings of the temple. They'd drawn blue and white war paint across their faces in lines and dots. Reuben stood amongst them, straight with shoulders back. A chieftain ready for war. They mounted their horses—satchels attached to their saddles, alongside their cloaks in case the weather turned.

"Are you sure you want to come with us?" His brows furrowed.

"I came here to strengthen my abilities, and that is what I intend to do." I gained a few raised eyebrows and smirks from the crowd of soldiers.

Although they might disagree with my decision, I needed to do this so one day I might bring a new age of peace to Arogath. It was my duty as queen, and I couldn't have left my kingdom for nothing.

I slipped my foot into the stirrup, then hoisted myself onto a horse left for me. We galloped along the path between the craggy mountains, towards a narrow stream that was lined with small shrubs and tall scattered trees. A warm orange glow reflected in the water. Its beautiful light reminded me of Arogath's sun. Did the two worlds share the same sun, or did many stars separate them?

We slowed when we reached the water's edge.

"Is this water safe to drink?" I glanced over my shoulder at Seth who rode behind me.

"The water flows from the springs in the

mountain," he said. "It's as fresh as it comes."

"I'll be quick." I dismounted, kneeling on the muddy bank. With cupped hands, I lifted cold water to my lips. Makdou's piercing red eyes glared at me from the water. I jumped back, heart slamming against my ribs.

"Evalyn?" Seth asked. "Are you okay?"

"I could have sworn…" I said on a sharp intake of breath. "Yeah, it's nothing." With trembling fingers, I tucked my filled flask into my satchel, then mounted.

The path stretched onwards along the side of the stream until the water swelled into a lake.

The shoreline was rocky with gravel in shades of grey and white, dotted between the knobbly driftwood at the water's edge. Spindly-legged skimmers skittered across the lake's surface, geese plucked grass nearby, and plumes of dust floated among the weeds.

Farther ahead was a long dock with missing planks. An old, rusted boat left tied up swayed with the current. Trees bowed over the lake, casting reflections in the water, and the sunlight glittered off the waves.

We continued our journey beside the water and descended a narrowing path through the foliage. Twigs snapped and fallen leaves crunched under the horses' hooves. Every so often, the birds nestled amongst the trees chimed their songs.

Several hours passed and the sun reached its highest point in the sky between scattered clouds. Its heat beat down on us, forming sweat across my forehead, yet it was no match for the intense heat in

Arogath. At the edge of the last field, black smoke swelled in the sky.

"Over there." Reuben pointed to the smoke. "Stay focused—the Orcs may still be close or head in our direction. Offer aid to anybody who is injured."

We neared the village. Thatched huts smouldered and smoke rose from the towers. A hut in the centre, built wider than the rest, blazed, sending smog high into the air. Wheezing, I shielded my mouth from the fumes with my hands.

The soldiers tugged cloth from their pouches, then tied the fabric around their faces. Seth offered me a strip, and I fastened it around my face before readjusting my helmet.

Seth and Dmitri fixed their gazes upon the burning ruins of the village. We dismounted, then climbed over the remnants of a broken fence. Arms and legs poked from underneath collapsed huts.

The whole village was destroyed. A watering well located alongside the stone paths was caved-in and market stalls toppled. Wheat and grains, cinnamon, nutmeg, trinket boxes, candlesticks, pots, and pans were scattered across the floor. Human merchants had been stabbed or shot with arrows.

Mutilated people, with gashes from collarbone to stomach, lay like ragdolls. One female was crushed into the ground by large stone blocks, surrounded by her own blood.

I wanted to escape the gruesome scene. The stench of corpses and burning bodies could not filter through the cloth covering my mouth and nose, for which I was thankful.

The soldiers spread out to search the village for survivors or Orcs who might be lurking. I followed Seth and Dmitri, staying close. Although I wielded a weapon and could summon magic, I began to second-guess myself.

My fingers trembled at my sides. Vivid images of the pain and horror my own people had suffered at the hands of the Orcs plagued my mind. Ascal ripped from his horse at the Badlands. People mutilated and hung in the forest, burned in their homes, and killed out on the paths for all to see. Waves of nausea turned my stomach. I needed to keep myself together, for the good of my end goal.

We reached the end of the huts where a small mound appeared. Corn growing in the open space around the mound had been hacked down and burned. Two bodies hung from a tree. Their limbs were severed.

The soldiers freed the dead Humans from the tree, laying them to rest on the floor nearby. Reuben pulled me away.

"I'm fine." My gaze darted from one corpse to another. "It's just—"

He touched my shoulder. "All this pain and anguish you are consumed with can be turned into strength."

My vision blurred, and my lungs tightened. Seething, I glared at the Orc flag planted into the ground of their conquered territory. "We should bury the dead."

Before anyone could even move to collect the bodies, the ground shook, sending grumbling sounds around the settlement. A glowing green light illuminated deep cracks in the hard ground. Soldiers screamed as they fell through the gaps and disappeared into the green light. I leapt back and gripped a nearby tree.

"Don't let it touch you," Reuben called over the crackling of the remaining fires and the churning ground. "We need to retreat now! There isn't anything we can do for them. The realm will care for their souls."

The ground continued to glow. The magic spread around the village until the whole area pulsed a bright green.

"Damn it." Dmitri bashed his sword against a tree trunk. "We're too late."

"Too late for what?" I asked.

He let out a deep sigh. "It's a sign of their conquering. They destroy a town, post a flag, and inject their magic. We don't know how they got access to it."

"A territorial threat." Seth shook his head.

"That's one way of putting it." Lilith growled as she appeared by his side. Her skin was pale as ice and contrasted with her dark hair and emerald eyes. She bent and scooped up a tiny soft doll covered in ash. She wiped it away and stared at it with drooping eyes. "They've destroyed so much."

"Then we need a better strategy." Dmitri shoved his sword into its scabbard, then crossed his arms over his broad chest. Thick ridges and scars of previous battles covered his unprotected biceps.

"Fight fire with fire." Lilith tucked the doll into her pouch.

Once we buried the dead, we mounted our horses, and Reuben led the way back through the open fields and trees, before we headed up the steep slopes to the temple overlooking the water. Nobody said a word as they rode around the lake. Next to the main entrance was a small silver plaque engraved with *Temple of Peace, training grounds and home to the northerners.*

"Freshen up and meet in the Armoury for training afterwards." Reuben slipped from his saddle, then retreated, shoulders slumped, to his prayer room.

~ * ~

That evening, I made my way to the library in the west wing of the temple. The room echoed with the sounds of my footsteps on the concrete floor. Leather-bound books covered the shelves lining every wall. A rectangular woven rug lay in the centre, silencing my footsteps when I crossed it. A candelabra stood on the table positioned in the middle of the rug. The orange glow of flickering flames of candles and sconces collided with the moonlight streaming through the square windows.

What did the books contain? There were no Mages in this realm, so none would contain spells. Why had I come to the library? I would find no comfort.

My thoughts turned to Felix as I rested against a bookshelf. How could I be angry at him when he had no magic to use against Makdou? Even the great High Elves and Sofia's High Priestess abilities were no match for her.

But Felix had one duty—to escort me to safety

and he *chose* to stay by my side as we fell in love. Gripping the smooth surface of the shelf, I sighed. He couldn't have done anything more, and I had to let my rage go, let it transform into something useful.

I plucked a random book from its shelf, then flicked through its pages. It contained images of weapons, detailed descriptions of their functions, instructions on how to use them, and guides for how to repair them if damaged.

"You know you won't find what you're looking for here." Reuben's voice resonated through the room.

Startled, I stumbled into the bookcase. He lingered in the doorway, leaning against the frame.

"I know." I placed the book back onto its shelf, then flexed my fingers, waiting for my heartbeat to steady. "There's something comforting about it. Something familiar."

The faces of my friends flickered in my mind, and with it, a sting of pain, a tightening in my stomach. We'd survived enough horrors to last many lifetimes and seal the bond of family. Yet the reliance and trust I'd bestowed on them shattered the moment Makdou reached me. My love for Felix was enough for me to make peace with the fact that he hadn't been able to stop Makdou, but I wasn't quite ready to let go of *all* my anger. The Elves and the guards of the Citadel should have been better prepared for an attack against their queen and heir.

"You know what you need to do. Train hard and focus on what is important to you," Reuben said in a smooth tone. "You have your armour now.

There's nothing stopping you."

I stared at the dust-covered stone floor. Did some part of my mind deny me the right to accept the truth? I needed the physical dexterity that would allow me to continue surviving such brutal wars. As much as Swynvale's magic lulled me into tranquillity, the death of my son, my own blood, would forever haunt me.

"I'm sorry for what happened to you, Evalyn, so very sorry," he said in a few octaves above a whisper. "Let the realm's magic help you to heal."

Tears welled in my eyes and slid down my cheeks. Rueben held his arm out. I backed away, blinking rapidly. My breath lodged itself in my throat.

This was real. The pain. The loss. All of it.

"This grief you suffer through alone can be eased by the realm," he said.

He was right—the magic *tried* to help me.

"If you improve your strength, stamina, and discipline, your magic will also strengthen," he added. "After all, that's what you came here for, and I will keep reminding you for as long as it takes."

He dipped his head, then headed out of the room, leaving me in silence.

Later in the evening, I trudged down the west wing, through the courtyard, and into the training room.

I stood in the corner with a sword in my hand, flipping it and unsure what to do. I'd carried a blade with me for months, but I'd never received serious training. I learned how to defend myself firsthand in battle.

"Don't fear the training, Evalyn," Reuben said on his way to the door. "Remember why you crossed through the portal. Remember your purpose and let it fuel you. You will be strong because of it."

"My Mage magic isn't enough. If—*when* I return home, I'll need to be ready to fight Makdou."

"We will provide you with all the skills you need. Your swordsmanship will be the very best," he said.

I smiled to myself, imagining Xurek's grin as I slashed through training dummies with accuracy.

Reuben patted my shoulder, then left the Armoury. After a glug of water from a stein and a snack of meat and bread brought by other soldiers, I continued to train until the orange and purple glow of twilight dimmed the training room. I placed the sword on the bench and raised my fists.

"Fists in front of your face. Block!" Seth ordered as he backed me into a corner. He swung for me.

I dipped under his arm and grinned. "Like that?"

"Great, Evalyn." Lilith let out a cheer. "Dmitri, why don't you join in? Make it difficult for her."

Dmitri leapt into the fight and swung his right arm towards my face. I blocked it with my forearm whilst Seth jumped from side to side with his fists held in front of his face. Lilith coached me from the sidelines.

We trained until every muscle ached. Lilith directed me to the stuffed dummies, then handed me a sword.

"Imagine Makdou's face on the dummies," she

said.

With the thin silver sword, I slashed the cotton fabric, spilling the straw stuffing onto the floor. When blisters formed on the inside of my hands, I incorporated magic to find the right balance between melee and sorcery. The fiery balls of magic blew several of the dummies into nothing more than a pile of ashes.

When all the models were destroyed, I panted, staring at the mess around me.

'This is for you, my little one. I'm so sorry I failed you,' I mouthed so no one else could hear.

The destruction around me hadn't been a successful source of anger management. After a few moments, the realm's magic soothed me. Yet this time, the magic had form—an ethereal white substance, faint and hard to see. But I *could* see it.

I stared in awe. How could I see it in its full beauty? The magic wrapped itself around me in an elegant, light dance. My mood shifted until I became weightless, hovering a few feet above the floor. For a moment, I forgot my son's murder, my traitorous protectors, and the many horrors I'd faced in Arogath.

"Oh my," Dmitri gasped. Lilith and Seth gaped at me.

The magic soon faded, and I dropped to the floor.

"Well, that's a first." Seth raised an eyebrow, helping me to my feet. "The magic doesn't take form for anyone."

"Evalyn is written in the scrolls. It makes sense the magic would manifest for her," Lilith said. "We must tell Reuben."

"That's not necessary," Seth said. "He would have been expecting it."

"Let's go again." I jogged on the spot to keep my heart rate high. "I need to be ready. *We* need to be ready for the Orcs to make their next move."

"You're right," Dmitri agreed. "This is a waiting game—we need to utilise the time we have."

"Then what are you waiting for?" Lilith grinned, handing our steins to us.

I gulped several mouthfuls, then placed the mug onto the bench before resuming my position in the middle of the Armoury with my fists held in front of my face. "I'm ready."

The sensation of weightlessness lingered, but a small burning ember within me remained. The magic could not rid me of my grief.

# Chapter Three

Soldiers filed into the large hall, huffing and grunting as they squeezed past each other. They swarmed around a wooden table in the centre of the room. I stood on my tiptoes to look over the heads of people in front of me. Seth, Lilith, and Dmitri gathered around the table as Reuben leaned back in his chair with his brows furrowed and fingers pressed to his temples.

The pale dawn light filtered through the windows, illuminating the specks of dust floating through the air.

"What's going on?" I asked over the indistinct muttering, eyeing the parchment sprawled across the wooden surface. A map of Swynvale.

"Can you please let Evalyn through?" Seth asked the crowd.

The soldiers shuffled to either side of me and created a path straight to the map.

I got to see this beautiful, strange world laid bare in front of me. The continents on the map were much larger than Arogath's territories.

"We need a plan," one soldier said. "We can't sit back anymore. This is our time to fight back."

"We've received word from Firsthold." Seth huffed and scratched his head. He hunched over the map, pointing at the calligraphy writing of the settlement he'd mentioned. "The Orcs have installed magical beams."

I placed my hands on the table and looked at the continent we were on—Monalyth—Firsthold was a small settlement north of here.

Lilith glared at the map, her hands planted on her hips.

"I'm more concerned about where they found this magic." I surveyed the map. "Orcs don't have natural magic."

"How many more settlements need to perish before we do something?" a soldier bellowed.

"Silence!" Reuben scraped his chair back, stood, then strode through the crowd towards the table.

He picked up the mini temple statue positioned on the Temple of Peace and placed it northwards on top of the calligraphy writing of Firsthold.

"We depart in one hour," he said, voice cool, without moving his gaze. "Discuss amongst yourselves an appropriate route. I am going to make some black tea with a hint of cinnamon." Reuben glided out of the room.

Tea? On a day like this?

"Don't worry about him," Lilith said. "He quite often leaves us to make the plans ourselves. He says they're the best when we pull together and agree as a unit."

"There's a fork in the main route, just here." Dmitri pressed his finger onto the thin lines. "The fork will take us northwards around the left side of the lake and skirt around the forest. Firsthold is a few miles beyond this point. It won't be any longer than a day's travel."

"There are no other routes," she said. "The lake and the forest disconnect us from the other settlements up north, and the mountains disconnect us from the west and the east. Unless you fancy trying to *climb* the mountains, then this route will suffice."

The Temple of Peace was situated on top of the mountain in the northeast with more mountains rising behind it. A steep walled valley ran between this mountain and the one in the west. We needed to follow this route out of the valley to reach Firsthold.

"That's sorted then," he said. "Evalyn, are you ready for this?"

I lifted my chin, looking him straight in the eye. "No, but the Orcs will not wait, and neither should we."

The soldiers gathered in the courtyard with their weapons sheathed and explosives placed safe in their fabric bags. I stood, dressed in my armour, beside Seth. My hands trembled at my sides—how did the Orcs get a hold of magic, and how would we stop them?

He grasped my hands to stop them from shaking. "You'll be fine. *We'll* be fine."

After what we saw the day before, how could he be sure?

"Where are all the soldiers?" I scanned the courtyard, noticing fewer men than the day before.

"Some won't be joining us. They are in the Garden of Peace for recovery," he explained.

"Garden of Peace?" I parroted, raising an eyebrow.

"A magical garden. I'll show you later."

Reuben observed the subdued soldiers who remained silent, as they waited to embark on their next expedition. The grey clouds hung over us and a chill breeze nipped at my cheeks.

"We'll ride forth into Firsthold and find the magical beams," he said. "Destroy them if it is safe to do so, eliminate any Orcs, and stick together."

The soldiers exchanged no words. A hollow-eyed man stared at Reuben.

At Westwilde, Felix and I had helped bury the dead—those who'd perished in the fire. The war wouldn't get easier. Not here. Not at home. All we could do was persevere and fight for what we knew was right.

Reuben turned on his heel, then mounted his horse. The rest of us hoisted onto our saddles, then followed him on the sloping path, towards the lake. Dmitri, Seth, and Lilith flanked me in silence.

A cool breeze fluttered the loose strands of hair around my face. It made for a pleasant change from the scorching heat of Arogath. Birds sang nearby, but the clanking of metal and heavy footsteps filled the air as we descended the slope. The ride to Firsthold was long and tense with the soldiers marching in silence. Reuben hunched his shoulders, becoming rigid.

Beyond the mud path framed with yellow flowers stood Firsthold, a keep made of grey limestone, surrounded by a towering wall of the same material. We passed birch trees and continued down the gravel path towards the entrance of the settlement. Would we find another destroyed village with people impaled and brutalised by Orcs? I swallowed and steeled myself, preparing for anything.

Reuben hopped down from his saddle. "Keep your wits about you. We can't be sure the Orcs haven't stayed behind in anticipation for our arrival. They know what they're doing, and they want a reaction."

I prayed futilely to the gods of this realm, whoever they were, that the Orcs were gone. It seemed the gods of my own realm had abandoned me the night I was attacked by Makdou.

When I dismounted, I flattened my sweating palms against my legs. We formed a line against the stone walls. A low humming noise drummed through the settlement.

"What was that?" I glanced at Seth.

"I'm betting it was magic," he said.

I peered around the corner of the stone walls then jerked back.

"What is it?" Reuben asked, calm and steady.

"Orcs," I whispered. "They are patrolling the area. There are two through the entrance on the left, a few more by the keep, and some farther back. Maybe ten in total—I couldn't count them all. We can handle that."

The low grunts of Orcs stirred beyond the wall, and I tried to process a plan in my head of how we would defeat them. "They have the green magic too—the same magic we saw in the grounds of the torched village."

"I imagine it's what's powering the beams they have installed here. We must discover what they do, then put a stop to them. All of them. We must execute as many of them as we can," Reuben said.

How would we avoid casualties? Whilst the Humans were high-skilled combatants, I didn't want to risk their lives in a conquered settlement. Yet no other option presented itself. Blood would need to be spilled if we continued with our mission into Firsthold.

With a burst of confidence, I ran through the stone archway and entered Firsthold. I conjured a large ball of fiery magic within my hands and prepared to launch it at an Orc who had its back to me.

The soldiers overtook me and charged with their swords held high into the small gatherings of enemies. I sent the ball of red light hurtling through the air until it collided with the leathered skin of an

Orc. He exploded and fragments of my magic set two nearby Orcs alight. Black dust rained onto the ground. I retched at the stench of burned flesh and bones.

Uninjured civilians surged towards the remaining Orcs with their dull, worn metal swords. They drove their swords towards an enemy's belly. The swords snapped on impact. The beast yanked one of the local villagers up, roared into his face, then tore his limbs off.

Blood spurted across the faces of the other civilians. They ploughed their broken swords into the beast's face, blinding him. The Orc roared in pain and swung his arms out, sending the villagers crashing to the ground.

I hurried through the keep, palms poised upwards, prepared to cast the next ball of magic. The Orcs thrashed their battle hammers into limbs, crushing them into the ground. The screams chilled my spine. I curled my hands into fists and pierced my palms with my nails.

"We have backup!" one of the villagers called. "Stay together. The soldiers received our message. Our injured have fled to the crypts beneath the fort to recover. We are not trained combatants but those who are fit enough have stayed to fight."

"Duck, Evalyn," Seth yelled.

I dropped to the floor as an Orc swung his axe. Seth parried the attack with his sword. Dmitri aimed his mace straight for the enemy's bare chest.

I scrambled to my feet, then threw a bolt of red light into the Orc and watched as he turned to ash. "Let's keep moving."

Dmitri, Reuben, and Lilith flanked me as I made my way around the back of the keep. The beams holding the great balls of green magic were closer together around the back and much brighter than the ones by the entrance of the fort. They glowed a vivid emerald.

The air stirred around us in thick gusts. Was it the realm's magic, brought to life by the chaos around us? Perhaps it fuelled my powers that engulfed the Orc in flames.

"Clear." Seth appeared next to me, face bloodied, and armour scratched and splashed with the dark crimson of enemy and ally blood alike. "The last of the Orcs are down."

"Are you injured?" I scanned his body for any serious wounds, but his armour kept his flesh hidden away. I sighed with relief.

"I wear the blood of our enemies, Evalyn." He wore a deadpan expression across his face, then a slight smile tugged at the corner of his lips.

Lilith, deer-eyed and hair freefalling around her face, looked me over once, then her shoulders relaxed. Had she, too, been searching for injuries, expecting the worst?

"I'm glad we didn't come face to face with a larger clan of Orcs—this could have ended badly," she said.

"We should remain focused," I said. "We are alive, and we managed to save some Human lives, so we should be grateful for that. Let's get this over and done with."

She dipped her head in acknowledgement and flexed her fingers. I wanted to reach out to her, to comfort her, but how would she react?

"I'll rally the surviving villagers and check for injuries." She marched back into the keep.

I dropped my gaze to the floor beside my feet—the green light flickered in the thin grooves between the stones. The flow of the light pulsed towards me from the south, at the far edge of the keep, behind the castle. The streaming light fed the other beams, pumping through the ground and up their stands. A larger one in the middle fuelled the rest.

I stepped closer to the beam. How did it feed the surrounding ones?

"I've seen something like this before." I stared at the glowing green light in the tallest beam in front of me. "Back in Arogath."

"W-what is it?" Although his sword was now tucked in its scabbard, Seth kept his hand resting on the pommel.

"A portal. When I was at the Citadel, I discovered a spell book to open a portal, and that's how I found Swynvale," I explained. "The one I used to cross through had a purple centre, but I've been exposed to evil kinds. I have a hunch this is the same. Come to think of it, these beams may act as some kind of anchor."

"The beams are the anchor?" Reuben echoed.

Lilith jogged over. "The surviving civilians are okay, no grave wounds. They are terrified and shaken, and we need to help bury their dead. What have I missed?"

"Yes," I ignored her. "And you're positive it's just Humans and Orcs in this realm? This seems like Dark Mage magic. I've seen enough to know."

"Positive," Dmitri said. "Mages haven't existed here for a long time, and I thank Otis, God of Peace, for it every day."

I scoffed. God of Peace? *That* was a notion I couldn't wrap my head around. The concept of peace hadn't existed in a long time, which begged the question: why did Otis allow for such suffering? Why not just put an end to the Orcs' tyranny and be done with these endless wars? It seemed prayers fell on deaf ears everywhere.

"You're lucky." An image of Makdou in my chambers back at the Citadel flickered in my mind. "Let's hope it stays this way."

"You're one yourself." A flash of fear appeared in Lilith's emerald, bottomless eyes. Like Seth, she kept her hand resting on her blade. "A Mage."

Did she fear me?

"Calm, now." Reuben rested his gaze on her until her shoulders relaxed. "You know in your heart Evalyn does not carry the evil she speaks of. I suggest we take a trip through this portal."

Seth laughed, although without amusement. "You're suggesting we jump straight into something we've never explored? One way to get us all killed, Reuben. None of us have experienced a portal before, except Evalyn."

"It is true, portals have not been a part of our training. Evalyn is the only one to have any knowledge of them," Reuben said.

Their gazes burned into me.

Entering the portal could provide clues as to how it was being generated.

If this *did* have something to do with Dark

Mages, it would be connected to Makdou. She was one of the most powerful Dark Mages from our world, but what connections did she have with Swynvale?

"He's right." I stared at the green magic coursing through the cracks in the floor. "Going into this portal could answer a lot of questions for all of us. For Swynvale *and* Arogath. We'll enter the portal first and bury the dead after."

I focused on the central beam, rubbed my hands together, then raised my palms. The portal needed to be teased open, somehow. With closed eyes, I pictured the green orb stretching into a large, shimmery, emerald circle.

The natural magic of Swynvale stirred a wind through the nearby trees, growing stronger as it reached me and rustled my hair.

I sucked in cool air and opened my eyes. The magnified, intense green magic within the beams shone across the keep. The soldiers shielded their eyes from the light. Soon, the main beam shot out a pearlescent, swirling magic. The magic formed into a portal with an opaque centre.

"The realm is also in agreement," Seth said.

"It's not purple, so there isn't a realm on the other side," I said. "It must lead to another location in Swynvale."

"Who's going first?" Lilith cleared her throat. "If I die in there, I will come back and haunt you all."

Seth chuckled, stroking her shoulder with his finger and thumb. "We'll make it through. Together."

Their gazes locked on each other, then disconnected as quickly as they'd joined.

A smile tugged at the corners of her lips, softening her cool exterior.

I had to look away, for his words reminded me too much of Felix and what I had left behind. Despite the grief straining my fractured heart, I still yearned for him.

"I will go first." Reuben stepped in front of the portal, his voice resonating without a single tone of doubt. "After all, it was my idea. Evalyn, how do we cross?"

"Just as you would climb through anything—put your legs in first." I shrugged, remembering it'd worked for me.

Reuben cocked his head as he stared at the portal. Sighing, he reluctantly placed his right leg through. He stopped and looked over his shoulder. "No pain. My leg is still attached."

Seth laughed. I stifled the same reaction, but more so out of surprise.

Reuben continued, disappearing through to the other side. Seth followed with Lilith and Dmitri in tow.

"Stay here and guard the portal," I called to the other soldiers.

They nodded, lifting their swords a few inches higher.

I stepped into the ethereal form. My body disappeared, split apart, and reformed on the other side next to my companions.

I scanned my new surroundings. A cave.

Why would the Orcs of Swynvale utilise this

42

place?

The cave walls were slick with damp and were the colour of clay, stretching high above. Large white crystals hung from the ceiling in clusters, allowing droplets of water to slide down their ragged surfaces and puddle on the floor around my feet. A path stretched onwards through narrow, winding spaces. Reuben led the way.

Lilith lingered beside Seth and kept her arms tight across her chest. During our first meeting in the mess hall, she'd been tough, demanded answers. Yet recent events had stripped it from her. I'd been the same way, many months ago.

"I'll lead the way." Reuben journeyed deeper into the cave, towards a narrow tunnel ahead. "If you could provide a light, Evalyn, that would be useful."

Nodding, I produced a ball of brilliant white light, then sent it high above his head, illuminating the way for him.

Seth gave me a cheeky grin. "Full of surprises, aren't you?"

Although I offered a half smile, I couldn't reply to his playful comment. I'd grown used to the brutality of the Orcs, but I feared the great possibility their green magic had something to do with Mages. I needed to get a grip—I'd handled worse.

We followed Reuben through the cave, past the rock pools, and into the narrow tunnel ahead. It curved around and stretched onwards.

A low hum rumbled through the air, piquing my attention. I exchanged glances with Seth, whose frown deepened as we reached the next opening. The steep slope descended underground, and at the bottom sat an expanse of dark, bottomless, stagnant water surrounding a small island. A thick green slime floated on the water surface.

My white ball of magical light winked out, unnecessary in the presence of a magnificent green glow. A beam towered in the centre of the island, harnessing its magic, and illuminating the cave chamber and its water-slick walls.

"That doesn't look good," Lilith called over the hum of the beam. "Any suggestions on how to destroy it?"

Sofia and I'd closed the portal that once allowed the Ezen Riders into Arogath. It had taken a lot of strength from both of us, and I couldn't have done it on my own. Destroying the Ezen Riders had sent me into Elysium—the realm in between the living and the dead—the endless black, drifting, weightless *nothing*.

Reuben caught me frowning. My heart sank, fearing the favour he'd ask of me.

He nodded. "There is a way."

I shifted my gaze away from him. I didn't want him to tell them. Not yet. Taking in a steadying breath, I stared at the stalactites.

When I finally returned my focus to him, he said with unwavering certainty, "It is time. Evalyn. You must go back to Arogath and find Sofia."

# Chapter Four

I remained frozen in place. Reuben's words rang in my ears. I couldn't go home yet. There was still more for me to learn in Swynvale, and I wasn't ready to face the terrors I'd left.

"There has to be another way." I locked my gaze with Reuben's.

"There are no other ways," he said. "You know it as well as I."

"Will one of you please tell us what is going on?" Lilith placed her hands on her hips. "If there is a way to destroy this thing once and for all, then we need to know."

"Evalyn has destroyed a portal before," he said

as casually as he would if sharing news on the weather outside. "In Arogath, her home realm."

"We know what the scroll contains," Dmitri blurted. "Sofia—she's the other Mage, isn't she?"

"She is," Reuben said, maintaining unbreakable eye contact with me.

"Then what are we waiting for?" Dmitri asked. "Let's go get her and bring her here."

"Enough." How could they demand this of me? They knew what I'd suffered, how I'd barely processed what had happened. If I admitted to myself that my friends had been unprepared—that it wasn't necessarily their failure *or* their fault— then I would blame myself. If *I* had been stronger, ready, maybe I could have stopped Makdou and spared my son's life. Now they wanted me to go back?

I spun around, heading to the portal.

"We can't let her go," Dmitri said. "We need to stop Ev—"

"Hush, Dmitri," Reuben said. "Give her a moment to accept there is no other choice."

Their voices echoed behind me as I hurried through the tunnel. Soon, their footsteps thundered behind me.

I'd be damned if I went back. Not now. Not yet.

I climbed through the portal, leaving the cave behind.

Birds flew overhead, nestling in one of the trees outside Firsthold. Smoke filled the sky, and the remaining flames flickered and crackled. My fears, and death, had followed me, and I couldn't escape them.

The others emerged from the portal.

"Evalyn," Seth said in a soothing tone. "We would not ask this of you if we knew of another way." He placed his hand on my arm. "Reuben is right."

I wrapped my arms around my chest and lowered my voice to a whisper. Heat burned my cheeks. Shame, I realised. "I can't go back there. I'm not strong enough. I'm not ready."

"If we are to save this realm from the Orcs, then we need to close the portal," Reuben said. "If you are right about Makdou having involvement in this, then it is critical you go back to get Sofia."

"You don't understand," I ground out. "There are many horrors in Arogath, not just Orcs. You're rather lucky here. You don't have endless wars between Dark Mages and Orcs and every other damn species in their territory. If this portal scares you, Reuben, you wouldn't have lasted a day in Arogath. You know what happened in Southkeep."

"You can help us," he said. "There are no Mages here who can. You and Sofia can stop another war from happening here before this turns into a bloodbath. You can prevent our people from suffering the same, terrible fate that yours did."

"I've seen people hanging from trees, I watched bodies burn, and evil take form as the Ezen Riders." Water filled my eyes, and he blurred in front of me. "I managed to close the portal with Sofia's help, but it could have killed me. Do you know what the worst part was? Everything I did still wasn't enough. My people still suffered. *I* suffered. When I entered Elysium, I wanted to stay. Even though I was pregnant with my son, I wanted to stay a ghost…to disappear. And to admit that…to admit that I would be better off dead than to be a queen, to let my people have some other ruler, makes me sick with shame."

"Evalyn, please," he said. "I know this must be hard for you."

"Maybe we should go back to the Temple and discuss it there," Seth suggested.

I ignored him. "I can't save you."

"You are stronger than you think," Reuben said. "Look at all you have accomplished. You came here to be ready to fight Makdou and give your people a safe and free future. This is just one step in the process."

I clamped my hands over my eyes.

One, two, three…

Once my heartbeat steadied, I lowered my hands, then stared at him.

"I did not mean to offend you, Evalyn." His gaze softened. "I shall not deny I cannot empathise with what you have gone through—you have seen more horrors than I think my men ever have. You are lucky to have survived it. But you did not get by on luck alone—you had strength, determination, and a reason. This *must* be done. You have to go back."

I turned away, striding along the cobblestone floors of Firsthold and past the many corpses. My heart pounded, and my fingers shook at my side. Seth jogged and fell into step beside me.

"I'm sorry this is happening," he said. "I wish we didn't have to bring you into this, but we don't have anyone else like you. You know you were meant to come here, and we have given you another reason to keep fighting. I will remind you of it every day if I have to."

"It's too much," I croaked. "I don't want to return to the place where I was attacked, and my son murdered."

He remained silent as we continued down the gravel path. He sighed.

"When I was seven years old, a clan of Orcs skinned my parents alive, then burned my village to the ground before leaving. I saw it all from inside a hay wagon," he said, his eyes dark and hollow. "Reuben and his soldiers found me on a patrol the next day, and I have been living at the Temple ever since."

"I'm sorry that happened to you. I didn't know."

"I'm not trying to say I have experienced the same things as you, Evalyn," he said. "But we have all seen our own horrors, and if I had the chance to see my family again, I would."

The High Elves I'd grown to love—Kiirion, Valneris, and Theodas. An allied Orc who'd proven his loyalty on more than one occasion. And Felix— the man whose soul was bound to mine. They had all become my family.

"I can't forgive them," I whispered. "I will never forget the feeling of being alone, helpless, and unable to use magic to defend myself. A part of me died that night. A part I'll never get back."

"For what it's worth, I'm glad you're alive." He smiled. "And from what I've read of Felix in the scroll, he loved you. I imagine he still does, but he would grieve the loss of his child too. Don't let the man you love grieve alone. I'm not saying you did the wrong thing, but when you are ready, you will forgive them all, and yourself."

"I'll go," I said, voice thin and my body drained. "But I'll get Sofia, and hurry straight back."

"I can come with you, you know, if it makes it easier." He placed his hand on my shoulder.

"That sounds like a good idea." I touched his arm. "Thank you."

We continued our journey back to the Temple of Peace, through the trees, past the large lake, and up the rocky mountain. Swynvale's mountain ranges climbed high into the clouds, and snow blanketed the summits. Arogath was similar in some ways— home to steep peaks and deep valleys, but also flatlands stretching into dense forests.

"You can do this," he said. "I will be by your side the whole time. If you're doing this for us, then this is the very least I can do for you."

Back at the Temple, the soldiers dispersed to the recreational room, bathrooms, and bedrooms. Reuben, Lilith, Dmitri, Seth, and I entered a room where two soldiers withdrew a stack of chessboards from shelves while another filled steins with beer. Reuben took a seat opposite an opponent, then set the chess pieces onto the wooden board.

I gnawed at my bottom lip and tapped my foot against the floor. The quicker I got Sofia, the quicker I could get away. Flexing my hands, I straightened my back.

"Whenever you are ready, Evalyn," he said. "I will be here, waiting for you to return." He picked up a chess piece, then slid it across the board.

"As will I." Dmitri smiled. He approached me, then placed his hand on my shoulder. "You've got this. We believe in you."

"You're braver than I thought," Lilith said. "I'm sorry for judging you."

"There's nothing to apologise for. You can thank me when I return."

"I've decided to accompany Evalyn," Seth said.

Lilith's eyes widened. "Are you serious? You can't go."

Instead of arguing, Seth crossed the room, gathering her in his arms. He muttered something inaudible, then placed a brief kiss upon her lips.

With a curt nod, Lilith let Seth return to my side, in front of the portal. She crossed her arms. "Be safe," she said. "Both of you."

I nodded, heading to the throne room with Seth. With him waiting close by, I focused on the spell. A low hum reverberated against the walls as the white, ethereal, swirling form of the portal appeared once more. We climbed through. I dissipated into nothing as we travelled through the space between realms and reformed again on the other side.

Moments later, Seth reappeared at my side. "Where are we?" he asked.

"Lake Delendil. My home." My chest constricted, and my words came out on an inhale.

"It's beautiful." He gaped as he gazed at the high walls and the rainbow-coloured glass illuminated by the afternoon sun. "I've never seen anything like it."

"Come on." I grabbed his arm, then towed him

towards the door. "I want to make this trip a quick one."

"Sorry, I'll be serious now." He nodded and lost the grin from his face.

I led him down the wide-arched corridors and the curving staircase to the ground floor. "This place was destroyed the last time I was here. They must have been quick with the repairs."

The Elven guard at the main entrance widened his eyes as I drew closer.

"My queen." He rushed to my side. "You're home!"

"Where are my advisers? My friends?"

"They have spent many hours in the council room, my queen." The guard guided us towards the council room in the left wing of the Citadel. "They will be very pleased to see you are well—the realm has been restless without you." He bowed and returned to his station at the entrance.

Staring at the closed door to the council room ahead, I shook, overcome with nerves.

"The Orcs have returned to Zhah, Valneris. This is the closest we have been to peace between the Triads," Kiirion said from inside the room. "The Orcs will remain in charge of the Dark Triads."

"Yes, you are right," Valneris said. "However, nobody has seen or heard from Evalyn. True peace cannot be restored until she returns. She is the head of our kingdom—the Crown itself—without her, our words of peace mean nothing, and our people will lose faith."

Seth eyed me as I listened through the door. He frowned. "What are you waiting for?" he whispered.

"She will return when she is ready," said another voice I knew all too well. Felix.

Time seemed to slow as his voice echoed through my mind, working the knots out of my stomach. He was here. *So close.*

I pushed open the doors and entered the council room with Seth on my heels.

My Elven friends sat around the council table, accompanied by Felix and Xurek. They fell quiet, gawking at me. Seth tensed beside me, as if registering the hulking presence of an Orc. I placed a reassuring hand on his arm.

"Evalyn!" Kiirion rose, then crossed the room in swift motions. "You're home. Where in the gods' good realm have you been?"

I waved his concern away. "Where is Sofia?"

"I'm right here, of course," the soft, angelic voice responded. She stood next to the large window overlooking the lake outside. Although her beauty was as radiant as ever, dark circles had formed under her eyes. Her silver hair hung limp over her shoulders and had lost its bright shine. "I'm glad to see you safe."

"Where have you been?" Aneirin, my father, bellowed as he stormed through the doorway. "And who is this man?"

"I have been in Swynvale—another realm much like ours." I glanced at him. "This is Seth, a soldier who can be trusted."

Felix's gaze burned on me while he remained fixed on the spot. My heart pounded. I held his stare for a moment, then glanced away, overcome with a conflicting need to both run from the room and throw myself at him.

"Evalyn," he said, voice strained.

"Please, don't." My voice was small, fragile—the complete opposite of what I wanted to portray. "I need to do this. I *need* time." I let those words fall heavy on those surrounding me. They would not convince me to stay. I wouldn't allow it.

Letting out a shaky breath, he crossed the distance between us, then dragged his hands through his hair. The others remained silent. "I'll let you have your time, but I won't sit here and watch you disappear again."

He left without another word.

I blinked back tears and flattened my trembling fingers against my legs. I would make things right with Felix, but now wasn't the time. "Sofia, I need you to come with us to Swynvale. The Orcs of that realm are much like our own, and they are using some sort of green magic to harness a portal."

"An anchor?" Sofia raised her eyebrows. The High Elves glanced at each other. "It can't be."

"You can't close another portal, Evalyn." Kiirion placed his fingers against his temples, a deep frown creasing his eyebrows. "The last could have killed you."

"I know. That's why I need Sofia to help me."

"I think we got lucky last time, Evalyn." She shook her head. "Even more so, you are lucky to be alive—"

"You don't understand. If it is in any way connected to Mage magic, we need to stop it. Maybe Makdou is in contact with them in

Swynvale—she may be behind all of this." I appealed to her logical side—if I spoke plain and true, she would see reason.

Seth remained silent at my side.

"Interesting thought," Valneris said. He was the oldest of the High Elves, and although his striking cheekbones were lined with the marks of ageing, he was as beautiful as ever. "How can we be sure she even has access to other realms?"

"If I had access, then she could have too." I huffed. I didn't have the time or patience to answer these questions. The Orcs grew stronger, and so did Makdou.

"She is your *true* enemy, Evalyn," Xurek said. "Why are you away fighting someone else's war?"

"The Orcs are our enemies too." I placed my hands on the ornate glass and ruby table. "If they hadn't challenged the Dark Mages, tortured them, and drained them of magic, then the Dark Mages wouldn't have rebelled against the Orcs, and my child would not be dead. I can't shake the feeling that Makdou is behind this." I turned to Sofia. "Will you help me or not?"

She glanced out of the windows at the gardens before she turned, then walked towards me. "You are my queen. I will do as you command."

"This is something I have to do." I watched her. "I wouldn't ask you if it wasn't necessary. I am asking you as a friend, not as your queen."

"Either way, you have my service," she said.

"If you must do this," Kiirion said as I placed my hand on the door handle. "Stay safe and come home soon."

I nodded, then left before I didn't have the strength to.

Seth, Sofia, and I hurried through the Citadel foyer, past the entrance and up the main staircase to the library where the portal awaited us.

"Evalyn," she said. "Are you sure this is the right thing to do?"

I wanted to wrap my arms around her, my friend, and promise her everything would be okay, that I'd made the right choice. But I didn't know how I could return to Arogath and be the queen I was meant to be without discovering the truth about the green magic.

"I do want to come home, Sofia." I sighed, rubbing my temple. "The people of Swynvale are much like us—spending their days fighting against evil that never seems to end. They suffer like we do. They watch their villages burn to the ground like we have done. This is the way of things for them, as it has been for us and my people. I can't stand idly by when they have directly asked for my help."

"Okay." She clasped my hands in hers. "I'll do this for you. I will stand by your side as your servant, and as your friend." She smiled.

We returned through the portal together. Surrounded by the black void, I drifted, weightless. A face pierced the blackness. Silver hair. Red eyes. A slim pointed nose. Makdou. She sneered.

My heart rate skyrocketed, and as I fell through time and space, there wasn't a single thing I could do.

*Calm down! It isn't her.*

56

As if a ghost, I watched myself step into the same portal. *How can I be here and within arm's reach at the same time?*

"Evalyn," Sofia screamed. "Evalyn, give me your hand!"

I snapped my attention to her. "How are you standing there? Y-you weren't there two seconds ago." I trembled, adrenaline shooting through my veins.

"Evalyn, Seth and me—it is Seth, isn't it? We've been here for a few minutes, waiting for you to come through the portal." She gripped my arm and steadied me.

"That was the most uncomfortable experience." Seth shook himself, grimacing. "I hope I never have to do it again. I want to keep my feet firmly on *this* ground. Evalyn, are you okay? You've gone pale."

"I just saw myself enter the portal." I stared at its shimmering surface. "We've been gone for an hour or so, but it's as if I never left...ah, my head hurts."

"Steady on, let's go back to Reuben and the others, then you must rest." Seth faced Sofia and offered an awkward half-smile. "Welcome to the Temple of Peace. This is Swynvale, one of the most beautiful places you'll ever see."

"It was the middle of the day in Arogath. How much time has passed since you left this place—Swynvale?" she asked.

I glanced out of the window at the same sunny, radiant sky I had left behind an hour, or possibly, a few moments ago. "Sofia, I'm serious, something isn't right. I saw her—Makdou—in the portal."

"Shhh." She rested her hand on my arm. "Portals

can take a lot of energy out of you. Don't fret about it. It could be nothing."

I nodded, hoping she was right.

"Evalyn…" Seth muttered.

"Yeah, I know, we should get going." I turned to see him pointing, open-mouthed as someone stumbled through the closing portal.

# Chapter Five

"Felix?" I frowned. "What are you doing here?"

He came to me at once, taking my hands in his. "I said I wouldn't watch you leave again, so I decided to come after you. I couldn't bring myself to leave you, so I remained outside the council room door and hurried through the portal after you walked through."

"I told you I needed time," I said. Despite the ache in my heart, his presence warmed my body. A familiar comfort.

He was here. With me. In Swynvale. He carried the same pain with him, and now I faced him. Would he hate me more for leaving him? Or worse, for not apologising for it?

"Evalyn." His voice cracked, and the muscles in his face strained.

"I'll be outside," Sofia whispered as she ushered Seth outside the room with her. She clicked the door shut.

"I know you need time." Felix cupped my cheek, and I couldn't help but lean into it. "But please don't shut me out. We stick together, no matter what. We can't let Makdou tear us apart, otherwise she wins."

I pressed my lips together in a tight line as a painful lump formed in my throat. Him being here brought everything to the surface, threatening to break the feeble floodgates holding back my emotions.

When I finally opened my mouth to reply, he tucked a piece of hair behind my ear. "Don't say anything yet. Listen to what I say—it might help to take away some of your pain. We can get through this together." He caressed my cheek. "We have been through so much, and we will get through this, too. There's no need for either of us to face this alone. You need time to heal—I understand that— but the gods know I need it too."

Despite my best efforts, I couldn't fathom why the gods would care. It seemed Xetis, God of Endings, and Ytia, God of Birth, were at odds with each other. How else could they stand for the death of an innocent child—and a violent death at that?

I cursed them, unable to bring myself to worship the gods who'd let Makdou tear my heart out when she took the most precious thing life could have offered me.

"You know why I left. The pain of losing a child—it's consuming. You couldn't prevent it. *They* couldn't prevent it. Right now, I cannot forget it, but I can forgive you. It wasn't your fault—not really. It never was. The blame lies solely with Makdou, but it doesn't make it any easier to accept. My heart broke into a thousand pieces, and I had to get away. I feel this deep-rooted pain—a crushing yearning to hold a child I know I never will. I know what I would've named him too." I imagined the small, round cheeks and hazel eyes of our baby. "Ascal. For the High Elf who sacrificed his life for us."

"Ascal. A lovely name." Felix smiled. "I won't let anything hurt you, Evalyn. Not again."

He'd made this promise before—to protect me, as a knight of the Eyrie, as a friend, and as a lover. But I had to trust in *us*, for my heart kept pulling me back to him. The ties between us trembled and buckled, but they would not snap.

I wrapped my arms around his neck and drew him against me. A wave of warmth washed over me as his arms locked around my waist. And for a moment, nothing else mattered.

We broke our embrace when the door clicked open, and Sofia and Seth stepped inside.

I glanced at Felix from the corner of my eyes—he looked at me too, and his lips curved into a warm smile. The embers of the love I felt for him, somewhere deep in my chest, reignited.

"Sorry for the interruption, but we need to find the others," Seth said.

I hurried through the corridors with Seth, Sofia, and Felix in tow. Flickering torches lit the way with their orange glow. My heart thumped at the possibility of us being gone much later than I'd suggested. What damage would it do to our plans to stop the Orcs' magic?

Seth sped around a turn, then entered a room with maps strung along the walls. Soldiers played chess and sipped beer from their steins—the way we'd left them.

"Seth?" Lilith, who'd been in a match against Dmitri, flung her chair back, rising to her feet. "How did you get there? You just left…wait. Why are you back so soon?"

"We spent an hour or so in Arogath." Seth glanced from her to the soldiers gaping at us.

"You've only been gone a few minutes." She gasped. "How is this possible?"

"A few minutes? Is that all?" I arched a brow.

"Of course," she said. "How extraordinary. I thought you'd be gone for hours but this…*this* is marvellous."

"How so?" I tilted my head to the side.

"This works in our favour, don't you see? We haven't wasted any time at all."

"Perhaps it's time I introduce you to Sofia." Seth placed his hands on Sofia's shoulders and nudged her forward. "After all, she is the reason we left."

She stretched her arm to offer Lilith a handshake. "A pleasure."

"Nice to meet you. I'm Lilith. Who've you brought along with you?" Lilith gestured to Felix.

Seth pulled her to his chest. "Why, this is the

famous knight of the Eyrie, Felix."

"Wow, I didn't realise. I apologise," she said. "I know a lot about you."

"You do?" Felix raised a questioning brow.

"I'll explain later." I rested my hand on his arm.

Lilith leaned into Seth, and she let him coo and fuss over her.

*She has a soft side after all.*

"I'm astounded—you can cross from one world to another, and it costs us a few minutes." She beamed.

"We must think of the issues this may raise," Dmitri said from his seated position. "Jumping from one timeline to the other—it's dangerous. We don't know what damages it can cause, and we cannot be frivolous."

"I knew this would happen," Sofia whispered to me while the others continued their debate over portal travels. "Do you realise you have been away from Arogath for six weeks? This is serious. We're jumping around from realm to realm—timeline to timeline—as if it's no big deal."

Six weeks? I'd been here a matter of a few days. "I don't have a choice, and that's what I've been trying to tell you. What I'm dealing with here— what all these soldiers are dealing with—is serious. They don't have magic like you and me. We are their hope."

"Let's all calm down. We will gather in the morning to discuss our next steps," Dmitri said, interrupting me and Sofia's separate conversation. "Can we trust that you will help us?"

"I will help you." Sofia eyed Dmitri who sat,

dark and brooding, in his chair. Her gaze lingered for a moment too long. I nudged her, and she snapped back to me. "What?"

My stomach rumbled. "Shall we get some dinner?"

One of the tables to the left crashed into the stone floor, sending the chessboard and pieces flying across the room. Reuben yelped as he fell to his knees. His opponent grabbed him, then cradled him into his arms.

"Reuben!" Lilith hurried to Reuben's side, weaving through the tables, then clutched his hand. "What's wrong?"

"M-my chest," he gasped. He slipped into unconsciousness and slumped onto the floor.

"What's happened?" Seth demanded as she held his wrist between her fingers, checking his pulse.

"I don't know!" She propped his limp body against her lap. "Can someone bring me a warm compress, please? Anything to help him wake." She fanned his face by flapping her hands in front of him. "He was fine…the green magic…it must be that. Is anyone else injured? Suffering from a tight chest?" When the soldiers replied with shaking heads, she beckoned to one of them. "Take Reuben to his chamber to rest."

"I'll take him now." Seth reached for Reuben. Felix rushed forward to help his new acquaintance.

"No, Dmitri is right—we don't know what damages the portal will cause to you, to all of you." Lilith sighed as two soldiers hurried their master out of the room. "Go. Eat and rest. You can see him tomorrow, and we will find a way to help him."

# Chapter Six

I left Sofia to wander the Garden of Peace with Dmitri while I headed back to my room with Felix. I hadn't questioned Sofia on the way she'd traded flirtatious glances with Dmitri, but I did want to know more about that later. For now, I was desperate to be alone with Felix, to share my pain with him. He was the only person in this world who could truly understand what I'd gone through, because it had happened to him too.

Even though I'd been desperate to escape the Citadel, having Felix with me here, in Swynvale, eased some of the grief weighing down my chest. While it would never leave me—I was pretty sure my grief would be etched into my mind and soul for the rest of my existence—bearing the weight of it with him made it easier.

As soon as the door was closed behind us, he drew me against his chest. I buried my head against him, inhaling his warm cinnamon scent. There was a sense of urgency in the way he touched me, the way his hands roamed the length of my back, up to my neck. And I needed him too.

There was a truth between us, in the way we held each other as if we might fall from the earth itself. Our touches were our bridge back to one another, while simultaneously being our escape. A few moments of pleasure instead of pain.

So when his lips crashed down upon mine, I didn't pull back. Instead, I welcomed his tongue against mine in its hungry exploration.

The headiness of the kiss overwhelmed me, and my body turned molten. His hands roamed my body, sliding up my sides, one to cup my breast, and the other to slither into my hair.

I wanted him closer, to be one with him in a way that mended both of our broken souls, even if temporarily. But an intrusive thought speared my mind.

"Felix," I breathed. "Maybe we should wait. The others—they need our help. What happened to Reuben is awful."

He leaned back and studied me with a serious gaze. "I know, and we *will* help them, but right now, everyone is going to bed or doing their own thing for the evening. There's nothing we can do until the morning."

## Severance of Minds

My mind was at war with itself. He was right—there *was* nothing I could do, and we wouldn't be able to set a plan in motion until the following day. But staying awake half the night tangled up with Felix wouldn't exactly help, either.

I rested my forehead against his, letting my heart rate calm and my breathing level. Flattening my hands against his shirt, I said, "Hold me tonight."

The corners of his lips tilted into a smile, then he placed a warm kiss on my forehead and smoothed my hair with his fingers. "I'll do anything you want, Evalyn. Whatever will make you happy again. So long as we do it together."

I blinked back the burning sensation in my eyes, for there was a rawness—an ache to his voice—and I would stop at nothing to ensure his happiness too.

So he took me over to the bed, and with the lightest of touches, helped me out of my clothes until I stood in nothing but my undergarments. In swift movements, he ripped off his own shirt and shuffled out of his breeches, then he threw back the covers.

Climbing onto the mattress, he tucked me against him, my head resting against his chest, the steady sound of heart lulling me into a state of peace. And it was enough, for now, to chase the demons away.

———⌣———

Birdsong filtering through the ajar window woke me some time past dawn. My leg was thrown over Felix's, and my arm draped across his chest, fingers against the fine dark hairs.

I traced light circles against his skin, and he stirred. With a groan, he drew me tight against him and buried his head in the hollow of my neck.

"I refuse to get up yet," he grumbled, voice muffled by my hair

I stifled a laugh, feeling no immediate desire to detangle myself from him, either. But a knock on the door had me groaning and throwing on a robe. "Who is it?"

"It's me." Sofia's sing-song voice carried through the heavy wooden door.

With a quick glance over my shoulder to ensure Felix had drawn the covers over his body, I cracked the door open and welcomed her inside.

"Apologies for the intrusion." Sofia's gaze briefly flicked between me and Felix before returning back to me. Crossing the room, she plopped into the armchair beside the dresser. Stray pieces of silver hair hung around her face, the rest tied into a bun.

Daylight streamed in through the gap between the thin curtains, illuminating the small dust particles floating in the air.

"It's probably a good thing you came." My cheeks warmed, but I cleared my throat. "I wanted to thank you again—it must be hard for you to trust these people."

"I don't," she admitted. "I trust *you*."

"What's it like? Back home?" Curiosity got the better of me. Not only that but abandoning my kingdom in the face of overwhelming grief filled me with shame. My people needed me, and I vowed to myself that I would go back when the time was right, when *I* could make things right. "I heard the others talking about peace in the realm. It seems like an unfathomable reality."

"A relative peace *has* been found in Arogath although the fear of the Orcs regaining power and a desire of dominating the Territories will always remain." Felix shifted into a seated position on the mattress, lifting the blankets to cover most of his exposed abdomen. "It's not the same without you, Evalyn. We need you—the Territories need you. I'll speak freely because I love you. This is someone else's war you're getting involved in."

"He's right," Sofia added. "I understand why you're here—what you want to achieve—but it's dangerous staying here for too long. We don't know the affects it'll have, as I've mentioned. Plus, the peace we speak of in Arogath is tentative, and with Makdou still on the loose, I doubt it'll take much to disturb it."

"It's all connected." I motioned with my hands to get the point across. "Makdou, the Orcs of Swynvale. Everything. I can't return home until I understand how powerful she has become. If she's behind the green magic here, then I'm not strong enough to defeat her, and my people deserve a real solution."

Sofia rose, brushing herself down. "I promised I would help you, and I will. Perhaps it's a good thing Felix came through the portal. You can heal together."

"I like the sound of that," he said with a note of

joy in his voice.

I peered at him over my shoulder, and the look of pure love in his eyes made my heart burst. "Me too."

"While we're here, maybe there's something I can do to help. I can enquire with Seth about a position as a soldier. Put my skills to good use. The gods know I could use a distraction," he said, although his burning gaze lingered on the hem of my robe.

I ignored the mentions of the gods and instead, chose to focus on the positivity in his voice. Sitting beside him on the bed, I leaned my head on his shoulder and absorbed his warmth, his familiar and homely scent. Everything I'd loved about him. I couldn't fight it. I didn't *want* to fight it.

"Good idea," Sofia broke in. "He knows what he's doing and having another sword-wielding soldier around won't hurt. We need all the muscle we can get when it comes to fighting Orcs."

We should see the others and figure out a way to help Reuben. The quicker we can get this done, the quicker we can go home. I hope we don't miss too much time in Arogath. Meet you outside in ten minutes?"

I nodded, already making my way over to the fresh stack of clothes that had been brought by the servants the previous night.

Sofia left the room as I chucked a clean pair of breeches and shirt to Felix. "You'll find armour and weaponry in the Armoury. I'll take you there before we meet the others, but we'll have to be quick—I doubt they'll want to waste much time."

Felix shifted to the edge of the mattress, then made quick work of getting dressed. "I've been wondering: how did Lilith know about me?"

"There's a scroll. It contains everything I've ever done. Reuben believes I could've changed the prophecy when I entered Elysium, which is why I'm here now."

"Do you trust him?" He shoved his feet into his boots, then rose.

"Yes. I have no reason not to."

"Not yet," he said with a hint of caution in his tone. Despite the hardness of his voice, his touch remained gentle as he tucked my hair behind my ear.

I leaned into his touch, relishing the warmth that spread from his fingers and through my cheek. "Come on. We should go."

With a swift nod, he clasped my hand, and we met Sofia.

---

Seth accepted Felix's offer to join The League, and he was given a set of leather armour, which did wonderful things to his physique, accentuating the corded muscles in his arms and thighs.

Sofia snapped her fingers. "You're gawking."

I blinked several times, and Felix chuckled.

"Lilith will be gathering the soldiers any minute now." Seth finished strapping his swords to his back, then headed for the door, leading out of the Armoury. "We should make a move."

The rest of us set about a quick pace, following Seth to the hall.

"The green magic has infected Reuben," Lilith called across the main hall as the soldiers filed in through the doorway. "It is taking his energy, and he grows weaker."

"Does anyone have suggestions on how to help him?" Dmitri asked, standing tall beside Lilith as Seth weaved through the parting crowd to take his position beside them.

"This is the first time we've seen anybody infected by this parasitical magic, so we have no idea what effects it will have on him, and how much time Reuben has before…" Lilith shook her head. "I won't even utter the words aloud, as I refuse to let them become reality."

"How can you be sure it was magic?" I weaved my way between soldiers until I found a spot near the front, Felix and Sofia by my side.

"It is all we can think of," Lilith said. "It *must* have something to do with the magic at Firsthold."

"If so, wouldn't others be affected?" I tilted my head to the side, feeling the weight of a dozen stares on me.

"I'm not sure," she said, voice thin and flat. "He is in his chamber, sleeping, and hasn't woken once."

"Is there something you can do?" I cast a glance over my shoulder at Sofia.

She was a High Priestess, a form of Mage who had an extraordinary ability to heal others. Perhaps she knew something that could help Reuben.

She brought her bottom lip between her teeth

before speaking, "I've never healed one infected by this form of magic, let alone in a different realm. My magic might have a different strength, or it may not work at all. It will be unpredictable."

"It's worth a try, right?" I arched a brow. "I know you don't know these people, but I need to help them. Especially considering everything my own people went through—if I can prevent other innocent people from being killed, tortured, or tormented by the Orcs or Makdou, then I will."

"I'll try." She sighed. "On one condition. When this is done, promise me you will come home."

I did need to go home. If there was any connection between the portal in Swynvale and Makdou back in Arogath, then destroying it would weaken her connection to the Orcs of this realm. Felix placed a hand on the small of my back. An act of reassurance.

Composing myself, I allowed myself a moment to contemplate her requirements. "Deal."

Why was Makdou forming alliances with the Orcs of Swynvale? She despised Orcs. "Do you think Makdou is using the Crimson Kiss as control over the Orcs?"

"It's possible," Sofia said, "and a terrifying idea." She stepped closer to Lilith, leaning towards her ear. "I may be able to help."

Lilith gave a cautious nod. "Go on."

"I'm a Mage, like Evalyn," Sofia said in her soft, velvety voice. "I have the ability to heal many wounds, even grave ones."

Her words caused the crowd to mutter amongst themselves.

Lilith raised a hand to silence them. "Please continue," she said with a glint of hope in her eyes.

"I healed Evalyn's mother—Mya—Eric, and Felix of grave wounds after our last battle with the Dark Triads of our world," Sofia said. "I've succeeded many times with my healing magic."

"How can we trust you?" Dmitri pierced her with a hard stare

"What she says is true." I smiled. "She is willing to try with Reuben."

He frowned.

I crossed the space between us, then placed my hand on his arm. "She is a good person."

My words seemed to reassure him, for the thick line between his brows softened.

"I must warn you," Sofia said. The candlelight created shadows under her cheekbones, making her look more Elven than Mage. "While I've a great deal of experience, I can't be certain I'll be able to stop whatever this magic is."

"I have a theory—it is Mage magic." I kept my gaze on Dmitri. "Makdou is the *only* Dark Mage we know of who can perform the Crimson Kiss spell. She may be using the *same* spell to control the Orcs of Swynvale. This could explain the portal and the channelled magic."

Sofia's gaze darted to me, and her eyes widened.

The Crimson Kiss and Makdou's power were already common knowledge—even the soldiers knew of the scroll and what she'd done to me.

"Evalyn, this isn't the place," Sofia warned. "You have no proof to support what you're claiming."

"Makdou used the Crimson Kiss spell to control my behaviour and murder my child." I ignored her and turned to face the crowd. "If she was able to open a portal to Swynvale like I was, then she may be using the same spell to control the Orcs here."

Murmurs rose from the crowd. This was my time to gain their trust. "If I'm right, which I'm certain I am, Makdou is a true threat to your realm as much as she is to mine. We need to make every effort to stop her."

I glanced at Sofia who didn't meet my gaze. Did she believe me?

"How do you suggest we break the connection between the Orcs and Makdou?" Dmitri asked.

"There's one option." Breath caught in my throat, and my heartrate soared. Adrenaline. "We kill her."

"Let me try to save your friend first." Sofia rested her hand on my arm.

"You know I'm right about this. I thought you'd understand."

"Killing her will solve everything?" She crossed her arms.

"We'll talk about this later." I waved my hand. "Not here."

"Will you come with me to assess Reuben?" Lilith asked Sofia. "The rest of you are dismissed until we have decided on a course of action."

"Of course," Sofia said, as the other soldiers filed past her. "Evalyn, are you coming?"

"Yes," I said, then turned my attention to Felix. "I shouldn't be too long, but maybe spend the time getting familiar with the way the soldiers fight around here—their tactics, how they work as a unit."

"I'll take him for a spar." Seth clapped Felix on the back. "See if he can win against me or Dmitri."

"Oh, I'll certainly try." Felix grinned.

I gave his hand a quick squeeze before falling into step with Lilith and Sofia as they made way for Reuben's room.

He lay unconscious on the bed with a thin layer of sweat forming across his forehead. Somebody had drawn the covers to his chin. A deep shade of red tinged his cheeks, either from fever or the heat emanating from the fire crackling in the hearth.

Unlike his fine jewelled chair, his chamber furniture was scarce. A wardrobe rested against the left wall opposite the window and a dressing table sat beneath the windowsill with vials of ointments and potions resting on the surface.

I crossed the room and picked up the vials— attempts to heal his ailment, no doubt.

"I used those vials twice through the night, but I'm not sure if they had any affect or not," Lilith said.

If Sofia could destroy a portal, then she could prolong Reuben's life.

Lilith clutched Reuben's still hand and she locked her jaw. Her eyes glistened with tears, but they didn't fall.

"He looks like he's sleeping. He doesn't seem to be in pain." I left the vials on the dressing table and went to the foot of the bed.

Lilith shook her head. "The green magic is doing *something* to him. It's not causing any symptoms other than an elevated temperature, but I cannot rouse him."

"How did the green magic get inside him?" Sofia stepped closer to assess Reuben. She drew the sheets, then inspected his skin—an olive colour with a hint of pink. "His blood seems to be travelling around the body fine. There are no gaping wounds or festering rashes."

"I have no idea." Lilith shrugged. "He was fine when we walked back from Firsthold. He started his game of chess and…fell to the ground—you saw it. He hasn't woken up. We searched the grounds this morning to see if there was any trace of invaders or clues of how he'd fallen into his slumber, but nothing."

"Curious." Sofia placed the back of her hand on his forehead. "Did he eat or drink anything when he got back here?"

"What are you implying?" Lilith asked, a sharpness to her voice. "You think one of us had something to do with this?"

"She isn't implying anything," I said. "She is doing an assessment."

Lilith gave a curt nod. "Let's be quick about it."

Closing her eyes, Sofia raised her hands above Reuben's body. She muttered foreign words, her lips moving in the form of a spell, while I propped up his pillows and tucked in his blankets to keep him warm.

Still holding Reuben's hand, Lilith observed the spell until Sofia stepped back from the bed.

A faint, gold glow materialised from Sofia's palms and cascaded down and infused with

Reuben's body. She kept her eyes closed until the light disconnected from her palms and the spell came to an end. "I've performed a healing charm that will dull any internal pain or discomfort he may be experiencing. It will keep him hydrated and will attempt to draw the dark magic out of him," she said. "However, I can't be sure it will awaken him from his slumber or cure him completely."

"Thank you," Lilith whispered, "for helping us when you owe us nothing and we have nothing to give to you in return."

"My queen asked this of me, and I accepted," Sofia said. "I'm glad to help where I can."

"We should let him rest. We have a portal to close." Lilith opened the chamber door for us.

"Indeed, we do." I tucked my hand in the nook of Sofia's arm, then strolled with her down the corridor as Lilith shut the door.

"I must apologise, my queen," Sofia replied. "I've doubted you and your purpose in Swynvale. You've done so much for your people, and I should've expected you to do the same for other innocent lives."

"You don't need to apologise, but I need your guidance." I pressed my lips into a thin line. "The thought of closing another portal is terrifying. How can we be sure I'm not lost to Elysium?"

Sofia patted my hand. "I'll be with you the whole time. We'll figure this out together."

# Chapter Seven

Later in the day, I grabbed a tray of bread and meat in the mess hall, then carried it over to a vacant table. I slid onto the chair as Felix strolled through the door. Briefly, he scanned the room until his gaze met mine. I waved him over and, after grabbing his own tray of food, he sat opposite me.

"Lilith is holding another meeting this evening to discuss our next steps for closing the portal in Firsthold," I said, then told him about the beams and the green magic.

He grimaced. "Orcs and magic are a formidable pair."

"Indeed." I stabbed a piece of meat with my fork, then popped it into my mouth.

Felix tucked into his own meal, then when he was done, he wiped his mouth with a napkin. "How are you feeling?"

I slowed my chewing, wondering how best to answer. If our relationship was going to survive, we needed to communicate, to deal with the grief together, and not shut each other out. "I'm okay, considering. I think it'll be a different matter entirely when I am back home—back where…it happened."

He stretched across the table and covered my hand with his. "I know. But you are never alone. Not with me. And not ever again."

Smiling, I entwined my fingers with his. "Neither are you. But enough about me—how are you coping with it?"

Peering out the window for a moment, he watched the birds fly from the branches of a nearby tree, then returned his gaze to mine. "It's hard some days. And the reality is, we will probably feel this way forever. It will never truly leave us, but I've thought about it, and I'm glad it won't. I *want* to remember it—our son. I want to think of him for every second of every day, as a reminder of why I get up and do what I can to protect those I love and those who need it the most.

"We will never be the same again—the version of us before our son's death is long gone. But we can use this pain to shape who we *will* become going forward. Be the leaders and protectors we need to be to ensure the good people of Arogath don't suffer the same fate."

I blinked through the tears that had formed in my eyes. His words were beautiful, capturing how I felt in its entirety. There was nothing I could say other than, "I love you. With every ounce of who I am, and that will never change. I hope you know that."

"I do." His gaze softened. "And you know I feel the same."

With a final squeeze of his hand, I rose from the table. "Come on. We should join the meeting."

We headed to the main hall where Lilith surveyed the crowd of silent soldiers. She cleared her throat. "I thank you all for your patience. This green, *foreign* magic isn't something to be taken lightly. If what Evalyn has said is true, then we are up against an enormous threat." She paused for a moment—the soldiers watching her with unwavering attention. "Firstly, we must escort Sofia and Evalyn to Firsthold, so they can close the portal."

Dmitri, who stood at the front of the crowd, beamed at her, and knelt on one knee. He thrust his sword in front of him. "For The League!"

The other soldiers followed suit, cheering the same words.

Warmth spread through me. Their loyalty reminded me of those who'd sworn their allegiance to me in Arogath, and the duty I had as their sovereign.

I smiled at Lilith. "May I address the soldiers?"

"Of course," she said.

Facing The League, I pushed my shoulders back. "I want to thank you for trusting and believing in me. While most of you know my life from the scroll, I am still a stranger to you. In front of you, I promise I will do everything in my power to help you before returning to my own world."

The soldiers placed their hands on their hearts and chanted in unison, "We swear our sword, shield, and life to The League. We pledge to protect each other, the vulnerable, and the unarmed. We promise to fight and spill our blood if need be."

I whispered the words to myself, now a part of something bigger, something whole. Flicking my gaze to Felix, pride radiated through me as he, too, spoke the vow.

---

An hour later, Lilith, Seth, and Dmitri rode their horses at the front of the travelling soldiers.

I patted my mare's neck gently before readjusting my grip on the reins. Felix and Sofia rode either side of me. Together, we passed the tied-up boat bobbing in the water.

Sofia gazed from the glistening lake to the snow-covered mountain tops. Her mouth opened as an eagle flew across the sky, its wings transitioning into purple as it soared by. "It's so beautiful here." She gasped. "I can sense it—the realm's magic. It's like a current."

"You get used to it." Dmitri chuckled, casting a glance over his shoulder at her.

She blushed and looked away.

Along the sunbaked road, yellow flowers bloomed, marking the path leading to the entrance of the Firsthold fort.

Orc corpses, covered in dried blood, decayed on the stone floors through the entrance. Their banners were torn and scorched from the soldiers' fire.

"Keep an eye out. Make sure the surviving civilians are locked inside the fort." Lilith dismounted.

The soldiers followed suit, then dispersed through doors and passageways between the buildings, market stalls, and destroyed vegetable patches. "I suspect the Orcs will come back as soon as we start tampering with this portal, if what you say is true, Evalyn."

"If they do come back and they *are* under the Crimson Kiss spell, they could be lethal," I warned.

She grimaced.

We neared the rear of the fort. The portal's ethereal surface shimmered.

Sofia pointed to the beams glowing the emerald light of foreign magic. "The anchors of the portal."

I nodded. "There was a large centre beam, right where this portal stands, before I opened it."

"This one isn't like the one we destroyed. If anything, this could be harder—the anchor is strengthening the portal." Sofia edged closer to the beams to inspect them.

"Rather you than I." Seth shrugged.

Lilith nudged him. "Let the ladies do their work in peace. They are doing us a service, after all."

Sofia faced me. "You must listen very carefully, Evalyn. If you reach Elysium again, fight to return to the living world. The more times you go there, the harder it'll be to find your way back."

"I will," I promised, my tone steady, measured.

There had been a time when I'd wished to stay in Elysium—I could've done so if I'd given myself over to the weightlessness of the afterlife, but I had a purpose—a duty to fulfil. I kept my chin high, and my muscles tightened in readiness.

"You can do this. I have faith in both of you," Dmitri said, and his gaze lingered on Sofia.

A deep rose tint returned to her cheeks.

"Don't worry, this will be done in no time," I said. If we could do it once, we could do it again. "For The League." I could honour the soldiers of Swynvale who'd fallen the previous day through those words. If I were to succeed, my actions would cement their trust. "For my friends, new and old."

The soldiers, including Felix, gathered around. Together, they'd ensure the civilians' welfare.

"Do you remember what to do?" Sofia said to me, her gaze unwavering. "You must let our magic intertwine, then we'll aim it at the portal."

Flattening my hands against my breeches, I nodded. The portal glowed and swirled, and its low hum rumbled through the fort.

"Don't let go." She clasped my hand.

My brows furrowed as I focused on creating a ball of red magic in my free hand. She, too, created her brilliant white magic. "Ready?"

"Ready."

I threw my light forward, urging it towards the portal. Sofia's spell intertwined with mine and formed a sturdy stream of white and red magic.

The power poured from me—the portal hissed and crackled, flickering in and out of existence as our spell fractured it.

My strength dwindled. With twitching muscles and blurred vision, I fought to continue.

"You're strong enough to do this again, Evalyn!" Sofia shouted over the loud-pitched squeal of magic. "Stay focused. You can do this."

Concentrating on her words of encouragement, I ignored my aching body and thrust my hands in front of me, forcing the red stream of light to shatter the portal. The anchor beams buckled, exploded, then evaporated. Although my sight darkened at the corners, I focused on the green hue of magic in the cracked ground. Slowly, it faded.

My legs gave way, and her hand slipped from mine.

"Are you all right?" She hoisted me from the stones. Her gaze scanned my body. Felix was at my side in an instant. As I brushed the specks of dust off my breeches, he unscrewed his cap from his flask and gave it to me.

"Thank you, both. I'm fine." I sipped the water. "I didn't see Elysium."

"We shouldn't be risking it at all." A muscle flared in Felix's neck as he gave Sofia a pointed look.

"She's just doing what I asked her to," I said. "And I'm doing what I must. Have faith that I can survive this."

"She's right." Sofia smiled. "It means you're getting stronger."

Despite Sofia's words of reassurance, Felix frowned. I rested my hand on his arm. "I promise I'm fine." Then I shifted my attention to Sofia. "I don't know if it has anything to do with this realm's natural magic, but I won't argue with it."

"What about you?" Dmitri asked Sofia as he ran his hand through his hair.

I stifled a laugh. "She's the stronger of us both."

"I'm fine." Her gaze flicked from him to the floor, then back again. "Thank you." She tucked a loose, silver curl behind her ear. Her face brightened as her gaze met his.

Allowing her a moment to adjust to her new attention, I turned to Lilith and Seth.

Lilith placed her hand on my arm. "I can't thank you enough for what you've both done here."

"One less string in Makdou's bow." I tilted the corner of my lips into a slight smile.

"We should head back. I'll check in on Reuben." She waved for us to follow her back to the horses, left to graze on the grass outside the fort's walls.

---

Back at the Temple, the soldiers dispersed to either the mess hall for their evening meal or the bathing rooms. Seth approached me, Sofia and Felix at my side.

"Are you all free for a moment? I thought I could show you the Garden of Peace," Seth said, stuffing his hands into his pockets.

"We're headed for dinner, but I can join you. Shall I meet you both afterwards?" I asked Sofia and Felix.

"Sure, I'll save you some stew." Felix smiled,

then slipped away with Sofia in tow.

Seth motioned to the courtyard outside. "Follow me. We tried our very best to heal those wounded by the green magic."

He led me through a stone archway and into the garden. White tulips and lavender were planted into flowerbeds beside yellow rose bushes. Dragonflies flew here and there, bees flitted through the flowers, and spider webs glinted in the light from the setting sun. A frog leapt from the slick rocks into the pond beside the flowers and crickets chirped in the grass. Shadows drifted across the garden as clouds moved overhead. Injured female soldiers lounged on stone benches around the garden.

He pointed to the pair of women who sat at a wooden table playing a game of chess. "See those two there? They're almost ready to return to their duty and serve."

The women laughed among themselves. One blurted her disapproval when the other made a move, which put her at risk of losing the game.

"I'm glad they have a safe place." I touched a blooming tulip, then bent to inhale its floral scent.

"Do you have somewhere like this where you're from?" Seth said. "In Arogath?"

"The Citadel gardens are beautiful, but there's something different about this place. Perhaps it's because it doesn't hold the same memories." I let go of the tulip.

He patted me on the shoulder. "Come on, let's get some food."

Once we'd eaten, I waited in the mess hall with

Felix and the other soldiers while Sofia accompanied Lilith to Reuben's chamber. A while later, they returned, beckoning us into the large hall where the maps were displayed. Lilith slipped into her position at the front of the room.

Moonlight gleamed in through the windows, its white glow mixing with the warm light of candles.

Sofia found me in the crowd.

"What's wrong?" I leaned close to her and whispered.

"It's not good." She shook her head.

Dmitri loitered close by, occasionally flicking his gaze to Sofia, although I wasn't sure she'd noticed.

"There's been no change to Reuben's condition," Lilith addressed the crowd. "Sofia's healing spell has stopped the fever and has continued to prevent any exterior deterioration from occurring, but we can't be certain no long-term effects could occur as a result of the magic."

"What do you suggest we do now?" one soldier asked. "The witch's magic doesn't seem to have done anything at all!"

"Do not insult our guest, Kirah," Lilith scolded. "Sofia has done all she can, and you all witnessed what they both accomplished at Firsthold earlier today."

Kirah, a bold-faced woman, scoffed.

Sofia glared at the female soldier. Dmitri casually stepped forward to block her view. He smiled at Sofia, and her tense shoulders relaxed.

"I will not tolerate any slander directed at our guests," Lilith said. "We should be focusing on finding a way to wake Reuben."

My eyes widened as I remembered his words.

*'There is a legend amongst our people that tells the story of a Great Mother Tree—a tree with extraordinary healing abilities. Such a treasure needed to be concealed from our enemies.'*

"There is something else which may help him." I cleared my throat, my body thrumming with anticipation. "The Great Mother Tree."

# Chapter Eight

"**D**oes such a thing exist?" Seth frowned. "Reuben sure loves to tell a legend or two, but there's no proof it's real."

"You speak of a myth whose existence has no legitimacy—it has never been discovered in history nor is there any evidence to suggest it does exist," Kirah said with a brash tone.

"The story of the Tree's powers has been told for hundreds of years," Sofia said, disregarding Kirah's comment. "It's something we should at least consider investigating."

"How do you know about it?" I raised an eyebrow at her.

"My research and training as a High Priestess led me to find the stories of its abilities to heal all ailments," she said.

Kirah crossed her arms, glancing from us to Lilith, perhaps looking for support. "You are going to need to provide proof."

"Reuben isn't the sort of person to talk of stories unless they have a deeper meaning. Something here could help him," Lilith said. "Even if it leads to a dead end, it's worth it."

"Why don't you tell us more?" Dmitri asked Sofia.

"I've been thinking about it a lot since I came through the portal into Swynvale yesterday," Sofia said. "There is something about the natural magic which makes me think it could be true—I don't know any other world to have such powerful, natural magic that has a form of its own and doesn't require Elemental beings."

I doubted she had travelled to other worlds to know for sure what natural magic occurred where. She'd spent many years as a slave in Southkeep before making a home with Aneirin in the underground network across the Great Sea. She relied on ancient scriptures and her Mage intuition.

Her expression remained neutral as she continued in a cool tone, "I don't know Reuben and his life has no bearing on mine, but I know Evalyn. She's connected to this world now—I care a great deal about her, and I will do whatever it takes to protect her and those she cares about."

I smiled, her loyalty warming me.

"Lake Delendil of Arogath has the ability to

absorb deceased bodies and allow their souls to cross into Elysium." My voice echoed across the crowd. Sofia glanced at me. "There are magical beings who live in Arogath. Mystical events continue to surprise me. Look around you— Swynvale is filled with natural magic—a power that has a mind of its own. The existence of the Tree is plausible."

She beamed. "Evalyn and I *know* magic. It's worth the time trying to find it. Could you imagine what it would do for your people if we did find it? Think of all the lives you could save."

Lilith placed her fingers to her chin. "It is a risk, but I cannot deny it would be life-changing for us. For Reuben, and for the other soldiers who were blasted by the magic. The Great Mother Tree could offer a permanent solution—a cure."

"Is there somewhere in this realm where the natural magic is at its strongest?" I asked.

Felix remained a strong and sturdy presence at my side. "That's a good point," he said. "In Arogath, the natural magic took its form in Elemental beings at the Galae Pools, Highland Trees, and the Vesuvius Caves. Could the same principle apply to this realm?"

"Reuben once told me the natural magic flows east, so I'm assuming it is east of here..." Lilith responded with a shrug. "But you can't travel alone, not in the middle of a war."

"I'll come," Dmitri said. "Our friend—the very man who has housed us for many years—lies in what could be his deathbed, and we are standing here debating. Even if we search for the Tree and we find nothing, at least we tried. He would be proud."

"His pride isn't enough," she said. "We won't be able to send all our soldiers on this mission. Some must stay at the Temple to protect it and the nearby settlements from Orcs, should they invade again."

"Hey, Sofia." I faced her. "We could do a location spell."

"It could work." She raised a finger at the idea.

"Everyone, move back," Lilith ordered.

The soldiers did as they were bid, forming a circle in the middle of the room.

Seth wandered to a table pushed to the far side of the hall, then dragged it into the centre. The table displayed a large map of Swynvale, with the Temple of Peace in the mountains on the left side of the map. He pointed eastwards, where several different forts were located, amongst ranges of mountains and lakes.

"Swynvale isn't like Arogath—the Orcs aren't separated from us." He placed his finger on one of the red 'X' marks hovering above the forts. "Over the last few years, we have patrolled these areas. All of them house Orcs."

Felix studied the map. "You know these lands. Show us the safest route—the less we run into the Orcs, the better. We can't draw attention to ourselves."

"There's plenty of woodland that conceals the path we'll be riding along. And even when we're in the open, it won't be for long. We'll rest at allied forts where possible," Lilith said.

"Yes." Felix nodded. "I suggest we limit the

number of fires we light on those nights. Whoever goes out to hunt will go in groups. No one will be left alone. Have another team of soldiers who'll take watch while the rest of us sleep, then rotate who's on shift. Keep eyes and ears out for Orcs at all times."

"Agreed." Lilith smiled.

"Ready?" Sofia took my hands and gave me a nod of reassurance before we uttered the enchantment in the foreign tongue of the Noble Ones.

We'd used the same spell in Arogath to locate the Dark Mages' portal and it'd worked the first time. I hoped, with every fibre of my being, we'd have no issues with it this time.

Would a spell linked to Arogath work in a different realm altogether? I wasn't too sure.

The spell continued, the foreign words rolling off my tongue and shaping into a soft, elegant tone. My magic flowed through my veins, tingling my body, and raising the hairs on the back of my neck. The spell halted, the magic snapped, and our link broke.

She stared at me, open-mouthed. "What in the realm just happened?"

"It didn't work." I huffed. "Although, I can't say I'm surprised—it's a different realm. Maybe some of our spells don't work here."

"I don't think that's the case." Frowning, she placed her fingers on her chin. "Something's blocking our location spell, perhaps a counter charm?"

I drew a blank. "Can you elaborate?"

"This Tree has been a legend for hundreds of years, right? If it truly possesses the qualities we believe it to, then maybe someone doesn't want us to find it. They'd want to keep it protected," she said.

"Can you undo the counter charm?" Lilith asked. "This really is our only option. I don't know how else we'll save Reuben."

"I can, but it requires a lot of energy," Sofia said. "I'll need to rest after undoing it before Evalyn and I retry the location spell."

"Of course," Lilith said politely.

"Can I help?" If I could do anything to lift some of the pressure currently resting on Sofia's shoulders, I would.

"In fact, you can," she said. "Close your eyes, focus on the words I say, and let your magic bond with mine."

"Okay." I obliged, clasping her smooth, soft palms.

Against closed eyelids, I focused on her foreign words—a spell I didn't recognise, although some of the sounds were familiar. A tendril of warmth sprouted from my chest, gradually enveloping me. It anchored me to Sofia, our magic woven together like fine threads. The connection went taut, strained, and the warmth turned to raging heat. Beads of sweat formed on my hairline.

Moments later, she let go, staggering back. Dmitri caught her by the arm and steadied her.

"Thank you." She glanced at him, the lit candles highlighting the straight bridge of her nose.

"Come on, sit down." I guided her to a nearby

chair, easing her into it. "Shall I fetch you some water or food?"

She leaned back. "No…I'll be okay. I need to keep still for a moment."

"Why has it affected you more than me?" I knelt in front of her and stroked her arm.

"The spell takes more of my magic," she said in a sleepy voice. "Magic required to reverse powerful spells will latch itself onto the strongest host, which is me." She sucked in deep, raspy breaths.

"Don't say anymore." I grabbed her a cushion from a bench at the back of the hall, then propped it behind her back. "Rest."

I stayed with her while she slept for a few hours. Felix had left to spar with some of the soldiers after I'd reassured him that we'd be fine on our own.

When Sofia stirred, she rubbed her eyes and stretched. Dmitri had brought her a tray of food, leaving it on a wooden table beside her. He'd peered into the room every now and then, to which I replied with the same reassurance I'd given Felix.

Sofia tucked into her stew, mopped up the last drops with a chunk of bread, then set the bowl aside. "Right. I'm ready to try this again." When Dmitri popped his head around the door, she motioned to him. "Get Lilith, please."

He nodded, disappearing in a flash.

"Are you sure?" I helped her out of the chair.

Sofia straightened, stretching her arms. "Yes. You know how to do this."

When Lilith and Dmitri returned, I connected hands with Sofia. Magic buzzed through me, and our mind's eyes became one, searching for the

Great Mother Tree. The vision blurred as it whizzed around the world in a haze, trying to locate the Tree. The spell froze and hovered at times when it thought it had found the Tree, then changed direction and continued its speedy search around the world.

After a few tense moments of following the vision through valleys and settlements, across lakes and fields, we halted in a large stone settlement built beside a jagged cliffside next to the ocean. Beyond the settlement walls, grasslands stretched for miles.

Vines climbed their way around the yellow bricks and towards the peaks of the towers. Humans weaved their way through the busy streets, and armed soldiers guarded the gated entrances.

The vision flickered to the far end of the edifice where the grounds stretched out, and before the walls were reached, a large and beautiful tree stood as tall as the towers. Large peach-coloured tendrils hung from the branches, and the sight of it alone brought a warm sensation to my stomach.

The vision disappeared, and with wide eyes, Sofia looked at me. We'd never been to this place before, but within the sights of the spell, it was as if we'd been there a thousand times.

"Meridian." The settlement's name rolled from the tip of my tongue, although I'd never heard of it before. The spell had given me the answer.

"The Tree exists?" Lilith gasped. "Truly?"

"Yes," Sofia answered. "Have you been there before? It's heavily guarded, as you would imagine."

After her initial amazement subsided, Lilith frowned. "You must be right about the counter charm. Seeing as the Tree exists in Meridian, it would've been marked on the map and the myth would've been proven long ago when the civilians first settled there."

"Reuben must've been right about Felix's ancestors hiding the Tree from plain sight." I jerked my hand up.

"Wait, what?" Sofia asked, baffled.

"I'll explain another time." I waved the matter away.

"Fine, but I want to hear all about it. At least we can plan our journey. We have hope of saving your friend, and the other soldiers too," she said in a gentle tone.

"Agreed," Lilith said. "We don't know how much time Reuben has left, nor do we know what affects the green magic is having on his physical and mental self. Meridian is as far east as you can get before reaching the sea, and it would take two weeks to get there at best. We might've found the tree, but we still need to consider a way to break the spell that's concealing it from the human eye. Taking Reuben with us will only slow us down. *If* we can make it to the Tree and reveal it, we'll have to find a way to secure some samples. Bring them back to cure Reuben and the others. I'm going to sit with Reuben. Are you coming too, Seth?"

"Yes, I'll be right there. Thank you for your help—we do appreciate it." He nodded to Sofia and me, then left with Lilith.

The soldiers dispersed from the hall. Sofia and I

were alone.

She placed her fingers to her lips and stifled an astonished laugh. "I can't believe it's real. I tried the location spell many times in Arogath to find it. Of course, it didn't work because the Tree is in *this* realm."

"Do you have any suggestions on how to lift a concealing charm?" My voice echoed in the empty room. "I've not practised any myself."

"Yes, I know a few counters," she said, "but I've never tried them on a concealing spell that's been standing for possibly a millennium."

"You're certain there's no other way?"

"Not as far as I'm aware, no. I've tried my High Priestess healing abilities—nothing's working." Sofia shrugged. "I think we should go home first and explain what's happening. I'm going to be here longer than expected."

"I can't go back, not yet anyway," I said. "I've promised you I'll return, and I will, but I can't go back to our friends, and my people, just to leave them all over again."

"Fine." She embraced me. "We have each other for now, and that'll be enough."

# Chapter Nine

**B**ack in our chamber, Felix drew the curtains. Then he turned to face me as I leaned against the closed door. His gaze wandered along my neckline, up to my lips, then finally, he met my own gaze.

He drew his bottom lip between his teeth in what I could only determine was hesitation. And I understood why—it had been so long since we'd been together in the way we both needed so desperately. The last time, we'd conceived our son, and now, after months of separation, grief, and heartache, we found ourselves alone. Such privacy made my heart pound and my fingers tremble.

Closing the space between us, he traced his

fingers over my cheek with such tenderness, I could've burst with love for him.

The soft glow of evening night filtered through the gap between the curtains. Even the gentle hum of crickets outside the window seemed to disappear, for all I could hear was my rhythmic breathing syncing with his.

Leaning in, he captured my lips in a tender kiss, and without hesitation, I cradled his face in my hands. The slight stubble on his jawline tickled my palms.

Energy built inside me, but not like the wild beast thrashing to be released like it had before. No, my magic *purred* beneath each of his touches.

The kiss deepened, and my lips parted, welcoming his tongue against mine in a gentle, almost tentative exploration. He snaked his hand into my hair, holding the back of my neck, and my skin tingled.

Arching my back, I leaned into him and tilted my head to the side, giving him access to my neck. His lips left a warm trail on my flesh as he worked kisses down the column of my throat, to the slice of my collarbone poking through the hem of my shirt.

His hands slipped beneath the bottom of the fabric, roaming the planes of my back. With splayed fingers, he drew our bodies flush, and my core tightened.

A low moan bubbled up my throat as warmth spread through me, making each of my nerve endings sing. His movements were slow, gentle, yet excruciatingly precise. My body was on fire, but I would happily burn for him.

"Felix," I whispered, dipping my fingers into the corded muscles of his shoulders, for fear my knees might give out beneath me.

"Yes?" His voice vibrated against my skin as he nipped the tender hollow between my neck and shoulder.

"This gentleness—I can't take it." I trembled against him. "Despite what we've been through, I won't break. Don't treat me as if I will."

He drew back, a frown between his brows, and his gaze searched mine. "I know you won't break. If anything, when you're with me, I want you to feel like you're invincible." He took my hand in his and placed it over his steadily beating heart. "Together, we get to find ourselves again, despite all that we have lost. Because of you, my heart still has a reason to beat. I cannot bear to breathe the air that you do not inhale. When I take you in my arms, it is akin to holding the entire *world* in my hands. You're everything I want and more, and the last thing I want you to feel is that I'm treating you like some fragile doll."

I tilted my chin higher, heat flaming in my cheeks and spreading through every crevice of my body. "Then show me."

He spun me around, and I gasped. In painfully slow movements, he ran his hands up the flat surface of my abdomen, then cupped my breasts. The friction of my undergarments against my nipples had me tipping my head back against his chest. I closed my eyes and focused on nothing but him.

"Stay still," he whispered in my ear as he hooked

his fingers in the waistband of my breeches and undergarments, then drew them down the length of my legs. "Don't move a muscle. Promise."

"I promise," I breathed, fighting against the urge to squirm beneath his touch.

When he rose to his full height, he pressed his chest against my back, giving me support as he hooked my left thigh with his hand and lifted it.

Cool air nipped at my most sensitive part, but the chill was quickly chased away by his fingers working against me. I closed my eyes and swallowed my rising moan.

He raised my thigh higher, spreading me for him as he drove his fingers inside me. I bit down on my lip, suppressing my cries of pleasure. With my weight distributed between my one foot and him, I lost all sense of place. My body *floated*, flying higher and higher with each thrust of his fingers.

"Felix," was all I managed to say, my mind foggy as I chased my release.

But he withdrew, and I dug my fingers into his wrist, guiding him back.

Chuckling, he pressed lazy kisses on the nape of my neck, then bit the shell of my ear.

"*Felix,*" I said again, this time more insistent.

"Tell me what you want." He tickled my thigh, drawing closer to where I wanted him the most.

"I want you to touch me." I trembled. "I want you to make me feel *alive.*"

"I would happily do that, even if it was the last thing I did," he said.

My answer seemed to satisfy him as he worked his fingers against me, building in speed, sending me hurtling towards the edge, and the release I so desperately needed.

"Out there, to the rest of the world, you might be a queen, a saviour, but in here, you're *mine*." His voice was gravelly and commanding. "Now come for me."

And I shattered against his hand, my body vibrating and quivering. There was something seriously hot about the way he'd spoken to me, and it made me want to please him in any way that I could. But I wanted him to tell me this time.

I turned to face him, then kissed him, deep and slowly. When I leaned back, I said, "I like it when you talk to me like that. With you, I can be whoever I want, *do* whatever I want."

His eyes burned with a predatory hunger. "Get on your knees."

So I did.

Tilting my head back to fix my gaze on his, I drew my shirt over my head, then reached behind my back and undid the laces of my corset bodice. It took me a while, but he cupped my cheek with his palm and stroked my skin.

When I was done, I tossed the last of my clothing aside, then batted my lashes.

"Gods," he muttered, slithering his hand through her hair. "You are the most beautiful woman I have ever seen." His gaze travelled down my body before returning to my face.

"You have finally gotten me on my knees, Felix," I said innocently. "Whatever shall I do down here?"

"Oh, I think you know," he said playfully as he

unbuttoned his breeches. He released his hard length, stroking it with his hand.

"Say it," I said with deviance, which sent a thrill shooting through me.

"I want you to take me in your mouth." He ran his thumb over my bottom lip.

Licking my lips, I wrapped my hand around his length, and gave him one last look from beneath my lashes before running my tongue over the tip. His fingers flexed in my hair in response, but his touch remained gentle.

"Don't look away," he said with what I suspected was the last of his restraint.

My body coiled itself into knots as I took him into my mouth, driving him deeper. He tipped his head back and groaned.

I flicked my tongue against his tip as I sucked, picking up momentum. His hand wound around my hair, gently urging me onwards. All the while, his dark, hungry gaze remained fixed on mine.

Knowing full well what would drive him crazy, I reached between my legs and slid my fingers against my aching spot. I groaned around his hardness, sending vibrations through him, and he trembled.

"Gods *damn it*," he growled. His grip tightened on my hair, and he drove into my mouth, deeper and faster. As his own speed mounted, I did the same, spurring us both towards release.

I grazed my teeth against him, and he erupted with a deep growl. Another wave of ecstasy crashed through me, and I trembled as he pumped into my mouth a final time. Each of his breaths were loud and ragged, as he lowered to the floor in front of me. We held on to each other, waiting for our heart rates to steady.

"I think my heart just exploded out of my chest." He grinned, cupping my head in his hands.

I burst out laughing, for the first time in as long as I could remember. And it felt good.

---

The next morning, Felix helped the soldiers prepare the carriages for departure, loading them with food, water, and spare swords and shields for the long journey ahead. An additional string of carriage horses was readied and brought along, to swap with the ones in harness when they tired. A blacksmith joined the company in case one should throw a shoe, or a wheel broke on the road.

I filtered through the crowd in the courtyard where Lilith dished out further orders. "Don't forget furs—the nights will be cold, and we should expect to be sleeping under the stars if we aren't able to stay at taverns or forts. Ensure there's plenty of bandages and medicinal supplies packed, too, in case Sofia needs to leave us at any time."

Men obeyed, filing out in all directions.

"Is there anything I can do to help?" I asked. Dark, puffy circles had formed under her eyes.

"Everything is in order," she said. "Dmitri and Seth will be along shortly—they're gathering dried meats, fruits, and bread for us to take on the trip."

I drummed my fingers against my thighs, for

lack of a better thing to do. "Have you seen Sofia this morning?"

"She's with Dmitri." Lilith kept a straight face.

Silence hung between us.

"Right then." I turned to leave. If Lilith wouldn't delegate a job for me to do, I'd help the soldiers gather any last supplies for the journey east.

An hour later, the soldiers gathered outside the Temple with the fabric-covered coaches suspended between two horses. A coachman held the horses' reins, ready for the impending departure.

Seth climbed into the first carriage, Lilith sliding in afterwards.

She poked her head out of the window. "You may use the rear carriage, Evalyn. Have Felix join you for company. Dmitri, will you be riding with us?" She glanced at him as he double-checked the supplies were fastened securely in the coach opposite.

"Uh." He ran a hand through his hair. "I'll meet you there."

"Suit yourself. The men with us will occupy the last two carriages," Lilith said. "We shall meet you at Langhurst."

The coachman tugged on the horses' reins, and the wooden wheels rolled along the path, sending small stones shooting into the air.

Langhurst? Perhaps this would be our place to camp for the night.

"We best get a move on," Dmitri said.

Inside the coach, I eased onto the bench beside Felix. He drew me against his side, draping an arm around me. His cinnamon scent filled my nose and reminded me of home.

Sofia and Dmitri hoisted themselves into the carriage, then plopped onto the opposite bench.

Dmitri thumped the wooden structure, then the coachman clicked his tongue, and the carriage jolted along the path, leaving the Temple behind.

Little conversation was exchanged in the first hour of the journey, although Dmitri and Sofia edged closer together. They glanced at each other—her face brightened, and he returned a smile. His hand lay on the bench between them, his fingers pointed towards her leg.

I wasn't entirely sure what was going on between them—if anything—other than my own suspicions, based on small, yet somewhat, intimate acts shared.

If something truly *was* developing between them, ought I say something to Sofia? We would leave Swynvale one day, and Dmitri behind with it, alongside any possible future they may have. My thoughts spiralled further—how would he react?

He and Sofia lived two worlds apart, and I had no idea whether he would leave behind everything he knew to come with us—to our world. And selfishly, I hoped *she* wouldn't leave *me*. I needed her. Her friendship and her talents.

Shaking my head, I rid myself of my speculations. If such an eventuality should happen, I'd be there for her.

"Evalyn?" she said, tearing me from my internal monologue. "Are you all right? You're frowning."

I glanced at her, smiled, and absent-mindedly swept strands of hair out of my eyes. Felix's steady, rhythmic breathing as he dozed was a comfort beside me. "I'm fine, I…got lost in thought."

"Have you heard of Langhurst before?" she asked.

"No." Although grateful for the change of topic, I couldn't ignore the pang of worry inside me. Everything about this place, aside from the Temple, was unfamiliar. "We'll stick together."

"Always." Her words held an unwavering certainty.

Dmitri placed his hand on her knee, keeping a neutral expression about the face, perhaps to not alarm her.

She peered at me from the corner of her eyes— her lips parted. I nodded with encouragement, and she relaxed back against the bench rest.

The carriage rocked from side to side, stones crunching under the wheels as it rolled along thin, winding paths. Along the way, we stopped a few times to stretch our legs and allow the horses to drink at the nearby river.

By midafternoon, the coach came to an abrupt halt and sloped to one side.

The coachman clomped from his seated position at the front. "Could one of you offer a hand? The blasted coach has gotten itself stuck in the mud."

One by one, we dropped onto the muddy road beside a river. Further ahead, the other carriages waited. Several men jogged towards us. They assisted Dmitri and Felix as they tried to shove the carriage out of the mud. Beads of sweat lined their foreheads, and mud splattered their breeches.

Seeing as pushing alone wouldn't solve their

problem, Felix and Dmitri placed logs underneath the wooden wheels while the coachman tugged the horses' reins in the front.

"We'll have to stay a while so we can swap out the horses," the coachman said.

Once the carriage was out of the mud, Felix and I wandered along the riverside. The coachman guided the horses to the water's edge to drink, while Dmitri checked the carriage's structure for any damage caused by the mud.

I hooked my hand around Felix's arm, and we strolled along the riverside. "Do you remember when we played in the river together?"

"Of course. I gave you a bath." He grinned.

"You mean you splashed me." I nudged him.

He cupped my cheek. "We *will* have moments like that again."

I rested my hand over his. "With you by my side, I know we'll see the end of this, and I never thought I'd say that, at least I didn't when I left you. I have a purpose here—a way to destroy Makdou, but I'll also set the people of Swynvale free if I'm right about her having something to do with the green magic."

"I will help you in any way I can if it means we avenge our son." He rested his forehead against mine, and for a moment, our troubles washed away with the water trickling over stones.

---

The carriages came to an abrupt halt some hours

later, the overwhelming scent of smoke wafting through the windows. Covering my hand with my sleeve and pressing it against my nose and mouth, I stuck my head out. I widened my eyes at the plumes of smoke rising to meet the clouds.

The thudding of footsteps and the hollers of men rent the air as soldiers scrambled out of their carriages.

"What's going on?" I threw a brief glance over my shoulder to Dmitri, who let go of Sofia and pushed the door open. Hopping down, he held his hand out for her and me until our booted feet hit the dusty road. Felix came up beside me, taking my hand in his.

"I'm not sure." A muscle feathered in Dmitri's jaw. "But we're about to find out."

Lilith joined the crowd of gathering soldiers, her gaze darting from the black clouds of smoke to Dmitri's face. From behind the swarm of people, I couldn't make out exactly what was on fire, but when she moved farther ahead, she clamped a trembling hand over her mouth, silencing the strangled scream bursting from her throat.

Seth was at her side in an instant, one hand wielding his sword, the other pressed to the small of Lilith's back.

"What's on fire?" I asked Dmitri as he, too, came to a halt.

His eyes widened, and all the muscles in his face turned to stone. He was at least a foot taller than I, so I suspected he could see far atop the heads of those blocking us from whatever burned ahead.

"Dmitri?" Sofia asked in a gentle tone, resting a

hand on his tense arm.

"They've gone too far," he ground out. He unsheathed his sword in a swift movement, his knuckles turning white.

"Who?" I asked, trading glances with Sofia.

She bit her bottom lip, keeping her hand on his arm. Perhaps this was her way of offering comfort in a circumstance where there wasn't much else she *could* do.

"The Orcs. Who else?" His words were hard, icy, and delivered a brutality that made her jolt. She dropped her hand.

He stalked over to Lilith and Seth at the edge of the gathering crowd. As I fell into place beside them, the Temple engulfed with flames filled my vision. My breath was lost somewhere in my lungs as my gaze roamed over the crumbling stone as if something had rammed into the right-hand side of the monumental structure at the bottom of the valley.

The wild, out-of-control fire had spread to the nearby houses, and without a significant amount of flowing water to douse the flames, it would likely continue to rage into the night. The sight of it shocked me to the core, rooted me to the spot, and my chest heaved. Images of piled corpses—murder victims of the Orcs left to rot on the road—burned in my mind's eye.

Dragging in ragged breaths, I clutched Felix, relying on his sturdiness to keep my knees from buckling.

"What are you waiting for?" Lilith whirled around, fixing a venomous stare on the soldiers as her voice broke. "Go down there and save whoever you can. *Help* whoever you can. This village will fall by sundown, and any surviving villagers need to get out."

Felix quickly kissed me on the head, then jogged after the soldiers who swarmed down the bank, navigating their way between the raging fire spreading across rooftops. As she took a step forward to join the soldiers, Seth gripped her arm and stopped her.

"You can't," he said. "If you go down there, you risk your own life."

"I cannot stand here and do nothing while the Orcs destroy the Divine Temple," Lilith retorted, her voice venomous.

"It is already destroyed." Seth cupped her cheek, wiping a stray tear that fell from her eye. Her bottom lip trembled. "There is nothing more you can do. The soldiers will escort the survivors to safety."

I turned away, feeling as if I was intruding on a private moment, and instead, placed my attention on the bank, watching and waiting for Felix and the other soldiers to return.

"Dmitri," I said carefully. "Tell me what I can do. Whatever Sofia and I can do, we will."

"Your magic will not restore the Temple." His chest heaved as he tore his gaze from the wreckage. "It is but another blow from the Orcs. To destroy one of our temples is an attempt to crush our spirit—our faith—and make us weak while they lay waste to everything we hold dear."

My heart twisted. Despite my own internal war

with *my* gods, I wouldn't wish such an atrocity on anyone—on any realm's faith.

Lifting my chin higher, I looked him in the eyes. "We will make them pay."

Dmitri relaxed his tense shoulders as he finally took Sofia's hand in his. "We will. And we will stop at nothing until we do."

Once the soldiers returned—the survivors set on the road to the nearest fort—we resumed our journey. Felix sat beside me, grinding his teeth, fire burning in his eyes. I rested a hand on his arm, offering him comfort, for I knew there were no words to quell the rage inside him, instigated by the attack on the Divine Temple. It was a trigger, a reminder of all we'd endured. All our own people had endured.

When the sun sank behind the mountain, casting a warm orange glow across the horizon, blending with the deeper blue of twilight, the coachman stopped the coach outside a small fort.

Dmitri scooted out from underneath the canvas structure, then held his hand out to help Sofia down. She accepted, then hopped onto the cobbles. Felix and I followed suit, and we gathered with Lilith and Seth at the front gates, while the last two coaches pulled to a halt.

"Welcome to Langhurst. This is where I grew up," Seth said.

At the wrought iron gates, guards hurried to haul them inwards upon recognising Seth.

"Seth," one guard said, his eyebrows moving skyward. "We weren't expecting you."

"Send for my mother and father, will you,

please?"

"Right away." The guard clomped into the main building.

We congregated in the courtyard inside the fort perimeter. The building sat against a backdrop of oak trees, a cloud of vibrant green leaves a pleasant contrast to the dull colour of grey stone worn from age and weathered by storm.

Archers stood, with their arrows stored in leather quivers over their shoulders. Lit braziers flickered, casting light and shadow across the cobbled floors of Langhurst.

Seth's face softened, his hand locked with Lilith's, and he smiled as he scanned the buildings of his home. I wondered how long it had been since he'd last been there.

"Brother!" A young boy tossed aside a bale of hay he carried, darted towards Seth, then flung his arms around him. "You're home."

"Oh, Jesse, you've grown so big and strong!" Seth swung his younger sibling around, settled him down, then ruffled his hair.

A slight woman with pale skin and sleek brown hair emerged from the structure—her lips parted with anticipation—and she rushed to Seth's side.

She scanned his facial features with her blue, welling eyes. "My darling, it's been so long. Oh gosh, what has happened? There must be a reason for your sudden and unexpected arrival."

"I'll tell you all about it in a moment. Where's Father?" Seth asked as a broad male, with greying hair tied back in a knot, thundered along the cobbles.

"Son, isn't this a surprise? Is everything all right? Who are these people you've brought here?" the man asked.

"Come inside, the sun is setting, and dinner will be served." The woman I deemed to be Seth's mother ushered us towards the building. "Seth, you can answer your father's questions while we dine."

Residents of Langhurst worked in the courtyard. Remnants of smoke from the blacksmith swirled in the breeze. Women shooed the last of the chickens into their huts, and the smell of dry straw and dust made my nose wrinkle. Soldiers greeted the men we'd brought from the Temple and offered their aid in unloading the supplies from the coaches.

Seth's mother turned to a nearby maid. "Have the guest rooms prepared."

She curtsied, then dashed up the wooden staircase through the entrance.

"Please, join us for food." Seth's warm mother rested her gaze on us. "I forgot to introduce myself. Excuse my ill manners; I wasn't expecting guests. My name is Theresa, and this is my husband, Stefan. Seth and Jesse are our sons."

"My name's Lilith—it's a pleasure to meet you and thank you for welcoming us into your home." She smiled at Seth's mother.

"Don't be silly, child." Theresa welcomed us into a large banquet room. "I'm glad I got to meet the infamous Lilith. I've heard everything about you in Seth's letters."

Lilith blushed.

Family portraits hung on the wall, lit by fire torches dotted either side. A large sword hung on a bracket above the crackling hearth. A wooden table stretched across the hall—a woven rug sprawled across the floorboards, fine silverware lay next to china bowls, and gold rimmed goblets were filled with deep, red wine.

"Please, sit," Theresa said.

When Seth returned with Jesse in tow, they took their seats either side of their mother. Their father sat at the head of the table.

"Introduce us to your other friends," his mother said.

"Well, you've read of my training partner, Dmitri, in my letters." Seth gestured to Dmitri as he slipped into an empty chair next to Sofia. "Then we have three rather interesting individuals: Sofia, Felix, and Evalyn—a story to be shared over dinner."

The servants served bowls of soup with a side of warm, crusty bread for starter.

"I look forward to hearing all about it. Now tell me, what has brought you home?" Theresa sipped her wine.

"The Orcs attacked our leader, Reuben, with foreign magic—channelled through portals. He's been unconscious for two days now," Seth said. "And many other soldiers have been afflicted."

"Foreign magic, you say?" Stefan tilted his head to the side. A frown furrowed his brows. "Perhaps we ought to have this conversation somewhere in private—out of earshot of the servants. We can't frighten the people of the fort. Not unless completely necessary."

~ * ~

After dinner, Stefan sent Jesse to bed, out of earshot of the conversation they needed to have.

"He's fifteen." Stefan placed his cutlery onto his plate after finishing his last bite of food, then wiped the corners of his mouth with a napkin. "With his young mind, I'm sure he'll be asking all sorts of questions. If you're all quite finished with supper, come with me to the reception room."

He led the way out of the banquet hall, through a long corridor and into a room at the end. Floor to ceiling bookcases lined the walls of this large room, reminding me of the Citadel library at Lake Delendil. A lit candelabra hung from the ceiling, illuminating many book spines, and sending those at the far end of the bookshelves into shadows.

"Make sure nobody interrupts us," Stefan said to the nearby maid as she finished plumping the cushions on the chairs.

"Certainly, my lord." She curtsied, then left the room.

My lord? If Stefan was the leader of this fort, and held a prestigious title, why did Seth leave to join the Temple to be a soldier? He could have gained leadership by following in his father's footsteps.

"Seth, you may now explain." Stefan settled into his seat, then created a steeple with his fingers and rested them on his knees.

Between Seth and Lilith, they shared the details of the green magic, the anchor beams, and the portal. Lastly, the story transitioned to the part Sofia and I played in destroying it, and Makdou's likely role in it all.

"It explains why you have scales and fiery hair."

118

Stefan's gaze rested on mine. "You're the Mage from the scroll, aren't you? From another world. Of course, you are. I've not seen the scroll myself—many of us haven't—but stories are told about you by those who've been lucky enough to read it."

"I'm not the one of importance here." I brushed away his sudden interest in me. "We're on an urgent mission to save Reuben's life. To find a cure for what's ailing the soldiers."

"Tell us more." Theresa sank into a seat beside her husband and gestured for the rest of us to do the same.

The maid returned, lit the hearth, then adjusted the logs with a fire poker. While the golden flames of the fire warmed the room, a tingle shot down my spine. A sense of urgency—one I couldn't suppress. Perhaps out of fear—I couldn't be too sure what lengths Makdou would go to.

I needed to take Reuben to the Great Mother Tree to heal him, find a way to destroy the connection between Makdou and the Orcs of Swynvale, return home and retain peace between the Triads, and find a way to protect those I love in the process. Not to mention my own sanity.

"I have a theory." I put my fingers to my lips. "If we kill Makdou, then we can sever the connection between her and the Orcs of any realm she's been able to reach. Killing her means no more harm will come to anyone in *any* realm. It might also see the end of the Crimson Kiss, seeing as she's the only known Mage to perform it in the last millennium."

"How do we kill her?" Stefan said in a stern, solid voice. "What needs to be done?"

I remained silent for a few moments, processing my thoughts. We needed to find Makdou if we wanted to kill her, and I didn't think she'd risk travelling through a portal to be in Swynvale when she didn't need to be. If I was here and she was *there*, in Arogath, then she could do what she wished without my interference.

"I'll have to be the one to kill her," I finally said. "As you know from the scroll, she has a personal vendetta against me. We'd have to return to Arogath, meaning we won't be able to help find the Tree until we return. I guess we should be thankful that time works differently in each realm."

"You won't be going alone," Felix said at once.

"Perhaps you can discuss the details in the morning. It's late, you've travelled far, and you must rest, all of you," Theresa said. "The chambers will be ready."

The guest chambers lined the right wing of the fort. The last room at the end of the corridor had been designated to myself and my friends for the night before we parted ways. I would have to leave Swynvale in pursuit of Makdou with Sofia and Felix, leaving Lilith, Dmitri, Seth, and the other soldiers to continue the journey to Meridian.

With the thoughts whirling around in my mind, I lit the candles in the chamber.

Felix climbed into bed, and I joined Sofia in front of the hearth. The flames of the fire crackled and danced, embers sputtered from the wood, hissing, and soon, his soft snores joined the chorus.

"I'm coming with you, you know," Sofia said abruptly. "Home—to find Makdou."

"What are you going to do about Dmitri?" I twisted in my chair to face her, full on.

"What about Dmitri?" She kept her gaze locked on the fire, its glow hiding the blush in her cheeks.

"I've noticed how you behave around each other. Little glances here and there, and the way he comforted you in the coach," I said. "You can't deny you've found happiness here. I've seen it."

"It's nothing." She waved it away. "It can't be anything. Not here, in a different world. As we've said, we'll be going back. It's just the way it is."

She wiped her eyes.

"Are you crying?" I leaned across and placed my hand on hers. "I'm sorry, I didn't mean to upset you."

"You are right—he *has* brought me happiness in this foreign world, but there is nothing more to it." She cleared her throat. "Please, my queen, don't speak of it."

# Chapter Ten

When the sun rose from behind the mountains and birds chimed from their nests in the trees, we gathered outside the living quarters. Lilith accepted a bag full of warm bread, meats, berries, and seeds from Seth's parents. A larger bag contained extra blankets and wineskins of water.

"Thank you again for your hospitality," I said to them.

"Thank you for bringing our son home to us, even for just a night." Theresa smiled. "You are welcome here anytime."

"Evalyn, I wish we had more time with you, to learn about you." Stefan wrapped his arm around his wife. "And I wish you all the best. Stay safe."

"It has been an honour meeting you." I shook his free hand.

The guards ordered families inside to clear space for the portal. Children watched from the windows. The birdsong halted.

Sofia and Felix stood by my side. Time to return to Arogath.

"We will see you soon, Evalyn," Seth said.

"I *will* return." I smiled. "The portal I'll create will take us back to Arogath. As soon as Makdou is defeated, I'll see you again." Not to mention, there was one less threat against my own people.

I locked hands with Sofia and Felix so we could travel through the portal together.

Closing my eyes, I concentrated. The ethereal, rippling surface of the portal appeared in my mind's eye. I focused on its hazy surface until the hum of the portal filled my ears. I peeped through one eye. Nothing. No portal.

"Sofia." I tugged on her hand. "I think we have a problem."

She adjusted her gaze on the empty space on the cobbles in front of us. A frown creased her brows.

"What's going on?" Seth asked. "Why isn't it working?"

"Who wants to bet Makdou is behind this?" Felix let go of our hands, then crossed his arms over his chest.

"You haven't had an issue conjuring a portal before," Lilith said. "At least from what we've read in the scroll."

"Felix has a point." An unshakeable dread

flooded my body. "She must know."

"The Dark Mage?" Theresa clutched her husband's hand tightly.

"She's clever—perhaps she knows we've figured it out by now. She'd be one step—if not more—ahead of us." My blood boiled, and my heart thumped. I dragged a hand over my face. "The last thing she'll want is to find me back home in Arogath on the hunt for her. Just as she's creating portals here, and *especially* if it's true she's using the Crimson Kiss on the Orcs."

"Why the Orcs of another realm and not the ones in her own world?" Stefan said.

A pulse pounded in the side of my head. "I...don't know. It looks like we'll be coming to Meridian with you, after all. At least, until we manage to get a portal up and running."

"We best get a move on," Seth embraced his parents. He climbed into his coach with Lilith, and the rest of us followed suit.

The guards hauled the gates inwards, and the carriage rolled out onto the road. Langhurst fell into the distance behind us.

The next few days passed at a slow pace—we spent nights in allied forts, empty barns on the side of the path, or huddled together in the coaches with spare blankets brought from Langhurst.

One late afternoon, we stopped in a flower-rich meadow. Trees, only a few feet away, were scattered around the meadow's margins.

Felix lit a fire to warm us through the cool night. The soldiers set up camp nearby, with more firepits for roasting, and snares for food. Sofia and I nestled together in front of the fire and drew a coarse blanket over our legs.

"I'm going to help the men hunt before the sun sets," Felix said, placing a kiss on my brow. As he headed off towards the treeline with Seth and the other soldiers, Sofia and I gathered the furs and blankets, draping them inside each tent.

When the men returned with rabbits and pheasants, I set a pot, filled with water, on a metal rack above the flames. Grabbing the cubed root vegetables from one of the supply bags, I brought them to the boil. Felix gave me a warm smile as he sat on a moss-covered log and withdrew a blade from the belt at his waist. Along with the other soldiers, he skinned the meat, then hung them to roast above other fires.

After I'd eaten, I unscrewed the cap of my flask, tilted it to a wad of cloth, and used the damp fabric to wipe away the dirt and perspiration from my face, neck, and hands.

As night descended, the others retired to their tents, leaving me alone with Felix. The sky was cloudless, and stars gleamed like diamonds. My heart swelled, reminding me of the night he'd given me his necklace. I raised my hand to my throat, where the leather cord would've dangled, if Makdou hadn't stolen it.

Felix drew me to him, draping a blanket across our laps. Together, we listened to the crackle of the fire, and the distant chirp of crickets.

~ * ~

By the end of the week, our source of food from Theresa had run low, so the coachmen agreed to

125

take us to the nearest market to refill our supplies before resuming the journey to Meridian.

"This is denda—the currency everybody uses to trade in Swynvale." Seth drew shiny silver coins from his pouch, giving one to each of us. "Buy as much as you can carry."

I tucked my coin into the pocket of my breeches, then tucked my hand in the nook of Felix's arm.

Stalls lined the cobbled streets. Crates displayed fresh produce—bundles of carrots, beets, and onions, bags of potatoes, peppers, and tomatoes. Husks of corn lay stacked in baskets beside baskets of apples, pears, peaches, plums, and blackberries. Braids of garlic and bundles of herbs filled my nostrils with their fresh scents.

Further along the cobbles, merchants sold knitted clothing and dolls, while others offered jars of honey and beeswax products, and towards the end of the market, a vendor selling jewellery reminded me of the merchant sacrificed by the Undines and Nereids in Arogath. It had been the price for their ability to walk on land.

My stomach grumbled. "My gosh, I'm *starving.*"

"Me too." Felix patted his stomach.

"Meet back in half an hour," the coachman advised as he hopped down from his seat, then guided the horses to a nearby field to graze.

Sofia strolled with Dmitri further ahead, while Seth and Lilith stayed together.

Felix led the way, venturing into the marketplace. He glanced at me from the corner of his eyes. "We had a ceremony for our son, you know."

Although his voice had been calm and gentle, the mention of our child hit me in the chest, almost buckling me. I gripped his arm for support.

As if he could sense the thick lump in my throat, he said, "He is at peace now, and by the gods, he was beautiful with these big round eyes and a tuft of brown hair sprouting out the top of his head."

Tears welled in my eyes. "I will regret not being there for every day of my life. I'm sorry I left you to deal with your grief alone. At the time, I wasn't thinking clearly. I could do nothing but leave. Maybe one day, you'll forgive me."

"There is nothing to forgive." He searched the air with his fingers until they touched my cheek, and he cupped it in his palm. "We couldn't hold a traditional ceremony without you—it's not our right to light the arrow. We've had a headstone erected in the gardens so you may visit him when you return home."

I flung my arms around him and held him tight. His lips brushed my forehead, and the tiny cracks in my heart continued to heal.

---

After purchasing food for the remainder of the journey, we continued down the dirt path farther east. Shadows filled the coaches as dark rain clouds gathered in the sky. A storm threatened to break out.

Sofia nestled against Dmitri for warmth—he

draped an arm casually about her shoulder. Felix scoffed a wad of cheesy bread he'd purchased from one of the vendors, then offered me a bite even though I'd eaten my own. I smiled at his consideration but declined. Light rain tapped against the canvas—a steady, comforting tune.

Sofia and Dmitri remained silent in their embrace, and I contemplated their relationship. The previous night, she'd said nothing would become of them—nothing ever could. Yet she nestled against him, his arms tight around her.

We continued to travel by day and rest by night, avoiding any confrontation with Orcs who might be lurking or hunting nearby, which in itself posed an interesting question. Was Makdou keeping the Orcs hidden while she prepared to use them for something bigger—something bad?

I shuddered. Images of Orc hammers crushing Human skulls, terrorising innocent civilians, and Ascal being ripped from his horse and murdered in the Badlands haunted me. Finding my mother and Felix beaten and starved in the Southkeep prison flickered in my mind. The day would come when I finally put an end to Makdou. I hoped we would be ready for the fight.

Soon, the rain subsided, and the coaches came to a halt next to the riverside. In the distance, a large stone bridge led to the gated entrance of Meridian. The settlement, enclosed by high walls and shielded by trees, clung to the cliffside. Vines climbed the sandstone towers and buildings of Meridian, and birds flew overhead towards their nests in the gaps in the roofs. Most window shutters were closed for the evening and candlelight flickered through the odd few still open.

At the bridge, Lilith held out her hand to stop us.

"Evalyn, when the guards ask who we are, and why we're here, let us do the talking," she instructed. "I mean no disrespect, but they may fear you for being different."

I nodded and crossed the arching bridge with Sofia, leaving the coaches behind.

Felix grabbed a satchel from the carriage, placing the strap on his shoulder before catching up to us. "Some food in case our reception isn't as hospitable as we'd hope," he said as he came to a stop beside me.

Guards stepped forward and lifted their spears.

"Lift your hands so we can see them," one of the guards said, his voice deep.

We obeyed.

"Who are you and why have you come to Meridian?" the guard asked. He was tall, broad, and dark-skinned like Dmitri. He had a single braid plaited down the middle of his head and the sides shaved. "You look…familiar."

The guard looked Dmitri up and down, a frown creasing his brow.

"We are soldiers from the Temple of Peace in the Western Mountain Range," he said in a confident and smooth tone, ignoring the latter comment. "We have come to Meridian because our home is under siege by the Orcs, and we seek refuge here until it is safe to return."

Had the guards believed Dmitri's lie? More importantly, *why* had he lied?

"If your home is under attack," the second guard pointed his spear towards us, "why aren't more of you seeking refuge here?"

A good question. I tried to keep a straight face and flattened my hands against my thighs.

"The civilians fled in panic, seeking refuge at nearby Human forts," Dmitri said, expression neutral. "We decided to make the long journey to your beautiful home because we are in need of aid. We wish to speak with the Elders."

"Fine." The first guard lowered his spear, and the second stepped aside.

Together, the men hauled in the large iron gates. The metal groaned and scraped along the cobbles.

"Head to the top of the hill, and you will see the main hall. Don't speak to anybody until you have spoken to the Elders," the first guard instructed with a stern glare in warning.

We passed market stalls with haggling merchants, craftsmen and blacksmiths clanking metal, and women who sold fresh fruit and vegetables from their stands. The street widened, and we stopped at the top of the steep, winding hill to catch our breath.

"Are you okay?" Sofia asked Dmitri.

"I'm fine," Dmitri said gruffly, beads of sweat trickling down his face.

From atop the hill, I had a clear view of tall towers extending into the sky and smaller buildings tucked into the curve of the hillside. Each path between the buildings bustled with people who traded coins for food and fabric. Narrow wooden bridges linked the tallest towers, and guards marched along them with quivers of arrows jutting out from their backs.

Meridian looked like it had a century of architectural history and reformation. The vines clinging to the bricks and stones of the buildings added charm to the large and vibrant settlement.

Murmuring civilians surrounded us—we were strangers in their home. I kept my head down although it would do little to conceal my scaled face.

Felix stayed close, a protective presence at my side.

Had the people of Meridian learned the true story of my life? Not everybody had access to the scroll, so who would know I am who I say I am?

"Hurry inside," a mother ordered her child as she shot a wary glare at me.

Even the blacksmiths halted as I passed.

"We need to make haste," I said to Felix. "I'm getting death stares from the locals."

"I've noticed." His grip tightened on the satchel strap. "We'll get to the Elders and explain our reasons for visiting. One step at a time."

Every guard eyed us, tilting their spears forward, as we passed by.

I hoped the Elders, whoever they were, could make our stay more welcoming.

Seth stopped in front of two tall wooden doors, hesitated, and glanced at Dmitri. "I hate to admit it but...I'm nervous. We are surrounded by guards—what if this goes wrong?"

Lilith smiled reassuringly. "We have come this far. I'm sure the Elders will listen to us. They'll know about the scroll, so they'll recognise Evalyn's name. Perhaps they'll know more about it than anyone else in this settlement. Even though they know you're a Mage, they've never seen one in the flesh before, so they may be curious about you."

I nodded. "I'm ready."

Seth heaved the doors in, then stepped inside. Large portrait paintings of those I assumed to be the Elders, and their long line of ancestors lined the walls.

"It sure looks like the Elders have splashed out with their denda," Lilith said. "Let's hope they are as lavish with their greetings as they are with spending coin."

Torches, affixed to the walls with iron brackets, lit the hall. The orange evening sun shone through the windows of the main hall and the firelight warmed the air. Faint voices muttered to themselves in the room on the right of the corridor. Slowly, we filtered into the room, and lingered by the door, ready to make a quick escape if needed.

"We are *much* safer within the secure walls of Meridian, Xavier," a tall, dark-skinned man said in a tired voice. He dragged his hand over his crinkled face. "It would be foolish to venture outside for *your* desire to eat fish from the lakes."

"We are stuck within the walls of this settlement with the cattle we have," the slight man said. He was a few inches shorter than Xavier. "It would be great to bring something new and fresh into the settlement—other produce to trade."

The first man didn't reply as his gaze fell on me and my friends in the doorway. His mouth dropped as he stared straight into my eyes. I shifted my weight from foot to foot, unsure what to do.

The man peeled his stare off me and shifted it to Dmitri who stood beside me, eyes wide.

"Dmitri," the man said.

Sofia glanced at Dmitri with an arched eyebrow.

Xavier stroked his chin as he examined Dmitri.

"Father," Dmitri said.

Father? He had said nothing about his father in Meridian, but this would explain how the guard recognised him. He'd left a whole other life behind when he joined the Temple.

"We have been waiting for you a long time," Xavier said. "It's my greatest honour to have you home. Did you have any hassle from the guards?"

"None," he said, voice cold, unlike what I'd expect from someone who'd reunited with his kin.

"I can't say I'm not surprised to see you. It's been over a decade, my boy." Xavier remained expressionless.

What was their relationship like before Dmitri left for the Temple of Peace? Why had he left so young?

"Who are our guests?" Xavier gestured to us as we loitered in the doorway. His gaze landed on me once more. "A Mage?"

"Yes, this is Evalyn," Dmitri said. "How much do the civilians of Meridian know about the scroll?"

"They know enough," Xavier said.

If they knew enough, why did they stare at me? Was it because I looked different, or was Xavier's notion of *they know enough* really anything at all?

Sofia glanced at me and whispered, "Don't say

anything."

Felix opened his mouth to speak, but I placed my hand on his arm to stop him. We had to tread carefully.

"I'm Xavier, First Elder of Meridian, and who might you all be?" He clasped his hands in front of him. Not a hint of emotion marked his face.

"I'm Lilith," she said, then introduced the rest of us. "We've come here to seek refuge from attacking Orcs near our home."

"I see," Xavier said in an even tone. "Meridian is, indeed, the safest place to be."

The man, who'd been in conversation with Xavier about fish upon our arrival, cleared his throat. "A pleasure to make your acquaintances. I'm Lucien, Third Elder. I will leave you to your reunion."

"I will speak with you later," Xavier said. "This conversation is not over."

Lucien exited the room, waving away Xavier's remark as he did.

"You know the stories of Evalyn's life." Dmitri gestured to me. "Do you recall the name Makdou? We think she is behind a foreign magic responsible for the ailment plaguing some of our men at the Temple."

"Foreign magic, you say. That's a topic I certainly want to hear more about in the morning. Dmitri, I assume you remember where our cottage is? You could show your guests the way—I imagine you are all tired from your long journey from the Temple. I would have offered you larger lodgings in our main estate, but it is currently undergoing some renovations."

Dmitri stiffened and didn't seem to relax from his father's kind words. Sofia grabbed his hand to comfort him. Taking a step closer to his father, Dmitri shielded Sofia. Why didn't he trust his father? Something didn't seem right.

"We will be leaving now," Dmitri said.

He hurried out of the main hall without a further word. Sofia and I exchanged glances as we followed.

Outside, he leaned against the wall, and dragged a hand over his face. She touched his arm.

"Your father seems pleasant," she said sarcastically, her voice feather-light.

"He is not easy to like." Dmitri clasped his hand with Sofia's. "That's a story for another time."

"Why did you lie to the guards?" I couldn't help asking, even though it wasn't much of my business.

"I wasn't sure how my father would react to seeing me after all this time." He shrugged half-heartedly.

I decided to leave it there.

He led us to a well-maintained bridge past the main hall. The bridge stretched across jutting rocks separated by a narrow stream flowing between the buildings.

The cobbled paths curved up the slopes of the hill, weaving between towers, markets, and buildings. The smooth, almost shiny surface of the cobbles glinted under the setting sun—a sheen layer of water clung to the ground from the earlier rain.

People trod the paths, carrying baskets of

vegetables, pelts, and buckets of water into their storage quarters for the night. Men worked up a sweat in the blacksmith's forge or on the woodworking benches for the last stretch of their shifts. Mothers shooed their lingering children inside their homes. The hearty scent of stew and fresh bread wafted from the ajar windows.

Dmitri stopped outside one of the stone huts, then drew a small silver key from his pocket underneath his breastplate.

Had he kept his key this whole time? Although his relationship with his father seemed tense, there must be a part of him that wanted to return home, or at least, still cared.

He unlocked the door and pushed it inwards, showing a warm glow of burning candles within. We entered the home, and Dmitri shut the door behind us. He remained rigid as he eased past us and into the small living area. A fire danced in the hearth on the opposite wall.

A woman—her hair wrapped in a dark orange cloth—sat in an armchair next to the fire. A few black curls fell around her face.

"Mother." A smile tilted his lips. "I have spoken with Father, and he has welcomed me and my guests to stay here for the night."

"Dmitri," the woman said with wide eyes. "Are you okay? My visions have been faltering as of late. I could see you, but through a distorted lens, so to speak. Blood, Orcs, and Reuben—unconscious."

"Yes, Mother. We have come here for help," he said.

She opened her arms to him and held her son

against her bosom. He relaxed into her arms.

"This is Evalyn, Felix, and Sofia. From the scroll," he said as he let go.

"I am honoured to meet you." She crossed the room and took my hands in hers. "I am very sorry for the loss of your child. It must be so difficult for both of you." She bowed her head slightly to Felix.

"Your condolences mean a lot to us," Felix said. "It's been a difficult time. I have known no greater loss."

Tears welled in my eyes, and the fragile bindings keeping my broken heart together threatened to fall apart.

She handed me a handkerchief from her pocket. "What you have endured has made you both stronger. I sensed you on your journey, knew you'd be arriving soon, although my visions aren't like they used to be. Although, I must say, it'll be a tight squeeze with all of you staying in this house. Some of you might have to sleep downstairs."

"My mother knows most of the scroll," Dmitri explained. "She has...visions, if you will. She doesn't need to read it like we do. She knows when events happen."

I raised a brow. "Are you a Mage?"

"No, dear." The woman chuckled, creating crow's feet at the outer corner of her eyes. "I am an Oracle, much like the one you knew many months ago. Although, like I said, my visions aren't what they usually are. It's like they're distant, the picture isn't full, like it is too far to reach."

This raised my suspicions. Could Makdou be the reason behind the woman's faltering visions? It would make sense for her to want to remove any advantages against her.

"I never thought I would meet another Oracle." I smiled fondly, remembering Juliette and her funeral on the lake—the lit arrow I'd fired at the boat carrying her body. "The people of Meridian are lucky to have you."

"Please, call me Dierdre. I'm Xavier's wife— Dmitri's mother—and Second Elder of Meridian." She welcomed us around the hearth. "You must be starving. Luckily, I have already prepared your food—I knew you would be arriving."

She handed each of us a plate of meat and boiled greens, then reclined into her chair. Despite us all crammed into the tight space, it was still homely.

I prodded the meat with my fork, unable to swallow my suspicions. "It's possible Makdou is the reason why your visions aren't like what they used to be."

"I don't doubt it," she said, unphased. "From what I understand, she is a very powerful Mage, and it would benefit her greatly if an Oracle couldn't see her every move, wouldn't you agree?"

"Don't you think we should do something about it?" I frowned.

"I presume you already have a plan in motion to defeat her once and for all, no?" she said.

"Well, yes, but—"

"Eat, dear. We will discuss everything tomorrow." She relaxed against the back of her chair, and her twinkling gaze rested on me. "What an extraordinary day. The prophecy—it's real."

# Chapter Eleven

"Can you tell me more about your visions?" I asked once I'd finished my meal.

"Usually, I cannot escape them," Dierdre said, the fire casting its warm glow across her small, round face. "They come at any time—day, night, you name it. I see all sorts of things."

"Does it bring you some peace—to know what's coming and be prepared for it? I can imagine it's nice to see your son is safe and well." I sat my empty bowl on the wooden table in front of me.

The others remained silent as they scooped their boiled vegetables into their mouths.

"It is quieter than I would like." She laughed. "But enough about me now. How have you found your stay in Swynvale?"

"Remarkable." I struggled to find another word. "The magic is different. I can't fight its encouragement to be at peace."

"A blessing and a curse. Dmitri, you spoke with your father? I hope he was polite to you and your guests." She took our empty plates and placed them on the kitchen workbench.

"As polite as Father can be," he muttered. "Seth and Lilith are with the healers who are tending to Reuben. He has fallen ill from the magic plaguing our land."

"It's not very often I don't see these things, my dear. I am sure we, as the Elders, will gather tomorrow to speak of the matter. Lucien and Xavier have been debating trivialities, so this will give them something new to argue about," Dierdre said. "Enough chatter now. Take yourselves a cup of water and Dmitri will show you the way to the spare rooms. Who'd be happy to sleep downstairs? There are extra blankets in the cupboard."

"We'll stay," Seth said, bringing Lilith into an embrace.

The smell of roasting meat wafted through the whole house. It should have offered me comfort and warmth, yet the images of burning Humans in Arogath haunted me. Perhaps they always would.

"You must be exhausted," Deirdre said as Dmitri kissed her on the cheek. Her skin was aged and dull under the eyes, but her irises a fascinating hazel—bright and twinkling, young in soul. "It's fantastic to have you home, Dmitri. Koltin, God of Duty, has been kind."

"You know I cannot stay," Dmitri whispered, his eyes hollow. "There is much to be done."

"Of...of course." She waved her hand and hid her reddened cheeks from her son. She faced me. "You are brave, Evalyn, and courageous. I wish the world had more Mages like you and your dear friend, Sofia."

"Thank you," I replied, following Dmitri upstairs, Sofia and Felix trailing behind.

"My parents' room is there." Dmitri pointed to the larger room at the front of the house. "These two are spare and will do fine for us." He opened the door to the first room. "You three can have this room, and I will take the small room for myself. There is a washroom at the end of the corridor for you to bathe and change."

"Thank you for your kindness, Dmitri," Sofia said.

He smiled and left.

Once we'd headed inside, Felix clicked the door shut. A fire crackled in the small hearth on the left wall opposite the two beds. Our bags had already been brought up, presumably from the servants, who'd emptied the carriages upon our arrival.

I pulled back the blankets on the bed by the window.

"I'm going to change in the washroom," Sofia said. "I will refill the bath with warm water for you afterward, Evalyn."

"That's very kind of you," I said, and she slipped outside.

Clasping the curtain, I stared at the crescent moon drenching Meridian in silver light. Felix came up behind me, snaked his arms around my waist, and propped his chin on top of my head.

"While I do like sleeping under the stars with you, it's nice to have a roof over our heads," he said, his voice low and smooth.

Resting my hands on his solid arms around me, I leaned into him, and breathed in his cinnamon scent. "Yes, and I must admit, having you with me has been more comforting than I thought—for us to grieve together." I drew my bottom lip between my teeth. "A part of me regrets leaving Arogath—my people need me. I'm their queen, and I left them. And once we're done here, I'll make them a vow. Send letters to every corner of my kingdom to declare my return, and that I will *never* leave them again."

"You will make it up to them," he said. "Besides, the High Elves are presiding over important matters, ordering restorations to be completed in your name. Although the time difference between these realms does present an issue. Without you present, over an extended period, you might start to lose your allies."

"I know." I sighed, finding the truth in his words. "But I will do whatever it takes to gain their trust back."

Sliding out of his embrace, I closed the curtains, then went to the hearth and prodded the logs. A short while later, Sofia slipped inside the room.

"The bath is ready for you," she whispered.

I rested the poker against the wall. "Thank you."

Sofia lingered in the hallway. "I am going to stay with Dmitri…an hour or so."

She disappeared into Dmitri's room, and I smiled to myself. If anyone deserved a moment of peace, it was her.

———◦∽◦———

In the morning, Felix and I sank into the chairs downstairs. Dierdre had gone to the market stalls to purchase fresh bread, cheese, and meats. Footsteps thudded downstairs, and a rosy-cheeked Sofia entered the sitting room with Dmitri behind her.

"It's nice for you to join me at last." I smirked.

As the two new lovers squeezed on the wooden chest beside Seth and Lilith, Dierdre opened the front door and whisked inside. She clutched a basket filled with bread and ingredients for our morning meal.

"Ah, how nice to see you downstairs." She beamed. "I presume you slept well?"

"Yes, and I couldn't be more grateful for the comfortable mattress." I adjusted the cushion behind my back. "It's been a while since I've had such a good night's sleep."

"And we will fill your belly with a hearty morning meal before we gather at the main hall." She scurried into the kitchen, placed the woven basket onto the counter, then withdrew the warm bread, meats, and cheese.

I tapped my fingers against my knee. Felix stood behind me, massaging the knots in my shoulders.

The longer we stayed here, the more nervous I became. I'd no idea what the Elders would decide—would they even believe us about the Great Mother Tree? Or would our chance to save Reuben and the other inflicted soldiers be squandered?

Dierdre wore a tan floor-length cape with a linen dress underneath. She'd pinned her hair away from her face in preparation for the meeting. A string of beads hung around her neck.

She served us our meal, which I scarfed down quickly. Nausea churned my stomach. I couldn't stay in the house longer than necessary.

"It's time," she said after she took our plates.

As we left the house, I fiddled with the creases of my khaki shirt, wanting it to lie flat in areas it didn't.

Sofia placed a soft hand on my shoulder. A smile spread across her dainty face.

We followed Dmitri and Dierdre along the winding cobbled paths of Meridian and over the bridge towards the main hall. Several of the civilians took off their caps and nodded at her as she walked past. She acknowledged the gesture with a pleasant smile.

Locals bustled in the narrow streets, setting their stalls and the blacksmith hammered metal on an anvil—smoke from the furnace raised into the air in clouds. Nearby villagers moved aside to give her and us a clear passage through.

People filed through the hall. Some of them held scrolls and letters in their hands and dashed into a room on the left, while others navigated in and out of other rooms.

Dierdre opened wooden doors, revealing a large, circular room.

Around the perimeter of the room, sat a gathering of Humans from Meridian. Were they acting as a jury while the Elders decided what to do with us?

We took our seats in the centre of the room, the wooden chairs creaking under our weight.

Dierdre sank into a throne-like chair beside her husband, and they exchanged a warm, yet professional smile. Lucien, the man who'd challenged Xavier the day before, took his position by his side.

Xavier rose from his chair to face the crowd of people who formed a crescent-moon shape around us.

"I have gathered you here today to bear witness of the safe return of my son, Dmitri, and his friends, to Meridian," he said in a clear, crisp tone. "My heart is filled with joy and such gratitude that Koltin, God of Duty, has returned our heir to our sacred homelands."

The crowd cheered and clapped.

Heir? Why had Dmitri kept this a secret if he knew he would inherit a wealthy position as an Elder of Meridian? Perhaps it had something to do with their tense relationship.

"We must address pressing matters—Dmitri and his friends have brought news," Xavier continued, his eyes piercing those who looked upon him. "Very serious news, indeed. It seems Swynvale has a new threat—a Dark Mage from Arogath, who we have all heard of from the scroll."

Collective gazes from the audience fell on me. My palms sweated.

"The scroll does not show us the future; therefore, we must act with caution. The Crimson Kiss is an old, powerful spell." Xavier paraded around the hall, looking into the eyes of different Meridian residents. "Makdou used it against Evalyn to kill the prophesied child."

The crowd gasped and mutters filled the room, confirming they didn't *'know enough'* as he had put it. Felix took my hand in his and ran his thumb over my skin. An act of unity, and of comfort. The mention of the child we would never get to raise— to hold—was a blow to the heart, but I squared my shoulders and kept my chin high.

"People of Meridian!" He lifted his arms into the air, demanding order. "It is alleged Makdou is controlling the Orcs to reach Evalyn and kill the *true* prophesied one. As a result, the Orcs of Swynvale are acting more aggressively, connected by green, foreign magic."

Sofia rested a hand on my knee and squeezed it. An act of reassurance.

Xavier's words fell heavy in the hall, and the crowd quieted. Lucien stared at me, and I couldn't be sure if we had his support.

"May I speak?" I rose, looking at each of the Elders in turn.

Xavier narrowed his gaze a fraction. "Go on."

I addressed the crowd, shifting my gaze from one face to another. "We have come here in search of something powerful that will become sacred to the people of Meridian. In fact, it has been in this settlement for a millennium, and nobody has known."

"Evalyn, what are you doing?" Sofia murmured.

I smiled at her, then continued, "I have reason to believe there is something of great wealth hidden within Meridian."

Dierdre and Lucien exchanged looks. The crowd muttered amongst themselves.

Xavier raised a hand to silence them. "A treasure you say. Tell us more."

I flattened my sweating palms against my thighs. "Reuben—the leader at the Temple of Peace—has been infected by the green magic you mentioned. Sofia has tried to heal him with her spells, but it hasn't awoken him. It has stopped him from starving or dehydrating, but we have no idea what effect the magic is having on his body. Other soldiers have been impacted by this magic, but to a lesser degree. We have come here to find…the Great Mother Tree."

I'd said it. The secret was out. He shot a wide-eyed look at the other Elders. Lilith shielded her eyes and shook her head.

The hall remained silent as Lucien rose from his chair. grey hair fell around his face and grew from his chin in a shaped beard. His skin, while sun-kissed like all residents of Meridian, had dulled over the years and wrinkles creased his forehead.

He stalked towards us, keeping a straight face. With our hands still clasped, Felix drew me closer to him. My breath hitched, and my heart pounded. But I didn't baulk.

"The Great Mother Tree does not exist," he said levelly. "It is a myth."

"We *have* seen it, I assure you." I fought to keep my own voice calm and collected. "Sofia and I, when our magic is linked together, are able to produce an effective location spell showing us the location of anything, even if it has been hidden under a concealing spell for a millennium. It's been at the back of the settlement this whole time, and nobody has known about it."

"It is true." Sofia rose, facing the crowd. "The Great Mother Tree is real and when we reveal it, it's going to be the most sacred thing in the universe."

"If what you're saying is true, how do you plan on lifting the spell?" Lucien frowned.

"We know the correct counter charm," Sofia said. "But we are dealing with ancient magic, which will be difficult to undo. We will use this Tree to cure any sick or injured within Meridian. In return, we request samples to take back to the Temple."

"How do you suppose we deal with the threats Xavier has spoken of?" Lucien asked. "While I cannot disagree that the Great Mother Tree would be invaluable to us, what is the point if Makdou is going to destroy everything we have?"

"I don't think her intention is to *destroy* Meridian." I lifted my chin. "She wants me dead—"

"So, she will destroy everything in her path until she finds you." He narrowed his gaze on me and kept his hands locked in front of him. "Or am I mistaken?"

"Let Evalyn speak," Dmitri said in a sharp tone. "She knows the Mage better than anyone. She knows her strengths and weaknesses and can formulate a plan best to deal with her."

I'd thought of killing Makdou many times, but I had no plan. I couldn't risk them knowing it, either.

"As Xavier said…" I took a deep breath, then continued, "She is channelling her Dark Magic to control the Orcs of this world. I also suspect she is the reason behind Dierdre's faltering visions. We find Makdou, kill her, and her control will cease."

"Just like that." Lucien sighed and returned to his chair. "How do you plan on finding her?"

Telling him about our failed attempt to open a portal would be treading on dangerous ground. I'd have to be careful.

I cleared my throat. "I…was explaining the plan in much simpler terms, of course. At the moment, we are facing an issue. Makdou is blocking my connections to other realms. She's disabling my ability to create portals."

"If I'm not mistaken, Lucien," Dierdre raised her hand, "this meeting is not about the plan to defeat the Dark Mage but is about the roles of these good people while they reside in Meridian, and that question has been answered. They must focus their attention on lifting the spell concealing the Great Mother Tree."

"I am in agreement, Lucien. We should allow them to reveal the Tree first, then make preparations for finding Makdou," Xavier said, settling the matter.

"So be it." Lucien nodded.

"People of Meridian, please make our new guests comfortable. Be kind in your exchanges and serve them food and water in your taverns with your welcoming behaviour, as always. This will be the beginning of a new era." Xavier concluded the meeting, and the crowd applauded.

"You'll do fine," Felix said as we made our way along the cobblestone path, north towards the grasslands, and beyond, the hidden Tree. "Remember, I'm by your side. We've come so far, and you'll succeed at this. And you won't be doing this alone—You have Sofia."

I squeezed his arm, grateful for his reassurance.

"Do you think this will work?" I glanced sideways at Sofia.

"I hope so," she said. "I can't see any reason why it wouldn't. I mean, I've done this spell before, but on smaller things."

Lilith and Seth fell into step beside me. Sofia smiled as Dmitri took her hand in his.

"The High Elves would love Meridian," I said, nudging Sofia on the shoulder. "Can you imagine how they would react if they saw this place? It's beautiful. It's well protected and not as exposed as Lake Delendil."

"We can tell them about it when we go home," she said.

"Yes. I suppose we could." I allowed my mind to wander to those I'd left, and my heart ached. To soothe my guilt, I focused on what I'd said to Felix last night. I'd fight to regain my people's trust.

"Evalyn, the ground is moving," Sofia said as we trekked up the hill towards the back of the settlement.

A pulse vibrated through the ground, making my feet tingle.

"Yes." I gazed in awe at my open surroundings.

Wildflowers sprouted amongst the long grass, ample sunlight illuminated dry leaves trapped in grass mounds and glinted on the wings of butterflies and dragonflies as they fluttered here and there. Bees flitted through flowers, frogs leapt near a stream close by, and nesting birds burst out of the grass as we approached.

"The ground isn't moving." Seth frowned—his voice breaking me from my observations of nature.

"What about you, Lilith?" She answered my question with a shake of the head. "Strange."

The Elders trailed behind, declaring this an event they couldn't miss. They watched like hawks while Sofia and I positioned ourselves in the middle of the tall grass.

"You are both Mages," Dierdre said, "and that is the reason why you can sense the vibrations and the rest of us can't."

"Do you think we'll be strong enough to release this spell?" I gripped Sofia's hands. "What if I end up in Elysium again? How do we know I'll be able to come back this time?"

"Don't worry," she insisted. "Fight the urge to slip. You *are* strong enough to do this."

She closed her eyes and chanted a spell. I focused on my auric field, forcing my chakras to balance. My heartbeat steadied, and my magic fused with her, creating a beacon of light visible through my eyelids.

The rest of the world fell away as the magic cocooned us, and the image of the Great Mother Tree appeared in my mind's eye. Its peach-coloured tendrils, dangling a few inches above the ground, sparkled underneath the sunlight.

Sofia continued her hypnotical chant as the cocoon of magic grew thick and strong. The wind whipped like a relentless storm.

The cocoon jolted and the real world came into focus through its ethereal surface. The Elders ran towards the centre of the settlement as the thumping of drums thundered. I darted my gaze from side to side, trying to find the location of drums. In the distance, on the watchtowers. The soldiers stationed there must've seen something considered a threat. Why else alert the entire settlement?

Seth tugged Lilith in the direction the Elders went. Dmitri hurried after his parents, but Sofia yanked my hands, snapping my attention back to her.

"Concentrate on the spell!" she yelled, then resumed her chant. "We need to complete it. Don't let yourself be distracted or it will not work!"

My legs trembled, and my fingers shook. I gripped tightly onto Sofia's arms. My stomach knotted. My head spun. Pain seared through my body.

The urge to break the bond with her consumed me. Black spots filled my vision. Blind, I sank further away from consciousness.

Felix's shouts penetrated the roaring in my ears as I fell into the Beyond. Elysium.

# Chapter Twelve

Freefalling through the black void, I grew further away from Sofia and Felix's yells. Then silence. The thundering drums ended. The screams of civilians ended.

Darkness enveloped me, weightless and floating. Wisps of light pierced the veils of Elysium—spirits and ethereal beings, spending their eternity in the Beyond.

How could I be here? Although I hadn't been explicitly told, I'd presumed Elysium to be the afterlife for those who lived in my own realm. Yet it couldn't be true.

*'This planet is connected to yours in more ways than I can explain.'* Reuben's words rang in my

mind. These two worlds shared Elysium.

Floating in nothingness, I was alone. During my first visit to Elysium, Alinar had stayed, but she'd passed on now, no longer waiting to greet me.

I wondered what it would be like to pass through Elysium to the other side. I'd be reunited with my family—all those I'd lost. And I might not be able to return to the living world. The more times I fell into the Beyond, the more likely I'd have to stay.

My mind jolted awake, vibrant with activity—I needed to get back, *wake up.* I couldn't stay here or accept this weightless eternity or a possible reunion with loved ones. My duty lay with my friends in Meridian—*they* needed me. Felix needed me. I couldn't abandon him. Yet unfamiliar forces pulled at my core and urged me to stay.

*It is safe here.*

A low hum—the deep, rumbling energy of Elysium. The void drew me deeper into its layers in a way it hadn't done before. A musky scent filled my nostrils.

*This isn't normal.*

Another indistinct hum, a few octaves higher than the void's natural energy, travelled towards me.

My body tingled as I materialised.

"Mother?" a soft voice called from far away.

My attention piqued. I scanned the darkness for the owner of the voice.

A small child wandered through the veils towards me. A white aura glimmered around him.

My heart pounded.

I stared at the boy as he approached. "My…my

154

boy?"

"Why are you here, Mother?" He tilted his head.

"Do my…do my eyes deceive me?" I knelt to his height as tears fell.

He touched my face.

Shaking, I stroked his hand as he cupped my cheek with his tiny palm—I could *feel* his soft skin beneath my fingertips. He was real. My son. A rush of affection warmed me.

"I'm real, Mother." He smiled. "But I must be quick—I don't have much time."

"Are you safe here, my child? Are you with Juliette? Ascal?" The questions tumbled from my mouth as I scanned every inch of him. His hazel, almond-shaped eyes and tousled hair reminded me of his father.

"They look after me, I promise." The boy squeezed me tightly. "You can't stay here."

"I know." I pressed my head to his. He wiped the tears away with his small fingers. "You are your father's son. You are much like him."

"I'm like you too." He smiled, and a dimple formed on either side of his mouth. "I have Mage magic just like you, so I can age here, in Elysium, so that one day you would see me as more than your baby."

"Oh, my beautiful boy. You are *so* clever. Can't you come home with me?"

"I wish I could but please know, I love you so much." His eyes glistened with tears as he clutched on to me. "There is so much left for you to do."

"My smart, smart boy. I'm so sorry you were taken from me, and I couldn't stop it. I couldn't save you."

"You must go now, Mother. There's something I must tell you," he said, tone urgent.

"What is it?" I clutched his hands.

"Makdou—she's stronger than you think. You're the only one who can stop her but tolls it will take." His form started to dissipate.

"What do you mean? Tolls it will take on whom? Me?" I frowned, confused by his riddle.

"Please tell Father I love him. I watch over you from time to time, and I'm always with you. Both of you." His words echoed as his face slowly faded. "What…would you…have named me?"

"Ascal." I smiled.

"I shall tell him." He nodded, never once removing his kind gaze from me until he disappeared.

I awoke on the long grass at the back of Meridian. Felix drew me to my feet, wrapped an arm around me, then guided me towards the main hall. Sofia stayed at my side for the whole time.

With my blurred vision, I stumbled through the meadow. My feet numbed, and my head spun.

"We have to keep moving!" he yelled over the thundering drums. "Meridian is under attack."

"Did…did the…the spell?" I tripped over my feet. Sensation slowly returned in the form of pins and needles. "Where are the others?"

"No, it didn't work. And I don't know where the others are," Sofia said. "Our priority is getting you inside. You look as if you'll pass out at any moment."

As if lingering on the cusp of consciousness, my

eyelids became heavy, and my head lolled against Felix's shoulder. "I saw…our son."

He peered at me, and his lips parted. But the surprise was gone in a second as he hauled me towards the doors. "We need to get you to safety. Everybody has been ordered to stay inside while the soldiers determine the level of threat we are under."

I jolted awake as the booming drums reached a crescendo.

"Where are the others?" I asked again.

"Don't worry about them, Evalyn. They are fine. We'll get you inside first, and you'll see them once order is restored." With his spare hand, he shoved the doors open, guiding me through the corridor. "Make some room, please!" he called over the bustling chatter of those who'd sought shelter.

"You heard him," Sofia added. "Come on now people, make some *room*."

"What in the realm happened to Evalyn?" a familiar voice asked.

"Seth?" I blinked through blurry eyes at the man in front of me.

"You got it." He smiled. "Dmitri and Lilith are here, too. Here—there's some cushions you can lay on. Much comfier than solid wood."

"Felix…help me." I sucked in a ragged breath.

Sofia had already dropped to her knees, propping up the cushions as Felix lowered me to the floor.

"Let's leave them to rest." Lilith took Seth by his arm. "Evalyn, I hope you are all right. We will speak more of this once you have regained your strength."

"The spell was too strong for her," Sofia said.

I nestled against Felix's chest, the sturdiness of him calming me. Another drumbeat startled me.

"Sofia?" he asked. "Can you help her?"

"I'm…right here…guys." I curled my lips into a half smile, although I couldn't open my eyes.

"Evalyn." Sofia snapped her fingers in front of me. "Stay awake. Felix, keep talking to her. Say something, anything you can think of—you shouldn't find it difficult."

"You're going to be okay, Evalyn," he soothed.

Mind muddled, and my limbs heavy, I raised my hand and pressed it against his cheek. I blinked at him through a blurry gaze. "He's just like you."

He held me tight, surrounding me with his warmth, and kissed my head.

"Evalyn." Sofia shook me. "Stay awake. Oh, it's no use. I need to start the spell now. For the love of all that is mighty, can you *please* give me some room? I'm trying to save a life here."

"You heard the lady—back up!" Felix shouted.

The yells and demands faded as I drifted in and out of consciousness. A warmth spread through me, and my arms tingled. A healing spell. The magic wrapped around me like a cosy blanket. Distant voices drew closer.

"Hmm…" I grumbled.

"Evalyn?" Felix soothed. "Sofia, get her something to drink."

"Already on it." She tilted my head back and pressed a stein to my lips. The cold liquid trickled into my mouth. Water.

"You should've warned us the spell could have

cost you your life." Lilith dropped to her knees and clasped her hands with mine. "Although I'm very grateful for what you have done for us. Hopefully, the Elders will keep up their end of the deal and let us take samples."

"It's not the spell, exactly," Sofia said. "It's Elysium. Every time she goes there, she increases her chances of being *stuck* there, unable to return to the living realm. And no matter how powerful she is, she's drawn to that place. Her son is there."

"You've got to be kidding me." Lilith pinched the bridge of her nose and tilted her head towards the ceiling. "The first time you visited Elysium, you *changed* everything. You *rewrote* your own timeline. What in the gods' names is it going to do this time?"

"I have no idea." I shook my head. "But…I got to see our son. His name is Ascal."

"Named after the High Elf?" Sofia asked.

"Yes." I wiped newly formed tears from my eyes. "I wanted to stay there. He'd aged too—I wanted to stay with him, and I know I can never return."

Felix rested his head against mine. "He is wonderful, isn't he?"

"Beautiful." I rested against his chest.

Women kept their children entertained by singing songs next to candlelight. Children listened to the melodic tunes, holding on to fuzzy blankets draped over their shoulders. Men, who weren't trained soldiers, paced the hall as the drums thundered over Meridian.

Shouts and chaotic orders from guards outside

silenced the mothers' songs. How long would we be stuck inside? Had the Orcs breached the settlement's perimeter?

"We can't possibly be under any serious threat," Lilith said in her delicate voice. "They can't breach the walls. There are archers—hundreds of trained foot soldiers—the Orcs are deluded to think they can conquer this fort."

"It's not them making the decisions." I sipped the water.

The drums silenced. Murmurs filled their place.

"It's over," Lilith said. "The soldiers must've defended Meridian."

"We need to act quickly." Dmitri flexed his fingers to crack them. "Lift the spell over the Great Mother Tree, get our samples, then get out of here."

"Evalyn is *not* performing this spell again. It will *kill* her," Felix said, ice crackling from his voice.

"How else are we going to lift the damned spell?" Lilith's frosty tone met his with equal measure. "People are relying on it. Including Reuben."

I knew Sofia and I couldn't perform the spell without the other's support, so I could say nothing else but, "I'll get it done. Reuben is not going to die."

Sofia nodded. "We'll figure it out."

---

The wooden floorboards beneath me had lost their shine from extensive footfall. Floor-to-ceiling stone pillars stood in the four corners of the room, supporting the high-domed ceiling. An intricate painting covered the expanse—angelic ladies wearing flowing skirts, their arms stretched towards their husbands to return home from war. Armoured men, lances in hand, rode on brown horses to slay the Orcs. At the other end of the painting, blood coloured the field crimson, and horses rode alone. Fallen soldiers lay face down in the dirt.

I stared at the fallen men. Death was inevitable, and I couldn't stop it.

"We can't just sit here," Lilith huffed. "We've been waiting for hours."

"It won't be long now before we can leave the hall," Seth soothed her impatient demands and stroked her arm with his fingers. "The guards will want to ensure it is safe for us and the civilians to return to their homes."

"I understand that, but Reuben is getting weaker by the moment." She sighed. "He would do anything for us, if it were the other way around."

"The Great Mother Tree isn't going anywhere," he said. "It'll be fine."

I couldn't blame Lilith—I would've broken down the doors and fought my way through the guards until I had the cure in my hands if I'd needed it for Sofia or Felix.

Lilith sighed through her nose. "Your own family may be at risk, Seth. What if the Orcs had burnt Langhurst to the ground? What would you do about that?"

"Calm down." I thumped the floorboards until

they turned to look at me.

Lilith jumped to her feet. "Everybody outside the walls is in danger. You should know—your settlements in Arogath were burned to the ground for your reaction. Remember? It's in the scroll, I've seen it. Regardless of the Crimson Kiss spell, the brutal, monstrous ways of the Orcs are the same. If anything, it just—"

"Enough," Felix growled. "That's enough, Lilith."

If I could just sleep…if I indulged this conversation, perhaps they'd let me rest.

"We can't say Orcs aren't trying to resist the spell, though. Do you think they *enjoy* being controlled by a Mage? The relationship between the two is hostile," I said. "The Orcs drained the Mages of their magic to fuel their machines. The Mages retaliated against them."

"What are you getting at?" Dmitri dragged his hand over his face.

"Don't you get it?" I sat up straight. "The Orcs have *always* wanted dominion—in multiple realms, it seems. They will fight the Crimson Kiss as much as they can. They would never admit defeat to one of their enemies."

"Are they strong enough to break the spell?" Sofia asked. "Makdou managed to control even you—a strong Light Mage—and was successful. What makes you think the Orcs will be any different?"

"There is one of me." I rested against Felix's chest and looked at the high ceiling. "There are thousands of Orcs out there. They'd be strong enough to resist it."

A small fleck of the painting fluttered down, illuminated by the torchlight. It tumbled, light and weightless, until it landed on Dmitri's lap.

"Let's hope they are." He flicked the paint from his trousers. "I never thought I would say this, but the Orcs may do us a favour. If they break the Crimson Kiss, there's one less issue we have to deal with. We can find a way of getting you home to Arogath and put a stop to Makdou for good."

# Chapter Thirteen

Guards burst through the solid oak doors of the hall. The Elders thundered in behind.

"We are no longer under threat, and you may return to your houses. We will remain posted around the settlement for the night to provide extra security," one of the guards said.

The villagers filed out of the hall, leaving me and my friends alone with the Elders.

Dierdre paced the length of the room. Lucien reclined into his seat—not a hair out of place—seemingly unphased by the invasion. Xavier nodded to his son, Dmitri.

Was his gesture a sign of respect? They had a

strange relationship I didn't understand, although I was in no place to judge. My father was fuelled by his ambition to lead, and I'd been without a mother for almost twenty years. Cracks ran through my family as they did his.

"The Orcs have never breached Meridian." Lucien waved his hand. "They never will."

"How can you be so sure?" I leaned forward. "After what you know of the scroll, everything your own people have experienced with the Orcs, you think they won't give it everything they've got? Do you think the walls will stand undefeated forever?"

He clasped his hands in front of him and smiled. "You are new here and unfamiliar with our ways."

"Lucien," Dierdre warned.

He ignored her and took a step towards me. "While we know everything about you, you know nothing of us, the history of Swynvale, and the many wars the Humans and Orcs have fought over the last millennium. Your wars are different from ours. My point is, we have *never* fallen into the hands of Orcs."

His words hung heavy in the room. We'd defeated the Dark Mages and the Orcs in my realm, but with great difficulty, and I couldn't be sure I wasn't out of luck. Despite our hardships, the people of Arogath trusted me to lead them out of war and into a stable, brighter future. The Elders needed my help—I needed to gain their trust.

"Let's focus on the mission at hand," Dmitri said. "Now the breach has been resolved, we need to return our attention to the Great Mother Tree."

"Evalyn is too weak," Sofia said. "Her time in

Elysium could've killed her. We won't be able to lift the spell, not until she's rested, and even then, it still poses a significant risk to her life—one I'm not prepared to make."

The Dark Mages had once used Blood Magic to connect themselves with the portal in Southkeep to allow Demons and the Ezen Riders to pass through. What if I could use it?

"What is it?" Sofia said. "You're frowning. What are you thinking?"

"Blood Magic…yes…that could work. Perhaps there's a way I could use my blood to help."

"No way, it's not happening," Felix said, jerking his head towards me. "We cannot risk losing you."

"We risk my life every day; besides, they used Blood Magic for evil reasons." I rose, leaving the blanket in a puddle around my feet. "If I fuse my blood with Sofia's, we should be powerful enough to reveal the Great Mother Tree."

"How can you be so sure this will work?" Sofia fixed her stern gaze on me.

"Because I'm a Mage, and I have learned a lot from our enemies." The words left my mouth with conviction.

Seth straightened his shirt. "What are you waiting for? Let's go."

Purple tinges kissed the thin clouds stretching across the twilight sky. Pebbles crunched underfoot as we walked towards the grassland. Lupin grew in shades of lilac, indigo, and pink, and their florid scent filled my nose. Dmitri walked ahead with Felix, leaving Sofia and me to discuss other matters.

"He'll be fine, you know." I took her hand as she stared ahead. "I know you care for him."

"I wasn't thinking about Dmitri." She laughed. "Fine, you're right. Have you got a blade? We need to perform the ritual."

"I hope you know how to perform a Blood Magic spell." I drew a small blade from inside my right boot.

The metal glinted under the light of nearby torches positioned along the path. Deep sounds of clanking metal echoed from the blacksmith, and patrolling soldiers' footsteps thudded along the cobbled streets.

"I have knowledge of them," she said. "Although I've never had a reason to use them. This is going to be interesting."

With the Elders in tow, Seth overtook us. They spoke among themselves as they followed us through the flowers and grass.

Dmitri halted in the swaying grass ahead.

When I came up beside Felix, he took me to the side, out of earshot. "I still don't think this is a good idea. Blades and blood. It reminds me of you lying in your *own* blood, and I couldn't save you. What if this goes wrong? What if this is all a ploy from Makdou?"

Doubt festered in my mind. What if the Great Mother Tree wasn't really what we thought? He may be right—this could be another trick. Another thread in her tapestry of deceit.

"You need to stop blaming yourself," I said. "I wish you could've seen our son in Elysium— perhaps that would've brought you peace. He looks much like you. I must do this so the rest of us may find the same peace."

He gritted his teeth but nodded.

Joining Sofia, I positioned myself opposite her, with our friends surrounding us. The torches crackled in the distance. A chilled evening breeze stirred the grass.

My fingers trembled as I dragged the blade across the palm of my hand. The image of the knife plunging into my stomach burned in my mind. I winced at the searing heat of the cut as my crimson blood spilled from the surface.

I handed Sofia the blade. She sliced her palm, then gave the blade to Dmitri, who wiped the lingering drops onto his breeches. Our onlookers remained silent.

"You need to give me your hand." She held her palm in front of her as her blood pooled. "The Dark Mages used a different spell, and it would've taken all their strength to power the portal. We don't need something of such magnitude."

My heart hammered as I gripped her hand, the blood oozing out the sides of our pressed palms.

We closed our eyes, and I listened to her chant. It wasn't the same language we'd used to find the portal in Southkeep. I made a mental note to ask her about it later.

Rather than the soft, ethereal cocoon the revealing spell had conjured earlier, a swirling crimson spiralled around us. It resembled the great red bursts of light I created in battle.

The spell swirled high into the air in a storm cloud. Magic coursed through my veins, setting them alight. My body tingled with power. Time slowed. I understood the Dark Mages. After a millennium of conjuring Dark Magic, they couldn't break their addiction.

I focused on why I used this spell. Fear—the fear of becoming something I hated—couldn't overcome me. Instead, I envisioned my son's face and let it fuel my magic. The power surged through my body, burning my skin.

The charge of magic rose to a crescendo—deafeningly loud. Then, as if snapped, the sound subsided and with it the burning sensation in my skin.

The cocoon unravelled around us and revealed the Great Mother Tree. Long, peach-coloured tendrils hung from the branches and met the tall grass. The trunk grew tall with thick limbs sprouting to the sides. Each tendril sparkled with magic. I jumped back as a vine-like root twisted out of the ground between my feet.

"W-we did it," Sofia gasped. "We did it!" She clutched my hands and shook them up and down. "How magnificent."

"I can't believe it." I smiled at the Tree's shimmering pink hue. The hairs on my neck stood on end.

"It's the most beautiful thing I've ever seen." Lucien knelt in the long grass and traced his crooked fingers along one of the winding roots.

Villagers joined us at the back of the settlement. The Elders welcomed them.

"I—I can't believe my eyes." Lilith jumped. "We must collect vials from the healers. Seth, come with me quickly." The pair dashed through the gathering crowd.

"Guards, bring the ill at once. Find the sick—anyone who is being treated by the healers," Lucien ordered.

Dierdre and Xavier knelt beside Lucien, touching the roots of the trees as they gazed at the glowing tendrils. Civilians lowered themselves onto the grass. Mothers hugged their children and smiled, seemingly at the wonder they now shared Meridian with. A man wrapped a blanket around his child and looked at me.

"Thank you," he said.

My heart warmed. Sofia and I'd given the people of Meridian hope.

Seth rushed through the grass with a basket of vials rattling around inside, Lilith at his side.

"What do we do?" Dierdre asked. "To heal the sick?"

"I think there's something special about the roots. The people should touch them." I traced my fingers across the sturdy surface of the roots.

"You heard her." Dierdre beckoned the guards.

The guards helped the ill and frail through the crowd and eased them onto the roots. The sick fell unconscious as the light flooded them.

Sofia knelt on the moss beside me.

"Why didn't you say anything? You would know about the roots, right?" Surely, she would've had her speculations.

"I wanted you to trust your instincts, and you did—" She met my gaze and gasped.

"What?" I frowned.

170

"Your eyes are red. It's not something I thought would happen but—"

"What do you mean?"

"It's evil magic by nature." She gripped my arm. "We have to be careful."

My attention was caught by a pulsating current and light surged through the tree roots and tendrils. How could I transfer its healing magic to Meridian's civilians?

I rose, racking my brain of what to do next. Many gazes fixed on me.

I closed my eyes, and a low hum rumbled through the tree trunk and vibrated the ground beneath my feet. Gasps filled the silence. An image flickered before my eyes. A shape—a person—I couldn't tell. Its ethereal form glistened white.

The form chanted. As if compelled, the same foreign words fell from my mouth. They weren't the ancient words of the Noble Ones.

"Thank you for revealing me, Evalyn. After all this time, I can once again protect the balance of life," the Great Mother said. She pressed her hand onto my chest where my heart was. Her power rushed through her into me.

The tune ended, and I opened my eyes. My pulse rang in my ears, adrenaline flooding my veins. I dropped to my knees beside the closest unconscious civilian.

She fluttered her eyelids, squinted until her eyes adjusted, then stared at the purple clouds—a single eagle flying overhead. Lilith gasped.

Was the eagle an omen for the people's healing?

People from the crowd hurried to their loved

ones who had been healed by the Tree. They cried.

I couldn't decide if they were tears of joy or of mourning. If the Tree had been discovered sooner, many more people could've lived.

With a sharp syringe, Lilith punctured a tree root and lifted the plunger, the tube filling with a pale peach liquid.

"Fill as many as you can," Sofia said. "I can use it to make a tonic."

Lilith and Seth set about filling the vials, while Xavier gave orders to a nearby guard.

"Send scrolls to each house. Every man old and fit enough must be taken to the training grounds. Now we have revealed the Tree, we must protect it at all costs," he said.

"You did it!" Felix gathered me in his arms, a look of fierce pride in his eyes. "I'm so proud of you."

I pushed up onto my tiptoes and kissed him.

~ * ~

Once the basket was filled with samples, we made our way back to Dierdre's house.

Torches glowed in the distance, and joyous cheers rang through the settlement. An elderly man discarded his walking stick and skipped along the cobbled path with a young girl in tow. Her giggles created a warmth inside me.

Revealing the Tree had brought happiness within a couple of hours, I couldn't imagine what great things it would do for the people of Meridian over the coming weeks.

When we were huddled inside, Dierdre put the kettle on to boil, then made us each a mug of steaming tea.

Sofia held hers close to her chest. "I can't believe you did it."

"I couldn't have done it without you." I flicked my gaze from her to the families dancing on the streets outside.

"The Tree exists. Seeing the Tree in all its beauty—its phenomenal healing properties—who would choose to leave that behind?" she asked.

"I met her." The muscles in my chest and back loosened as I relaxed in my chair. "The Great Mother. She's real. The people of Meridian will be able to access her."

"We're one step closer to going home." Her lips curved into a slight smile, but she gazed past me.

I left Sofia to her thoughts and delved into my own. The Great Mother *loved* me. She guided me towards the light even though Blood Magic tainted my eyes.

Dmitri planted a kiss on Sofia's cheek as he joined them in the seating area, a brew in his hands. Her face turned pink.

Sipping my tea, I watched Dierdre open the back door. Chickens clucked as they scurried around the stone floor. Herbs were planted in ground beds, along with parsnips and leeks. Broad beans grew up sticks, and at the back of the garden, an almond tree stood in full glory.

Dierdre, with a book in one hand, lit the candle positioned on the table beside her, then lowered onto the bench. One gust of wind and the flame would blow out. Dmitri wandered outside to join his mother, beckoning Seth and Lilith.

With Felix's arm draped about me, we watched the fire dance until night fell, and the sparse candles in their iron bowls burned out. Wax droplets set down the length of the candle and solidified in a pool at the bottom.

Dmitri leaned close to Sofia. "You'll be going home soon."

Her eyes sparkled. She glanced at her hands and nodded. Tears fell from her eyes.

"I could come with you, see what your world is like," he said in a soft tone, almost inaudible.

I shifted my gaze to the fire in the hearth, giving them a little privacy.

"You would like it," she whispered.

I thought of home, and although many memories haunted my realm, I couldn't help the burning love within me. The way the sunlight hit the multicoloured glass of the Citadel at Lake Delendil, how it refracted across the water and mosaic bridge.

I swore I could smell the sweet, scented flowers in the gardens next to the water. The image burned bright in my mind as if I could reach out and touch them.

Felix reached out with his fingers and lifted my chin until our gazes met. "It is only a matter of time until we get to go home. Soon."

I smiled and rested my hand over his. "I know. And together, the thought of it is not so daunting."

———～———

The next morning, we strolled along the cobbled

path towards the hall. The scent of warm, crusty bread wafted from the bakery. A farmer herded goats through the courtyard, and horses whinnied from the stables. Women pegged laundry on the washing lines, and men left for work. The roaring of the furnace at the blacksmith could be heard above all, and the clanking of metal being beaten into swords rang through the settlement.

Dmitri brooded in the corner, keeping a fair distance from his father, while Sofia, Felix, and I took our seats. Lilith and Seth had gone to the carriages, to secure their samples to take back to the Temple.

"Now that we've rested, we need to find a way to open the portal back to Arogath," Felix said, his hand on my thigh.

"The last time I did that, Makdou blocked my access." I rested my knuckles against my chin.

"I know a way," Sofia sat straight, gaze fixed on me, "but you won't like it."

"Let me guess." My heart rate sped up. "This has something to do with Blood Magic."

"Yes," she whispered. "Unfortunately, it does, but what choice do we have?"

"No," Felix said instantly, his voice cold and hard.

I pushed back my chair, then paced back and forth. She was right, but my eyes had already changed colour. What was next?

She cleared her throat. "Evalyn, listen to me. You are my queen, and I wouldn't risk your life. Look at what we are capable of when using Blood Magic." She flung her hands into the air.

"I know what Blood Magic does. I've seen it, remember? I've seen the evil it can do. Let me remind you that the spell we used to reveal the Tree was *half* the magnitude of what the Mages did. Who knows what another spell will do to me? Didn't you say we'd need to be careful?"

"Can you think of any alternatives?" She tilted her head a fraction.

"I'm not doing it." I sank into my chair and stared at the fallen pieces of paint on the floorboards. "Don't ask me again."

"You must see reason," she implored.

"Sofia," Felix warned—a sharp edge to his voice. "She's given you her answer. Leave her be."

She shook her head, then left the hall, skimming past Dmitri, who lingered in the doorway.

If I could get my hands on some books—on any magical literature—I could learn another way to get out of here. I longed to be in the grand library of the Citadel at Lake Delendil.

I tapped my fingers against my arm. Why was Makdou making it impossible for us to travel home?

The Elders hurried into the hall. Dierdre stopped in the doorway to embrace her son, then returned to her husband's side. Xavier nodded at Dmitri.

"It will only be a matter of time before word gets out about the Great Mother Tree's existence. We can't trust everyone—who knows if we have infiltrators living in Meridian, someone controlled by the Orcs or Makdou?" Lucien said. "We need extra security measures—soldiers to patrol. Sentries positioned at every street, corner and courtyard, additional archers on the walls."

"It's a done deal." Xavier nodded. "The guards have already started their rounds of the village—men will soon be filing into the training grounds."

A beat passed before he shifted his gaze to me. "I suppose you will be taking my son with you on this mission of yours. Shame he hasn't accepted his legacy in Meridian. His home." He spoke of his son as if he wasn't there. "He would have been an Elder."

I glanced at Dmitri, who stood rigid.

As Felix accompanied me outside, I placed my hand on Dmitri's arm and smiled. "Let's get out of here." I lowered my voice to a whisper. "Dierdre, do you have a library?"

"Of course, we do," she said. "I will show you the way—"

"Don't do anything stupid." Xavier's voice rang sharp from behind. "We need you alive."

Felix shot him a glare.

Dierdre escorted us to the library as the others left the hall.

"Is he always like that?" I strolled beside her, through a long corridor with domed ceilings.

"Twenty-five years we've been married, and even *I* can't control his behaviour. Lucien can, although they bicker like siblings. There is respect between them, though."

We parted ways with Dmitri, who muttered something about finding Sofia. Felix, however, stayed with me.

Diedre led us down the west-wing corridor to a large room. An intricate painting covered the ceiling, yet this one didn't peel, suggesting it wasn't as old. The colours were vibrant, and the light illuminated the small details—a chain of beads around a woman's neck and an engraving along a man's sword.

"Can you tell this room is my pride and joy?" She beamed. "I come here every few days to find a story to read in the evenings. Whatever you're looking for, you'll find it here."

Aisles of bookcases filled the circular room. Daylight leaked in through the windows and drenched the room in a yellow glow. A servant wove her way through the aisles, dusting each book and shelf.

I gestured to the first bookcase. "Can you help get some of these books down?"

"Of course," Felix said. "Tell me which ones, and where you want them."

Scanning the shelf, I read the spines. "I won't be able to tell which will be useful until I flick through them. Grab a bunch of them, and put them on the table, please."

With ease, he did as I asked. When they were piled on the table, I flipped open the tome at the top of the stack. Its pages were filled with runes next to a vial of red liquid. Blood Magic. I slammed the book shut, then tossed it aside. "Not that one."

How could there be texts of Blood Magic in this realm? There weren't any Mages in Swynvale. Pressing my fingers to my chin, I considered how these books could've possibly found a home on a bookshelf in a world where they wouldn't be needed.

Regardless, I couldn't use Blood Magic, not if it meant risking my life. I'd need an alternative method of opening a portal. One that wouldn't taint my magic or harm me, Sofia, or Felix on our travel back to Arogath. It had to be discreet so, wherever Makdou was, she wouldn't sense us.

"What is it you're looking for, exactly?" Felix asked. "Maybe I can help."

"I appreciate your offer, but you don't know magic." I raised a brow. "But that reminds me. Did you know your ancestors were Mages? Reuben said they played a pivotal role in concealing the Tree."

His brows shot up. "No, I didn't. I'll have to check out the library in the Citadel when we return home. See if there's any mention of it."

"You might not find anything. They fled to Arogath to live Human lives. If there's any mention of your ancestors, I suspect it'll be here." I motioned to the shelves.

"Hmm, I'll have a look. Call me if you need anything." He headed to the aisles.

Someone knocked on the door. I turned to find Sofia lingering in the doorway.

Her lips curved into a smile. "I thought I'd come help you find another option."

"Why hasn't the Blood Magic affected you?" I frowned.

"I have High Priestess abilities." She shrugged. "It's instinct for my body to attack intrusive magic."

Her words hung in the air. She'd be fine while I…what would happen to me? Would I spiral out of control as the Blood Magic took root inside me? I couldn't let that happen, not when people needed me.

"Wow." Sofia gazed at the oak bookcases engraved with passages of foreign tongue.

The scripture was written in a language I didn't understand.

"This place is magnificent, and we thought we had something spectacular in the Citadel. Without understanding the language some of these books are written in, it'll be near impossible to find anything of use. We'll need to find someone who can translate. What do you have there?" She glanced at the booked tossed aside.

"Blood Magic, can you believe it?" I shook my head.

"How is that possible?" she asked.

After I filled her in about Felix's ancestry, she raised her brows. "Explains why he's nose-deep in a book over there. Can you even *understand* it?" She called over to him, amusement twinkling in her eyes.

"Not really." He laughed. "But there's a few books containing family trees. I'll see if I recognise any of the names."

"That'll be like finding a needle in a haystack." Sofia chuckled, then grabbed a wooden stool and placed it in front of the bookcase. Stepping onto it, she grabbed a book from the highest shelf. "I've never seen anything like this before." She flicked through the yellowed pages of the book in her hands. "The whole of Meridian's history must be in here."

I started down one of the central aisles. Many of

the book spines were scribed with the same ancient tongue carved on the wooden bookcases.

Scanning the spines of several books, I tried to decipher the words emblazoned on them. "This is Dierdre's personal library. Either she'll be able to translate, or she'll know who can."

"Well, we might as well work our way through these." Sofia hopped off the stool with a stack of books in her hands, then laid them side by side on the carpet. "We've ruled out Blood Magic. I thought about what you said, and you're right. After what it did to your eyes, we can't take any more chances—this sort of magic is addictive. It's a drug you won't be able to get off if you get in too deep. It'll send you on the same evil path as Makdou."

Breathing out slowly, I nodded once. "Exactly. There must be another way. We'll start by reading the texts we do understand and leave the ones needing translation for later."

Together, we dove into the texts, surrounded by thousands more books and not enough time.

# Chapter Fourteen

W e searched the library into the evening, and we were no closer to finding the book we needed. When Felix had given up on finding any reference of his ancestors, he went in search of Seth and Lilith to see if he could offer another set of hands in readying their carriages for departure.

A servant came in to light the candles dotted around the room, then lit the logs in the hearth. She placed a silver tray, with two bowls filled to the brim with stew onto the round wooden table in the centre of the room. Although I'd eaten the same hearty meal the night before, it would act as fuel through the long night ahead.

Slumping into the wooden seat, I arranged the cushion behind my back, then brought the bowl to my chest. I kicked off my shoes, sank my feet into the thick, woven rug, then scooped the warm stew and ate it as the fire warmed me.

I finished my meal and gulped a mouthful of water from the goblet.

"My head is pounding." I rubbed my temples as I stared at the ceiling.

"Well, you'll be pleased to know I've found something." Sofia slid the book towards me, tapping the page.

Clasping the nearby candle, I brought it closer to the text. Its inscribed title was written in gold and hadn't lost its shine over the years. The language matched the text written on the bookcases and spines.

"You certainly have," I said. "We can ask Dierdre if she can translate it."

Who'd written it and how had the ink lasted this long? Some pages contained diagrams of strange symbols or runes unfamiliar to me. Notations and drawings of circular devices covered every free space.

I flipped the book closed, then headed towards the doorway of the library. "I'm hoping I can catch her before she retires for the night."

"Shall I come with you?" She scooted her chair back.

"No—spend time with Dmitri. I'll figure it out, thank you." Before she could object, I left the room and hurried down the corridor.

I found Dierdre in the small war room off the

side of the hall. She sat at a wooden table displaying a map. In one hand, she clutched a book, and in the other, an ink-dipped quill.

"Dierdre?" I knocked on the door frame.

She glanced up from her work. "Ah, I thought you may come in search of me. When the others left, I chose to linger for when you would call upon me." The candlelight illuminated the tiny freckles scattered across her nose and cheeks. "You have a problem dear—you cannot read the text."

"Why didn't you tell me before?" I sank into the seat beside her.

"What difference does it make? Either way, you would find the book you need. I will be able to translate whatever spell will be of use to you."

"How will you know which spell I'll need? You don't perform magic."

"I'm not an idiot." She eyed me over the rim of her specs and set her work and quill aside. "I don't need to be a Mage to understand what the spells do."

"Of course."

"Now hush child, and hand me your book." She plucked it from me, laid it open in front of her, and scanned the pages. "Can you fetch me a piece of parchment from the cabinet?"

I brought her the parchment. Dipping her quill into the inkpot, she scribbled her translation. "This is what you're looking for, I'm sure of it."

She paused her writing three-quarters of the way down the page and tapped her fingers on it. I leaned forward to get a glimpse at the words, but her writing was too small for me to read under the dim lighting.

Once she'd scrawled the last curl, she put the quill aside, then handed me the piece of parchment and smiled. "You ought to bid farewell to your friends before you conjure the spell. I should imagine it'll take a lot of energy, and the portal will not hold for long."

Her footsteps echoed as she disappeared from the room.

I stared at the spell in my hands. The key to going home. I didn't know what I feared more—defeating Makdou or seeing my son's headstone. But it was time.

Heading out of the hall, I made my way over the rope bridge and down the sloping street. The washing lines hung above my head, and the water-slick cobblestones glistened under the torchlight. As night fell over Meridian, I wondered how much time had passed in Arogath.

When I reached Dierdre's house, I hauled the door inwards.

Dmitri and Sofia were cuddled next to the fire with mugs of tea in their hands. As I entered, Dmitri rose, then prodded the fire with an iron poker. Dark shadows circled his eyes.

Sofia placed her mug on the table. "What is it?"

"It's time. For us to go home—all of us." I swallowed, trying to rid the dryness from my mouth. Returning home meant facing my demons.

She froze, her eyes glistening under the firelight. Dmitri reached her side in two long strides and pulled her to his chest. I remained silent.

"Come with us?" she asked Dmitri in a low tone.

I hadn't expected her to ask him that. How could he leave everything he knew behind?

"There is so much for me to do here—so much responsibility." He stroked her cheek. "Yet I don't want you to go without me, knowing you'll be facing danger."

"What are you saying?" She clasped his hand and gazed into his eyes.

They should've had privacy, but we didn't have time for it. I tapped my foot lightly against the carpet. "I'll introduce you to my council, explain your presence, and you'll be accepted. I'm sorry to push you, Dmitri, but we need a decision. We don't have much time."

"I will come," he said, and a wide smile spread across his face. "I won't leave your side until this is sorted." He planted a kiss on Sofia's forehead.

"We'll go to Felix now, tell him it's time. Then we should cast a spell in the field at the back of the settlement, by the Great Mother Tree." I grabbed my cloak, draping it over my shoulders. "It'll give us plenty of space and nothing will be damaged if something should go wrong with the spell."

"Won't you need to say goodbye to anyone, Dmitri?" Sofia asked.

"My mother has visions remember—she knew this was coming." His gaze hollowed. "Even if they are fractured, she still has her feelings—her senses."

"She must be so proud of you," she said softly.

"Come on, let's head out." I headed outside, and the cool night breeze nipped my cheeks.

———————— ～✧. ————————

Once we'd bid farewell to Seth and Lilith, offering them a safe journey home and best wishes for healing Reuben and their soldiers, Felix and I led the way up the hill, across the wooden bridge to the stretch of long grass next to the Tree. Its tendrils swayed in the evening breeze.

I vibrated with anticipation, about to return home to those who'd become my family. My last visit was abrupt, filled with disdain towards the High Elves. My time away allowed me to heal and remind myself of my purpose. As queen, I needed to free my people of the evil lingering in Arogath.

A fluttering sensation stirred within me. I could almost taste the fresh air of Lake Delendil.

"Felix, could you hold this in front of us so Sofia and I can read the spell?" I plucked the piece of parchment from my pocket and handed it to him.

She and I held each other's hand and read the spell aloud. I stumbled over the unfamiliar words, but after practice, the chant rolled from my tongue. The magical cocoon formed around us in a pale peach colour, much like the tendrils of the Great Mother Tree.

We repeated the spell three times as required on the parchment. The cocoon evaporated. We waited for the portal to manifest. I jiggled my leg.

The ethereal circular shape appeared in front of us, hovering a foot above the ground.

"We need to concentrate on the image of Lake

Delendil to ensure we will travel there," Sofia instructed.

"I'll lead the way." I had more experience in travelling through portals, so it needed to be me. "I have the clearest image of Lake Delendil—it's my home after all. Keep hold of Dmitri or the portal may rip him apart. I will do the same with Felix."

Dmitri swallowed. "This sounds like it'll be a pleasant experience."

"You'll be fine," Sofia whispered, "just don't let go of my hand."

I clasped Felix's hand in mine, then we walked through the portal, leaving the swaying grass and the evening air of Meridian behind. As we floated in between dimensions, we became nothing, only consciousness.

We reappeared, whole, on the other side—the mosaic glass bridge in front of us.

A black sky hung over Arogath, and the water glimmered under the moonlight. Fire torches flickered from across the lake. Candlelight glowed in the Citadel windows.

Tears welled in my eyes.

"What's wrong?" Felix asked, touching my arm.

"I left with such animosity for my friends—for you." I wiped the tears from my face. "Now I return with love. Swynvale's magic has made me feel at peace."

"I know." He squeezed my hand. "You can pick flowers from the garden and lay them next to our son's headstone. He would like that."

"We'll do it together." I nudged him playfully with my shoulder.

"This place is remarkable. A whole castle made of glass and marble? Look at all those colours—I can only imagine how it glimmers under sunlight." Dmitri hurried ahead.

"You have a lot to see." She laughed as she jogged to catch up with him.

"At least they're happy," I said to Felix.

The guards in golden armour flung open the doors. The stone soldiers that once protected the lake against the Ezen Riders stood rigid in the entrance. How much time had passed since we'd disappeared into Swynvale?

"Evalyn?" Kiirion's eyes widened as I sped towards him. "You are home. I...I cannot find the words. What happened to your eyes?"

He pulled me into an embrace and smothered me. When he let go, Theodas and Valneris hugged me in turn.

"I will explain momentarily," I said.

"Are you okay?" Valneris asked. "How about you, Felix? At least the two of you were together."

"Fine, thank you." Felix bowed his head. "There's much to discuss."

"We can explain all this." I pushed the wooden door of the council room open. The ruby-encrusted table glistened inside. "Take your seats. I must introduce you to my friend. He can be trusted." I hurried through the introduction, eager to get to important matters.

"Locate Eric and bring him to us," Valneris ordered the guard, who stood nearby. "Try to pry Xurek from his training ground too. Tell him his queen has returned."

The guard exited the room.

Kiirion propped his arms on the table and waited. I reclined into my seat, while Sofia and Dmitri sat in the wooden chairs opposite me. Felix sat beside me, resting his hand on my leg. A servant placed goblets in front of each of us and filled them to the brim with red wine. I took a large gulp, needing to take the edge off before I revealed the mission.

The wooden doors burst open, and Xurek thundered into the room. Eric hurried in behind him. He'd grown a short beard of dark hair that camouflaged his angled jaw. Dmitri stiffened at the presence of an Orc, but when Sofia took his hand, he relaxed.

"I'm glad to see you well, Evalyn, but what in hell has happened to your eyes?" Xurek pulled back a wide-framed chair. He was a large Orc with wide shoulders and arms double the size of any normal sized Human.

"As am I, my—" Eric beamed, but when his gaze fell on me, his words fell short.

"I'm glad to see you both again." I clasped my hands in my lap. "Truly. I left this world in a great deal of pain, but I have been healing. While we have returned with matters to discuss, I want to apologise for leaving you—my people—at a perilous time, and I cannot thank you enough for looking after this kingdom in my absence. Do not fret about the colour of my eyes. I will explain."

My friends nodded, and I interpreted this as their acceptance of my apology.

"These last two months in Swynvale have

allowed me the time to heal and meet kind-hearted people who have helped me. And when Felix joined me there, it made the process easier. The grief will never end—not truly—but I know we can deal with it. While we were there, the use of green magic in Orc wars has made me fear that Makdou is using the Crimson Kiss on a large scale—influencing the Orcs of Swynvale and here."

"Wait. Two months?" Eric's brow creased. He leaned back against his chair. "You've been gone for two years."

A silence formed in the council room. All words escaped me. My breath lodged itself in my throat. Two years I'd abandoned my people. I looked at Felix—his face had paled, and a muscle feathered in his jaw. Even Sofia shook her head in disbelief.

"I-I don't know what to say. Two years—are you sure? In Swynvale, only a few minutes had passed when we came back from our trip here the last time. Wait, this doesn't make sense." I turned my gaze to Valneris. My voice broke. "Is this true?"

"I'm afraid so, my queen," he replied, his eyes hollow and dark. Fine lines formed underneath them.

I lifted my goblet to my lips and drank the wine in one gulp, then gestured to the servant. "More. I need *more*."

"Evalyn," Sofia said gently. She stretched across the table, resting her palm on my trembling hand.

I snapped my gaze to her.

What had I done? How could I explain this to my subjects? As if he sensed my thoughts, Felix took my hand in his, and rubbed his thumb against my skin.

"The Orcs have retreated to the Barren Territories." Kiirion unravelled the large map and rolled it across the table. He pinned it down with stone figures, then dragged his finger over the Badlands. "Since the near extinction of the Dark Mages, the Orcs have regained dominion of their land and haven't tried to overthrow the Fertile Territories."

His words echoed in my ears. My vision blurred. *'You've been gone for two years.'*

"Evalyn." Sofia shook my hand.

"What? Oh…yes. Sorry." I withdrew my hand and flattened it against my leg. "It's odd they haven't tried to regain dominion. The Orcs were brutal beasts, who loved to murder and torture people because they could. This makes me think this has something to do with Makdou and the Crimson Kiss."

"The main focus should be finding Makdou and putting an end to her," Theodas added. "Then we'll be able to tell how the blasted Orcs behave on their own."

I stared at the map—the thin line of barren land separated the two territories. My unmoving gaze caused the map to blur. "It has to be me. I must be the one to kill her."

"We will be with you when the time comes," Kiirion said.

I dragged a hand over my face as a heaviness settled in my bones. "Felix, will you come with me to visit our son's gravestone? I need a moment with him. We will resume this meeting in the morning."

Later that night, I parted with Felix to bathe. Afterwards, I retired to my chamber, closing the door behind me. I stared at the floor, tinged brown, in front of the fireplace. I knelt and traced my fingers along the polished floor. My muscles ached.

The memories of Sofia shouting at me as she clutched and tugged at my lifeless body—my blood pooling around me—begging me to be okay, swarmed my mind. Then blank. Darkness. Elysium. Everything else passed in a blur.

I frowned and gazed into the lit hearth. My memories were fragmented, scattered across the planes of my mind like spilled beads. A lump formed in my throat, and a tightness constricted my heart. Whirling around, I fled the room and headed for Felix's.

I clicked the door shut behind me, pressing my back to the wooden surface. My heart hammered. Felix glanced up at me from the bed, a night robe tied loosely around his waist. He strode over to me and draped his strong arms around me. Drawing me to his chest, he held me as I sobbed against him. He smoothed my hair away from my face.

"I'm sorry, Felix." His shirt muffled my words. "For everything."

"Shh," he soothed.

With my face pressed against his muscled torso, his heart pumped fast. "It's okay," he said, voice strained.

"When I saw our son, he was grown, and he's happy," I whispered, keeping his shirt bunched in my hand, for fear I might fall to my knees. "Safe. In Elysium."

"Happy," he repeated in a featherlight voice.

My stomach knotted, and a lump created pressure in my throat. Why was I nervous about our intimacy? We'd been alone together since I'd left, but not in the Citadel. Regardless of what happened, I needed him, yearned for him, and I hoped he wanted me too.

My pulse pounded in my ears as I stepped back, only enough to see his eyes, and the same bright desire burning in them. He ran his thumb over my bottom lip. As he traced his fingers down the column of my throat, I held my breath, focusing on nothing but the heat he left on my skin.

With my back against the wall, he positioned one of his arms beside my head. He pressed his forehead against mine, each of his breaths ragged. "Evalyn…"

"Yes," I said, a little abruptly. "My answer is yes."

And he needed no further encouragement. He ran his hand up my leg, hooking it under my knee, and I wrapped myself around him, enveloping him with my arms. There was nothing slow or tentative about our kiss. My lips parted for him, and his mouth explored mine, while his hands worked on the buttons of my shirt. As he did so, I shoved the robe off his shoulders, letting it drop to the floor in a puddle. I ran my fingers up the hard planes of his abdomen.

My stomach somersaulted.

"Please," I pleaded against his mouth. If one thing would bring us back together, fully, it was this. For he was mine, and I was his.

He groaned as he planted a kiss on my neck, yanking my shirt down from my shoulders. I tossed it aside as he worked on the buttons of my breeches. With my clothes discarded, he scooped me up, cradling me against his bare chest.

I cupped his cheek with my palm. His eyes were deep and bright, and although I felt as if I floated somewhere above my body, he kept me anchored, grounded.

He pulled back the drapes of his four-poster bed and laid me on the feathery covers. The curtain fell back into place, concealing us from the rest of the world.

Lowering himself, he hooked his arms around my thighs and hoisted me closer. He looked up at me with a mischievous grin and hunger in his eyes. "If I could have this view for the rest of my life, I would die a happy man."

My cheeks burned and gooseflesh covered my body. Not a single inch of my skin was covered, and I craved his touch everywhere.

"I could say the same about you." I let my gaze roam across the rigged surface of his shoulders and biceps. "You make me a very happy woman, indeed."

"Oh, I think there's at least one thing I can do to make you feel even happier." He ran his thumb across my sensitive spot, his breath a gentle tease, and he inched closer.

"Is that so?" I weaved my fingers through his hair, guiding him to where I desperately wanted him.

"Yes." His voice was gravelly with the remnants of his restraint. "I'm going to make you scream."

Before I had the chance to respond, he buried his mouth against me, suckling me into his mouth. The unexpected intensity of it had me arching my back off the bed.

He let go of one of my thighs, only to hold me pinned to the mattress while he ran his tongue against me.

I quivered, shooting my hands into his hair for something to hold onto.

With no room to squirm, I could only lie there, trapped by his arms, and take the mounting pleasure he gave me.

When he groaned against me, I moaned, relishing the sensation of vibration. I gripped his hair in my fist and hooked my ankles together behind him.

Moving his hands, he cupped my buttocks and lifted me off the bed, giving him better access. He speared me with his tongue, exploring deeper, and I could see nothing but blurry stars behind my closed eyelids. My entire body hummed.

My legs trembled uncontrollably as he urged me towards release. I kept my lips clamped tightly closed, for I knew it wouldn't take much for me to scream, just like he'd asked.

As if sensing my resistance, he shifted his weight, lowering me back onto the mattress, only to slide two fingers inside me, while running his tongue against my sensitive spot.

I moaned, tilting my head back as he pumped his fingers into me, mounting in speed. "Scream, Evalyn."

A shrill cry of pleasure tore from my mouth as release erupted through my body, setting each of my nerve endings on fire.

My eyes flashed open to see a burst of white sparkling light pouring from my body. The planks of the bed creaked and splintered beneath us, threatening to collapse. Panting, I couldn't care less who had heard.

"The servants won't be pleased to see we have damaged my bed as well as yours." Felix quirked a brow, then pressed a kiss to the inside of my thigh.

"I don't care," I said breathlessly. "Not even a little bit."

"For the next part, I think we should use the floor." He trailed tender kisses on my hip bone and up my abdomen, before running his teeth against my sensitive nipple.

"Felix." I ran my fingers up his biceps. "I cannot think straight."

"That was my intention." He hoisted me off the bed, ripping a giggle from my mouth as he carried me to the sprawling rug on the floor in front of the hearth. He grabbed the pillows from his bed, then positioned them on the floor.

"Lie down." Felix gestured to the pillows.

With the burning sensation of pleasure still coursing through my body, I tilted my head and said, "No."

"No?" He grinned. "Why not?"

"*You* lie down." I pointed to the rug.

With an amused look upon his face, he kicked off his trousers, then did as I asked. The orange glow from the hearth lit every crevice of his body.

I straddled him, holding his hard length. I ran my fingers over his swollen tip, which rewarded me with a groan of approval.

Reaching up, he palmed my breasts, running his thumbs over my nipples. Without taking my gaze off his, I lowered myself, inch by inch, onto him. He twitched inside me as I took my time to adjust to his length.

Placing his hands on my hips, he watched me as I rose and lowered in torturously slow movements. I couldn't fight my own smirk when he ground his teeth together.

"You're killing me," he said.

I pressed a kiss to the corner of his mouth, then whispered, "Good."

Growling, he let me ride him slowly, and my body hummed with pleasure. After a few moments, he gripped my hips harder and bucked his own to thrust into my deeper. We moved together, and fire erupted inside me as he increased his speed. A groan escaped his mouth as he pumped into me. I splayed my hands against his chest and threw my head back until we spiralled into release together.

---

I hugged the pillow as Felix prodded the fire with a poker. The golden light illuminated the contours of his naked body.

"I love you. Fiercely." The words left my mouth with unwavering certainty.

He turned to face me—the moonlight streamed in through his bedroom window and poured its silver glow over him. Crawling into bed beside me, he traced his finger down my cheek. "I've waited so long to hear you say those words again."

"No matter what's happened, what we have won't go away." I leaned into the palm of his hand. "We stay together."

"I can't tell you how sorry I am." He drew me in to press his forehead against mine. "It haunts my dreams, you know."

"Shh." I nestled against him. "It's okay. I don't blame you—nor our friends. It is the gods I hold in contempt."

He tucked me against his side and held me as we watched the fire flicker in the hearth. "The gods will set down challenging paths, test your faith in them, but in the end, everything you endure is to make you stronger."

I buried my head against my chest, suppressing my rising scoff. "If the gods chose to take away our son to make me stronger, then I do not wish to believe in them. My strength should not cost me an innocent life—*our* heir."

"You will forgive them in time," he whispered, stroking my hair away from my face. "As you have forgiven all those you love."

Instead of disputing his claim, I held on to him. If there was ever a chance I could forgive the divine beings for what they'd seen fit to allow to happen to me, it wasn't now. Perhaps I never would. I chose to focus on my love for Felix—at least I still had him.

"When you fall asleep," he said, voice still velvety from passion. "Do not let the memories haunt your dreams. Know our son is happy in his afterlife. Be content with it and know we will *always* have each other."

I brought his knuckles to my mouth and kissed them. He could single-handedly stitch the fragments of my heart back together. Drawing the covers to our shoulders, I scooted closer to him, and a while later, his breathing evened with sleep.

Quietly, I slipped out of his embrace, got dressed, and made my way into the gardens to find my son's headstone among the flowers. Kneeling, I traced my fingers along the engraving. "I wish you could be a part of our lives, my little one. We could've given you so much. We would have given you the world."

I cupped my palms together and produced a warm ball of magic. It hovered into the sky and separated into hundreds of lights illuminating Lake Delendil. "I'm sorry I couldn't give you a funeral, my son. If you can see me from Elysium, I hope these lights bring you peace."

Leaning back against the grass, I watched the balls of magic float across the heavens.

# Chapter Fifteen

Moonlight drenched the flower beds and rose bushes, grass swayed gently in the breeze, and the lake rippled. Past the gravel near the peonies, I slid onto a wooden bench overlooking the water.

Silence enveloped me. I fixed my gaze on the trees across the mosaic bridge, picturing the Badlands beyond.

A mouse scurried past my feet and dashed into the brush, snapping my focus away from the woods. I sighed and relaxed my shoulders. The lanterns I'd created diminished until one ball of magic remained, flickering against the black sky, then its light faded.

Valneris approached me. "May I join you?"

I nodded and scooted across the bench. "Sure."

"There is something I must speak with you about and thought it best to do so in private." He sank against the wooden backboard.

"What's on your mind?" My gaze travelled to the frown between his brows.

"This place is your home, Evalyn," he said. "You are my queen, but firstly, I think of you as a daughter. I promised myself I would not fail you as your real father has. It hurt me greatly to see you leave."

"I'm sorry for causing you pain, but I did what I had to do. I hope you can forgive me." A pang of regret stung my heart.

He placed a hand on my knee and smiled. "We have sent word to your father to say you've returned. He's helped with the rebuilding of the allied settlements over the last two years and is living in a small encampment just south of Bluefair Fort. Your mother is with him too."

"Thank you." What else could I say? My father took any chance he could get to gain some form of leadership. I'd left my mother for so long, shortly after finding her, which made it worse. "I suppose you want to know about my red eyes."

"It is a concern." He frowned. "What did you do?"

"Again, something had to be done—but it took Blood Magic to achieve. The eye colour is an unfortunate side effect."

"The magic is lingering in you," he said.

"Afraid so." I crossed my arms.

"Before I retire for the night, there's something I'd like to give you." He stuffed his hand into his pocket, then withdrew a velvet cloth wrapped around a circular object. He handed it to me.

I peeled the fabric back and the moonlight glinted on the metal surface of the bangle. The band was encrusted with rubies, and intricate engraving surrounded the stones.

"I had the blacksmith make it for you after you left. We cannot bring your son back, and I'm deeply sorry we couldn't stop Makdou. Accept this gift as a token of my love for you," he said, voice thin, almost a whisper.

Sliding the bangle on my wrist, I studied the engraving. On the inside, *daughter* was inscribed.

"It's beautiful." I traced my finger over the letters.

He squeezed my shoulder and smiled, then escorted me inside. "Get some rest."

I returned to my chambers, determined to face the demons still lingering there. Crossing the floorboards, I forced the images of my bleeding body from my mind.

---

When daylight broke through the coloured glass of the Citadel, I stirred. The morning heat warmed my cheeks. Gwendolyn entered my chamber, then placed fresh clothes on the bed beside me.

I undressed from my night robes, and my handmaiden helped me into a soft, white silk shirt.

The smooth fabric slid along my arms. She reached for a pair of cotton breeches and handed them to me. As I pulled them on, she grabbed a pair of leather boots, recently polished. I slipped into them and braided my hair.

"I'm sorry for your loss, my queen," she said as she made the bed.

Her condolences made me smile, but I couldn't stop myself from flicking my gaze to the stained floorboards in front of the mantel.

"We have tried hard to lift the blood." Her voice brought my attention back to her.

"Thank you." I touched her arm. "Truly."

I met my friends in the council room. Felix helped himself to a goblet of juice, as Elven servants dressed the table with the morning meal. Fruit bowls were placed in the centre of the table beside a plate of fresh, warm bread. We took our seats as the servants dished out the food.

"Morning all," I said. "I trust you slept well. And now that we are all gathered, I'll tell you about the Great Mother Tree." I sipped my juice, then placed the goblet on the table. "We located the tree in Meridian, Dmitri's homeland. At first, it was concealed, so we had to find a way to reveal it."

"I presume this will explain the change of eye colour, Evalyn," Kiirion said.

"Indeed." I kept my back straight, and my gaze steady. "A simple revealing spell didn't work. We needed to try something much stronger."

"What did you do?" He held his hand in front of him, about to pop some berries into his mouth. A frown creased his brow.

"You won't like it if I tell you."

He rested his grapes on his plate and leaned forward. "Evalyn…"

I glanced at Valneris, having told him the previous night. He raised a brow, as if to signal I must tell the others.

"What in the realm have you done?" Xurek's voice boomed.

"Blood Magic." I kept my tone level. "Our first attempt sent me back to Elysium and could've killed me. There was no other choice."

"Elysium?" Theodas held his hand up. "What do you mean *back?* Have you been there before?"

I sighed. "I was first there during the battle at Southkeep, then again when Makdou attacked me. The third time was when we tried to reveal the Tree. I saw my son. We named him Ascal." The memory of his round face and dark hair would forever be imprinted in my memory.

Kiirion's eyes glistened. The High Elves bowed their heads.

"I'm honoured you've named him Ascal," Kiirion said, "and you have paid great respect to him. He would've loved to meet your son."

"No other name would've suited him." Felix leaned across and took my hand in his.

I cleared my throat and sat straight. "We should focus on the matter at hand. I went to Swynvale with the sole purpose of turning my anger and hatred into something useful. That realm's magic, along with Sofia and Felix at my side, helped me deal with my grief. Now that I'm home, Sofia and I will return our attention to the library and continue our search for a defense spell. Before I adjourn this meeting, I would like you to send word to all our allied forces—make it known that I am home, and I vow to do whatever is necessary to regain their trust. I can imagine my relationships with our allies will be strained, seeing as I have not been present for far too long."

"Consider it done," Valneris said.

"Dmitri, perhaps you'd care to join Xurek and me at the barracks?" Felix asked.

"You bet."

As they headed out of the room, I made my way through the foyer with Sofia in tow. We climbed the stairs, heading for the library.

As I sat at the table, I stroked the spines of the books in front of me. Sofia and I had already plucked a dozen of them from their shelves, scattering them across the surface.

She peered her head around the aisle and cleared her throat. "I think I might've found something."

"Oh?" I arched a brow, and my heart rate sped up a notch.

"Follow me." She gestured, leading me into the next aisle. "I can read some of the titles—there's mentions of counterspells for all sorts of magic. Perhaps we'll find what we're looking for here."

I wandered to her side and peered at a book she laid open on the counter. "Good place to start, I guess."

Sofia grabbed a candle, shielded the light with her hand, then placed it beside the books.

Leaning against the counter, I scanned the texts. "If we'd known of this spell sooner, we could've saved my son's life. We would've been better prepared."

With a gentle look upon her eyes, she rested her hand on my arm. "No, it wouldn't have been that simple. The Noble Ones knew the Crimson Kiss existed—they would've created a defence spell and they most likely protected it in some way to stop the Dark Mages from finding out." Her brows creased. "And even if we did discover this sooner, you changed your timeline when you entered Elysium. Your son was never meant to survive. If the Crimson Kiss hadn't killed him, something else would've."

"Changing my timeline is Reuben's speculation at best—it's not concrete fact." A part of me refused to believe there would've been no hope for my son.

The corners of Sofia's lips turned up in a sympathetic smile.

Peeling my gaze from her, I flicked through the parchment of a leather-bound tome. The pages were rough against my fingers. Somebody must've documented something, *anything*. The Noble Ones, *someone*.

She removed a dozen books from the shelves and scattered them across the table and floor. She skimmed through each, then tossed them aside.

I sank on to the floor between the rows of bookcases, scanning page after page, until my vision blurred.

"Look!" Her eyes widened as she thrust a book towards me, tapping a page in a fast rhythm. "This spell is coded. It could be the one we're looking for.

It makes sense. If the Noble Ones didn't want the Dark Mages to discover this defence spell, they'd surely code it. There aren't any other spells like it in here."

"You think it's coded?" I tilted my head, studying the writing.

"Yes, see these different characters?" She nudged closer to me, pointing to the sharply angled shapes on the page. "They're symbols, not letters."

Drawing my bottom lip between my teeth, I waited for my mind to work its way through the fog and connect the dots.

Rolling her eyes, she grasped the book, then planted it square in the centre of the table. "I'm a High Priestess, so it would also make sense that my main talent is healing; therefore, I wouldn't know how to translate this."

"Sounds promising…" I wouldn't give a better response until I knew for sure we weren't clutching at straws.

"Surely, there's another powerful Mage we know who could decipher this." Sofia grinned.

I raised a brow. "Mother?"

"Yes!" she chirped. "She's been around a long time. She'd know what to do."

"Okay, even if my mother *can* decipher this, it's still going to be a complicated spell, right? Especially if the Noble Ones made it. How are we going to perform this? Are we strong enough?"

"It'll take days of practice, for sure, but with the three of us together, I have confidence we can do this." A smile spread across her face. She headed towards the doorway. "Evalyn, you should send for your mother. The sooner she gets here, the better."

---

The High Elves sat around the ruby-encrusted table in the council room. The Citadel was quieter than I remembered—no more Gnomes or Centaurs about, only servant Elves and guards roamed the ground.

"We might've found it!" Sofia beamed as she entered the room. "A chant, which will counter the Crimson Kiss, but we'll need to decode it first to be sure."

"Sounds promising." Kiirion's smile spread across his face, and his eyes twinkled, adding to his youthfulness.

Theodas placed his hands on the table. "Is this realistic? After what our queen has told us about her trips to Elysium, I am concerned to say the least. Let's not forget the red in her eyes." His gaze rested on me.

"We must send for my mother—she could be the only one who has the ability to decode it." I tried to keep my tone steady, although a fluttering sensation went through my stomach in waves.

"What do you mean?" Theodas leaned forward. "Is this some sort of riddle you need to solve?"

Sofia sighed, flipped the book open, then slid it across for the Elves to look at. "I suspect the Noble Ones did what they could to protect the spell. Evalyn's mother can help us."

"We *think* she can help," I corrected. "Let's keep

this quiet until we know for sure this is the right spell. I don't want to set anyone's expectations until we're certain."

Valneris nodded. "As you wish. We will send for your mother right away. I've also dispatched your requested letters to our allies."

"Thank you, and it'll be good to see her again." The last time I'd seen her, she'd been ghost-like and struggling to readjust to the real world after twenty years of imprisonment. My father, on the other hand, was a selfish man who desired nothing more than power.

"She wrote to you." Kiirion picked up a scroll, bound with a wax seal. "We've received a couple others detailing her whereabouts. She is safe, and now she knows you're home, she wants to return to the Citadel."

I leaned forward and grasped it. Peeling off the wax, I unravelled the parchment, revealing a long, curly script.

"We should be as discreet as possible." A frown knitted Valneris' brows. "If Makdou receives word of this, she'll attack Mya on her journey here."

The door banged open, and Xurek and Felix strolled in.

"We'll ride out to meet her," I suggested.

"We cannot risk your life again." Kiirion shook his head.

"What have I missed?" Felix frowned.

"My mother wishes to return," I explained. "We must go to her before Makdou finds her."

"The Orcs could attack at any time—we cannot risk you," Felix said.

"As we have just said ourselves," Kiirion added.

"I can meet your mother. This is the best option for ensuring Mya's safety. I will ride south tonight. Eric will presumably want to check in at Bluefair Fort, so he can accompany me," Xurek said.

"I agree." Felix rested his hand on the pommel of his sword at his waist. "The best option is for you to remain here, Evalyn."

"I will speak with him." I turned to leave, resting my hand on the doorway. "Every ounce of my body believes he will do everything he must to serve and help me, but it is time I give him something in return."

I hurried through the Citadel gardens in search of Eric. The sweet, aromatic scent of budding roses made me dizzy. A servant planted fresh tulip bulbs in the soil beds near the river.

I found him alone, sitting on a bench among the bushes. He tilted his head towards the sky.

"It's a lot colder than I would like." He peered at me from the corner of his eyes. "Bluefair Fort is used to persistent heat, and there's always a breeze drifting over the lake here. You'd think I would be used to it, having spent most of the last two years here."

I sat beside him. "I have one last favour to ask of you, then you may return home. To Bluefair Fort."

"What is it?" He shifted on the bench to face me.

"Accompany Xurek to meet my mother. Once she is with him, you may part ways. You've done so much for me—for the Light Triads—while I've been gone."

"Think nothing of it. My place is by your side."
An earnest smile spread across his mouth. "I will
continue to serve you—however it pleases you."

"Then it would please me for you to return
home." If I commanded it, he wouldn't deny it. "I
order you to return to Bluefair Fort—keep peace in
the south and check in on the Gnomes while you're
down there." I rose. "Find Xurek, prepare the
horses, and depart at your earliest convenience."

He stood, now eye level with me, then bowed
low. "As you command, my queen."

# Chapter Sixteen

Waking to the chirping of birdsong, I slipped out of bed and cracked open the window to let the fresh air in. Quickly dressing, I left the room in search of my friends.

I found them gathered in the foyer in front of the staircase. A servant handed Xurek and Eric satchels.

Xurek towered beside Eric, easily double his size and twice as tall. Although the Citadel was built with high ceilings and wide doorways, Xurek had to frequently duck to fit through. He clutched his hammer and swung it around—which I took as a sign of his readiness to embark on the journey.

Eric shoved his sword into its scabbard, then adjusted his satchel over his shoulder, shifting its weight.

"Evalyn, we're about to leave." He shifted his gaze to meet mine. "We're taking two of the horses. I know we only have a few, but it'll hasten our journey. Once I stop off at Bluefair Fort, I'll hand the mount to your mother for her to ride."

"I will see you again soon." I drew him into an embrace.

"When we finally get around to having this coronation of yours, my queen, *I* shall travel here." Eric laughed. "My sword is yours. Forever. You can call on me at any time."

"I know." I smiled and held back tears. I would not make him feel guilty for returning home. "Make sure you keep him safe, Xurek."

"Have you prepared a soppy goodbye for me too?" He winked. "Nobody will touch a hair on his pretty head. Not while I'm alive."

I laughed. "Bring my mother home to me."

"I won't fail you." He nodded.

Outside the entrance, the horses clomped their hooves on the cobbles, their misty breath spiralling in the air. Eric and Xurek climbed onto their mounts, then rode across the bridge and through the clearing between the trees.

Rubbing my eyes, I yawned. It was early—the sun barely broke the horizon—and I yearned for more sleep. "I'm going back to bed. Have the handmaidens wake me in another hour or so," I said to Kiirion, then headed up the staircase to my room.

Sprawling across the mattress, I traced a hand

over my chest, where Felix had planted kisses the night before. I smiled to myself and considered my coronation. Could I have him rule by my side? Would our lives be any different as husband and wife? I knew I loved him and hoped our union wouldn't change anything between us.

I closed my eyes, and a while later, I fell into a dream.

*Felix sat in an armchair near the fire, clutching a small child to his chest while I flicked through the pages of a magical text. The child giggled and flexed his fingers above the cosy blanket. He stretched his hand to touch Felix's face.*

*He cooed and stroked his baby's brown hair.*

*"Our family," he said. "I vow to love you both. Forever."*

*Then blood spilled from his eyes, dripped from his face, and pooled on the floor. The baby disappeared from his arms.*

*I screamed, leapt from my own chair, and clawed at the air as Felix disintegrated.*

Jolting awake, I trembled as a thin layer of sweat trickled down my forehead. My heart pounded.

I yanked the covers back and summoned my handmaiden.

"Your Majesty?" Gwendolyn frowned. "Are you all right?"

"A nightmare." I scraped my hair back with shaking fingers. "Prepare me a bath, please."

"Of course, Majesty." She curtsied before heading for the bathing room.

Climbing out of bed, I wrapped a robe around me. I took a few moments to steady my uneven breathing before following Gwendolyn.

As I headed down the hallway, I passed another servant who carried fresh bedding, presumably to change my sweat-sodden sheets.

The next few days passed in a blur. The sun sank behind the trees when Xurek rode across the mosaic bridge with my mother at his side. A warm glow cast across the sparkling lake and a breeze rustled the rose bushes. I pressed my fingers to the window of my chamber as I gazed at the woman coming here.

I hurried from my room, leaving the door wide open behind me. Downstairs, I glanced at Felix, who hauled open the doors, allowing a stream of golden light into the foyer. "I could see your mother from the council room window."

"Thank you. Come with me to meet her." I offered my hand.

Placing a kiss on my temple, he weaved his fingers with mine, and we headed out together.

The High Elves filed outside the Citadel as horses' hooves plodded towards us.

Mother's hair was the same fiery red as mine—a symbol of her strength and magic. The last time I'd seen her, she was weak and made little conversation. Her imprisonment had sucked the life and spirit from her, and I'd left her with Aneirin for the past two years—a man who put his own needs above others.

She wore dark cotton trousers paired with solid leather boots. Instead of furs draped across her shoulders, she'd donned a long-flowing, embroidered cape, which concealed most of her underlayers. The stitching was remarkable—an array of oranges, red, and golds worked into the fabric—fit for the queen's mother.

She jumped from her mount and patted it on the flank. Mother was striking against the harsh, angled features of the Orc towering beside her.

"Could you hold this a moment?" He handed her his heavy hammer while he unstrapped their bags from the horses.

As she neared me, Mother's eyes sparkled gold. "Evalyn, your eyes." She drew me into her arms and squeezed me tight. "What happened to you?"

"I've got a lot to tell you, but that's why I asked you to return. Come with me."

Taking my hand in hers, she brushed a strand of hair away from my face with the other. She pushed me to arm's length to study me. After a moment, she beamed. "I'm so glad to see you. It's been two years, and I only had a short time with you after you rescued me. I can't thank you enough."

"You don't owe me anything, Mother." I smiled. "I'm sorry I left, but I was—"

"Mourning, I know." Her eyes glistened. She flicked her gaze between Felix and me. "I'm so sorry for what you have both endured."

"We appreciate that more than you know, Mother. Now let's get you inside. You've travelled a long way, and you must be starving. Tell me how you found life at your encampment."

"Fine—I oversaw the revitalization of Rushdale Forest, Westwilde, and Bluefair Fort alongside your father. Can't say I'll miss the place, though. I much prefer Lake Delendil." She winked.

"How have you found my father's company?"

"Abominable, unbearable. He's a changed man, and not the man I fell in love with. I chose to come back to the Lake when I received word you'd returned. Thank the gods he's gone, but enough of that, I'll tell you later. Come, we must hurry inside. I ache all over from the ride here." She strolled through the entrance of the Citadel with my hand still in hers and Xurek following behind.

Even *I* couldn't bring myself to thank the gods for my father's disappearance. If they'd seen fit to allow me and my subjects to endure such suffering, I doubted they had any involvement in my father's absence.

When I reached out to that tether—faith—tying me to the omniscient beings I'd worshipped my whole life, there was nothing except coldness. Perhaps it was my own grief that prevented me from *feeling* them again, but their guidance was lost to me.

I cast him a glance over my shoulder. "I trust Eric arrived at Bluefair Fort without trouble?"

"We didn't encounter any hostility on the journey, my queen." His voice rang deep through the foyer. "He said he would write to you when he has settled."

"Good. Mother, I've missed your reunion with the High Elves, and I would love for us to gather to discuss our news." Instead of turning left to the council room, I led her to the right of the grand staircase, through an archway, and into a large seating area.

Kiirion stood beside the lit hearth, a scroll in

hand. "Evalyn, we need your signature on these."

"What are they for?" I leaned closer to inspect the writing.

"This is why I was in the council room." Felix gestured to Kiirion. "I was reviewing the mail we'd received from our allies. These scrolls are our drafted responses—they notify them of your return, and we ask them to ready themselves for Makdou's eventual attack."

Kiirion passed her the parchment, then scooped up the stack of other letters ready to be signed.

Valneris entered through the door with Theodas.

"My queen," Valneris said. "We've been preparing the soldiers and increased our security around the Citadel. We're still going to need those stone soldiers of yours, though."

"I'll ensure they're enchanted." I nodded once.

Xurek dipped his head and edged in through the doorway. He dumped the luggage underneath the window and sat on a large trunk made of solid oak.

Sofia came into the room, gesturing to Mother. "It's good to see you again, Your Grace."

It warmed me to have her close. I wanted to know more about her, and perhaps, I would find the time to trade stories with her.

"We need your help, Mother." I gestured for her and Sofia to sit. "We've been studying a chant written by the Noble Ones found in the library. It's encoded, and we believe you might be the only one who can decipher it, because of your extensive knowledge."

"Does this have anything to do with your red eyes?" Mother asked.

"I used Blood Magic to reveal a hidden tree, and this is the consequence. We were looking for a counterspell against the Crimson Kiss, and we found this charm. It could be our shot at defeating Makdou once and for all." Adrenaline pumped through me. I tapped my foot on the floor, eagerly awaiting her response.

"Can I see it?" she asked.

Sofia handed the book to Mother.

Lying it flat on her lap, she traced her fingers over the symbols. "Ah, yes. I've seen similar coding to this during the time I spent studying as a new Mage before I was captured by the Orcs." She pulled the paper closer to her face for inspection. "During my twenty-year imprisonment at Southkeep, I'd often decode passages like this for the Orcs. Perhaps they suspected there was something to counter the Crimson Kiss. I think they wanted a Mage under their control, for if their freewill was ever threatened by a Dark Mage strong enough to use the Crimson Kiss."

"You know of other passages like this?" I raised a brow.

"Many—the Noble Ones were very powerful as you know, but they weren't stupid," she said. "Fortunately, I never found *this* particular coding. Fancy that, the Severance of Minds has been at the Citadel this whole time, the one place the Orcs cannot go."

"Do you know the translation?" Sofia nudged Mother's shoulder.

"Spending twenty years looking at these symbols means I know them like the lines on my palms." She grinned. "It's a shield. It produces a dome over the people it is protecting. Their minds would be free of compulsion. However, there is a cost."

"What cost?" The hairs on my neck prickled.

"The caster's life will be shortened. It doesn't say how long, but it is common for there to be a price for such spells."

"Do you think Makdou would've paid a price for using the Crimson Kiss?" Felix edged forward from his standing position beside Kiirion.

"I'm almost certain," she said. "The spell would've likely affected her in the same way."

"If we presume it to be true, then Makdou's life is shortened." Sofia's lips parted with the realisation. "She could be easier to kill—she's not as young as she once was."

"It would certainly even the playing field. Let's have our morning meal, then gather in the library for practice." I used this as an opportunity to escort my mother to the banquet hall. Sofia fell into step beside us.

"Before you go," Felix passed me an inked quill. "Signature, please." He smiled. "Then I'll ensure they're sent on your behalf. Afterwards, I'll speak with the soldiers and discuss options for how best to track Makdou and put an end to her."

I scrawled my name across the bottom of each scroll before handing them back to him. "Thank you."

Leaning back against the chair, I rubbed my filled stomach. The room bustled with servants who cleared away plates, goblets, and cutlery.

I gestured for them to leave Mother's goblet and urged her to drink more. "You must be thirsty."

"I'm fine, child, don't worry." Nonetheless, she lifted her goblet to her mouth and gulped. "This is quite an astonishing place to live, you know. I might have to stay a while."

"I hope you do, Mother." I grasped her hand. "There's so much I want to learn about you. I've a lot to tell you too."

"Tell me about this Felix of yours." She grinned. "Of course, I've met him before, but it is different to hearing it from you directly. Does he treat you well?"

I squeezed her hand. "He's the love of my life. I'll admit, for a while I blamed him for losing our son. It took me a while to remind myself it wasn't him. Now I love him more each day. I went to Swynvale to heal—and I think I'm getting there. I've made allies there, and I've got a better understanding of Makdou's intentions. If I can stop her from using the Crimson Kiss against the Orcs, my people will finally have peace. And so will the people of Swynvale."

"I'm so proud of you, my girl. It was a pleasure to see my son-in-law earlier in healthier times." She leaned forward. "You are a wonderful queen."

We were not wed yet, but knowing my mother viewed him as such made my heart swell. "Thank you. You would do me the honour as acting council alongside the others."

"I will stay by your side for as long as you need me," she said. "Ah…I have something for you."

She rummaged in her pocket, then drew a velvet pouch and handed it to me.

I untied the drawstrings, then emptied the contents into the palm of my hand. A silver locket glistened under the light streaming in through the large windows.

"I had it made for you when you were gone." She smiled. "I know you don't remember much of me, but you're still my daughter, and I know you're suffering. Losing a child isn't easy, and I hope this will soothe your pain."

I unclicked the locket and gasped. Inside, my son's face shimmered. Tears welled in my eyes. "How did you know what he looked like?"

The gift reminded me of the necklace Felix had given me. Makdou had stolen it, using it to fuel her magic.

"Magic." Mother rose and rubbed my shoulder. "He will be with you forever. Now, let me put it on."

I wiped away my tears, then lifted my hair.

Mother fastened the necklace around my neck, then took my hair from me and flattened it gently down the length of my back.

"Come on, dear, let's go master this spell." She held her hand out for me to take, then cupped my cheek with her other palm. "I'll be with you every step of the way. We all will be."

As we headed out of the room, Sofia met us in the foyer. We ascended the stairs and followed the turning towards the library. As I passed Felix's chamber, I blushed, remembering our passionate night together. A fire burned within me, and every fibre of my being wanted to return to him tonight.

Sofia met us in the library. Daylight streamed in through the domed, multicoloured glass. Recently polished wooden furniture smelled of beeswax, and the cushions had been plumped for our use. A fire burned in the hearth, its warm light mixing with the glow of candles. A jug and three goblets were placed in the centre of the wooden table.

"We'll need to make sure we are well rested each day we practise this spell. It's going to take a lot of energy." Mother settled into a chair, then opened the spell book on the table in front of her. "On a different note, I can't imagine what long-term effects Blood Magic is going to have on you, Evalyn."

Sofia and I slid onto seats beside her.

"I've been back a couple of days, and nothing else has happened to me. It's not a concern. What we *should* be focusing on is this defence spell." I took the book from Mother. "Trust me. I will let you know if there's anything to be worried about."

"I do trust you." She smiled.

"What happened to the rest of the Light Mages?"

"There hasn't been a true colony since the time of the Noble Ones, many centuries ago." Mother clasped her hands in her lap. "There was no distinction between Light and Dark Mages back then. They all gathered in harmony at the place we know as Sanctum City. Eventually, divides and cracks started to form. People grew jealous over the powerful ones, the Noble Ones."

"Is this why the Triads used to visit Sanctum City, because the Noble Ones did?" The settlement was once a neutral territory, far north of the continent. It'd since been sacked in recent years by the Orcs. "Has anything happened to the area since?"

"No," she said. "It remains empty and abandoned. The Orcs withdrew their forces and returned to their own lands in Zhah and beyond. Perhaps Makdou is there. It's a free zone and would be useful to her."

"We'll use a location spell to be sure of it," Sofia said. "But even so, we mustn't assume it to be that easy. She's had plenty of time to prepare—she knows you're home, and she'll know you're searching for her."

"Even if she's using a concealing spell, we can lift it, right?" I glanced at her. "Just like you did to reveal the Great Mother Tree."

"I only hope it is as easy as this." Mother frowned. "Makdou is powerful. We can't forget this. She will have defences in play."

"We'll master the Severance of Minds first to guarantee it works before worrying where she is," Sofia said. "Evalyn, you need all your strength—we can't afford to lose you to Elysium again."

"You've been to Elysium?" Mother's eyes widened.

"I'm fine, I swear." I enunciated my words with confidence. "We're doing this."

Neither of them questioned me further.

Mother smoothed the edges of the yellowing paper, then pronounced each word loud and clear.

Sofia and I repeated them until we created the correct sounds. We carried on late into the evening until our heads hurt and the words all sounded the same.

# Chapter Seventeen

I slid my chair back, rubbed my temples, and sighed. My mind spun, and the foreign words of the spell jumbled.

Rising, I shook away the tingling sensation in my limbs. "We should check in with the High Elves before retiring."

The three of us met them in the council room. The High Elves, along with Felix, were sitting around the table, maps sprawled across the surface.

"Can you provide us with an update on your plans?" I settled into my own seat.

"We were discussing Sanctum City." Felix created a steeple with his fingers. "You and I were unable to visit like we'd originally planned two years ago. The Elves mentioned the Orcs have returned to their side of the Badlands, to Zhah, but our men have not begun any restoration works on the bridge to Sanctum City."

Kiirion gulped his wine, then cleared his throat. "We have not sent men that far north, my queen. In your absence, we have prioritised the rebuilding of destroyed allied homes."

"Understandable, and you have my gratitude," I said. "But an opportunity has presented itself—a truce between the Triads has formed and hangs in the balance. It's imperative we claim Sanctum City so we may prevent it from being seized by enemies again. Mother already suspects Makdou could be there right now—we could be too late."

"We've not seen Makdou in months," Valneris said. "If she *does* have control of the Orcs in Swynvale, then Sanctum City is the best place for her to conjure the Crimson Kiss spell through portals undisturbed. It makes sense."

"Which furthers my previous point—I've been gone two years, right? Surely, you would've considered sending a patrol to Sanctum City in case Makdou *was* there." I couldn't help the annoyance bubbling in my veins.

"I apologise, my queen. Many homes within the Light Triads were destroyed, and with it, many good folks were left homeless, starving, and bereaved among other things. We couldn't spread our resources or our men too thin."

An intense wave of guilt shot through my core.

"There's nothing to stop Makdou from doing whatever she pleases," Sofia pointed out.

"We can't waste any more time." I tapped the table. "First thing in the morning, we'll master this spell, while the rest of you finalise the plans for our travel north."

"Are we ready for this?" Sofia asked. "Are we truly ready? As soon as we've memorised the spell, we'll have nothing else in our way. We just need to conjure the Severance of Minds."

"I'm not sure we'll ever be truly ready," I replied. "Even when we know the spell, what's to say I won't be hindered in some way? She has my necklace, which is enhancing her magic. Perhaps there's a way we can sever the power in the runes."

"Great idea," she said. "I'll do some research and see if it's something we can do."

"Hey, I have an idea." I instinctively touched my new locket hanging around my neck. "Mother gave me this—could we enchant it? Surely, that could increase our odds against Makdou. Which reminds me, Mother, I found your talisman before we reunited. The High Elves swore it was yours—three emeralds fixed between claws, the surface scratched and dull."

Her brows shot up. "Well, I never thought I'd hear about my talisman again. Not to worry about me, though, dear. I only wore it when I was younger and not at my strongest in terms of abilities. I'll be just fine."

I nodded and unclasped my own necklace, then handed it to Sofia. "See if there's something you can do."

"Your love for each other gave your magic added potency. Perhaps I can add something of his

229

to it—seal it with a kiss." She winked.

———————◦~◦———————

The following morning, heat streamed through the coloured glass of the library. The air was stuffy and stagnant inside. A servant poured a jug of water into the hearth to diminish the fire.

"Please open the windows." I tugged at my collar, sweating from the stuffiness.

Once Mother, Sofia, and I had taken our seats at the table, I drew the leather-bound book towards me—the symbolic spell on one side and my mother's translation on a separate piece of paper positioned next to it. The calligraphy scripture of the ancient spell stood out against the pale parchment.

"Read it out again." Mother grasped the translation between her fingers and removed it. "Without assistance. You need to get this right, Evalyn."

I sighed. "Yes, Mother."

Uttering the words, I stumbled over the odd, clunky syllables.

We spent the rest of the morning learning each section of the spell until the curly writing was etched into my brain and the loops of each letter blurred in my vision.

My sweaty clothes clung to me. I gulped a goblet full of water, then stuck my head out of the window for a breath of fresh air. I needed a cool bath.

"Trust today to be the hottest day ever." I huffed.

"It's nearly time for lunch. Take some time to eat, then we'll reconvene this afternoon. Sofia, let me know as soon as you find a way to sever the magic in my old necklace and my new one is ready."

———————— ～～ ————————

Two hours later, I went to the gardens to spend some time with my son, before returning to the library.

The cloudless sky meant the afternoon heat beat down on me, and the palace grounds, with a relentless force. I wiped the perspiration from my forehead as a squirrel scurried along the stones and disappeared up a trunk.

I came to an abrupt halt. Sofia nestled against Dmitri on the bench amongst the flowers.

Dipping into the shadows, I leaned in. A fern branch flicked against my face, and I sputtered, swiping the leaves away from my mouth.

"If this works, will you stay here?" Sofia said with a low husk to her voice, which indicated it to be an intimate conversation, one I shouldn't be eavesdropping on.

But she was my closest friend. I knew she cared for Dmitri, loved him even, and I wanted to be there for her in any way she may need it.

I pushed the guilt aside and edged closer. If I knew what they discussed, I could prepare my answers for when Sofia eventually came to me. I stubbed my toe on a garden rock and clamped my hand over my mouth.

"I'm not going to leave you. In fact," Dmitri cleared his throat, "I would like to ask you a question."

I froze, hidden by the dark cloaks of the ferns, and a jolt of excitement shot through my body.

"What is it?" Her voice hitched.

"I didn't expect to find someone like you, yet Tilula, Goddess of Love, has seen it fitting to bless me with you. While we may worship different gods, I believe, either way, they would've led us to each other. I promise to stand by your side, to cherish, and love you. I'm yet to get a ring made for you, but would you do me the honour of becoming my wife?" He spoke steadily, filled with conviction.

She giggled.

I pressed my palm to my breast, overcome with happiness for my friend.

She leapt onto his lap and smooched him. "Yes. Always, yes! But we must tell Evalyn. The queen should know."

A mouse scurried across my foot. I swallowed a screech and darted out of my hiding spot. "No need to worry. Your…uh…queen is just fine."

I flattened down my robes, cheeks burning.

He grinned. "I'm also sure you heard everything."

"What were you doing behind the ferns?" Sofia laughed. "I would've told you anyway."

I relaxed my shoulders and smiled. "I know. When it comes to you and your happiness, I couldn't resist. I'm happy for both of you and congratulations are in order. I'll have the servants bring the celebratory champagne from the cellar and take it to your chambers."

She clasped his hand and, together, they rose. "I would like your blessing, my queen."

"Of course." I slung my arms around them both, drawing them into a warm embrace. After a few beats, I let them go. "You are welcome to marry and reside here. Now celebrate your engagement— enjoy the lit gardens, drink wine, dance to music— ask the servants for anything you desire."

"What about the spell?" Sofia asked me as she leaned into Dmitri, one arm wrapped around his waist and the other rested on his stomach.

"We will resume in the morning," I smiled.

"Would you care to join us?" Dmitri asked.

"I would love to, but I'm going to sit by my son's grave for a while. Today is for you—both of you. Tell the servants to bring you champagne and desserts for the occasion. I will see you both in the morning!" My voice rang like a song as I whisked past them towards the bench beside the headstone.

---

Later, in my room, no fire blazed in the hearth. The air was close and sticky, the heat of the day carrying into the night. A breeze drifted in through the ajar window.

Stripping out of my clothes, I slipped into my nightdress, then drew the covers and climbed into bed. Despite my best efforts to succumb to sleep, I tossed and turned, breaking in and out of sleep, throughout most of the night. Lake Delendil was at its highest temperature of the year. It was going to be a long night.

Just before dawn, I awoke again. Huffing, I shifted upright and tugged the cotton gown over my head and tossed it aside. I lay in bed, naked, a sheen layer of sweat forming on my head.

I drummed my fingers against my thigh, my mind buzzing with energy.

Shifting off the mattress, I redressed and tied my robe around me. I slipped my feet into my slippers, grasped a candle, then wandered to the library. The servants and handmaidens were still sleeping, but the guards patrolled the Citadel. One nodded to me as I passed him.

I tilted the candle to light two others, then placed the three of them in the centre of the wooden table.

Opening the leather-bound book, I flicked through the heavy parchment pages and landed on the Severance of Minds spell.

Flexing my fingers, I sucked in a deep breath, then cupped my hands in front of me and chanted the first verse. Adrenaline pumped through my body and a shiver of excitement bolted up my spine. The magic charged through me like a current, and an ethereal shield formed in my palms. While it only spanned a few inches, it *was* working.

I jiggled in my seat, and the shield disappeared. Grinning from ear to ear, I headed to the window and peered outside—the sun pushed through the horizon. Birds flew across the sky. Dawn.

My progress couldn't wait. I hurried out of the library and turned to one of the guards. "Awaken my mother and Sofia immediately. Call for the

High Elves and Felix as well. I have important news."

He nodded once, then strode down the corridor.

In my chamber, I stepped into clean cotton breeches, slipped on a blouse, then stuffed my feet into leather boots.

Glancing at my hands, I wondered what else I could do with my magic. I swirled my fingers in a halo motion above my head. Strands of hair floated and weaved together, clumping into a bun. Laughing, I adjusted it, and exited the room.

Downstairs, I flung open the council room doors. Shortly after, my friends joined me.

"What's wrong?" Felix asked, coming to my side. "Are you okay?"

"I'm great!" I beamed. "It works. The Severance of Minds *works*."

"You've performed it already?" Kiirion's brows shot up.

"I couldn't sleep—it's too hot and sticky—so I went to the library, and I created the shield within my palms. It was only small, but if I practise more and fuse my magic with Sofia and Mother's, it will be enough." I tapped my foot against the floorboards, eagerly awaiting the others to join me.

My mother entered the room and gripped my arms, scanning my body. "What's happened?"

"Nothing, I'm fine. I'm sorry I worried you." I clasped her hands. "Everything is coming together. I can perform the spell, Mother."

Her eyes widened. "Magnificent."

"We must perform it now—there's no time to waste." I steered my mother towards the staircase,

Sofia hot on our heels.

"Wait, I'm coming with you." Felix caught up with us. "If anything should happen to you—"

"Feel free to join us, but with the three of us combining our magic, nothing is likely to happen to me." I led the way to the library.

Inside, servants dusted the shelves and straightened the books. One neatened the drawn curtains and another poured water into our goblets.

Sofia hummed to herself.

I smiled. "Any thoughts on your wedding preparations yet? Once we've dealt with Makdou, we'll have the finest gown made for you."

"What wedding?" Felix tilted his head to the side.

"Dmitri and I are engaged." Sofia beamed.

"Fantastic news." Mother clapped, waggling her brows at me. "Perhaps you can hint at Felix too."

I laughed. "Settle down. Let's focus."

"Now we know the Severance of Minds works, we should get around to doing this location spell. If we can confirm for certain that Makdou is in Sanctum City, then we can depart as soon as possible." Mother swigged her water, then set her goblet aside. "If the three of us perform it, Makdou will be clear in our mind's eye and the words won't be misinterpreted."

"I agree." I clasped hands with them. "Let's begin."

We closed our eyes and chanted the foreign words of the location spell in unison. The melodic sound of our voices filled the room, echoing against the high domed ceiling.

A vision materialised. Peaked mountains sprung from the horizon—their tips covered in white, untouched snow. Situated halfway up one of the mountain was a derelict building surrounded by an iron fence. High towers stretched into the sky, competing with the jagged mountain range.

Broken windows sat between dark, crumbling stones. Moss and twisted vines grew up its length. The roof sagged, looking brittle and about to collapse.

My vision floated through the wrought iron gate, into the compound, and up the slippery, overgrown slopes towards the entrance of the structure. Large wooden doors stood before me, rotting from the rain it'd seen over many centuries—the copper door knocker green with age.

I wondered how it'd survived for so long, being bristled by the sharp winter winds of the north, day in, day out. Sanctum City had been left to decay.

A cool breeze stirred through the keep entrance. Whispering winds seeped through and chilled the inside. The staircase crept up the left-hand side of the foyer, rotten and covered with vines.

The vision glided up the staircase and across the landing overlooking the foyer. We came to a halt outside a room whose doorframe held no door.

Inside, Makdou stood in the centre. She held her hands high as she chanted the words of a portal creation. The same spell I'd used before. The sensation of rats' feet scampered up my spine.

Fear found itself in my stomach and formed lumps in my throat. Makdou was creating portals and performing the Crimson Kiss spell *through* them. Orcs stood on the other side, staring at her with blank expressions. She had full control over them, like empty vessels ready for command.

The image broke away, the spell snapped shut, and the three of us fell back against our chairs. Felix shot out his arm to steady me. We'd stayed there too long.

"You were right, Mother—Makdou is at Sanctum City." Triumph rang in my voice.

My heart pounded. I couldn't tell if I was excited we'd found her, or terrified I would soon face her again.

"Now all's left to do is conjure the Severance of Minds," Mother said. "Together."

I frowned. How many attempts would it take for us to produce the perfect shield? I'd been able to make a tiny version of the spell within my palms, and I hoped our magic combined would be more affective.

I flexed my arms and fingers and sucked in a deep breath. "Are we ready?"

"Are you sure you won't fall into Elysium again, Evalyn?" Felix kept his arm around me, searching my eyes with his own.

"I trust in us to do this," I said with as much reassurance as I could.

"Hang on." Sofia dug her hand into her pocket, then withdrew my locket. "Here—take this. It should behave in a similar way as your previous necklace. With this enhancing your powers *and* you being connected to two other mages, you'll be fine."

Clasping it around my neck, I smiled at the

familiar warmth of my love for Felix. "Thank you."

Mother and Sofia stood and held their hands out to me. We connected, forming a circle.

I glanced at the leather-bound book, splayed on the table, one last time. "We can do this."

My palms sweat against theirs, adrenaline coursed through me, and my magic surged.

Just as the words of the spell flowed from my mouth, a loud horn bellowed from somewhere outside the Citadel. I jolted, and my heart somersaulted. Felix was already at the window, craning his neck to get a look at whatever had caused the warning blare.

"Damn it," Mother shouted as our hands disconnected.

"What in the realm is going on?" I hurried to Felix's side, but he was already heading out of the library. "Felix, did you see something?"

"No, but it has to be something important," he said. "Come on."

Downstairs, guards marched to the entrance of the Citadel, Xurek and Dmitri hot on their tail. The High Elves fled from the council room.

"Guards?" Kiirion asked. "What's happened?"

"Orcs, gods be damned," Xurek cursed. "They've crossed the Badlands, and they're almost here. You need to get out of here, Evalyn."

"This can't be true." I shot a look at the High Elves. "You said they were staying put in Zhah."

"We couldn't expect the peace to last forever, not with what you said about Makdou controlling the Orcs," Kiirion said.

"She must have sensed our location spell." Sofia

rubbed her temples. "And could've commanded the Orcs to orchestrate an attack."

"How is that possible? The Orcs wouldn't be able to appear here in seconds." My mind raced as I fought to put the pieces together.

"She could've had Orcs stationed through the Badlands and the forests, or perhaps, something less conspicuous—she'd transport them through a portal." Sofia dragged her hand over her face.

Valneris clenched his hands into firsts, eyes glowering. "My queen, you three need to perform the Severance of Minds. Fast."

"We don't have enough time," Mother said. "Nor have we practised."

"What good is it doing us standing here? Come on. We have to try." I turned for the stairs, but Felix stopped me.

"Be careful," he said, his voice urgent yet soft. "I'll stay with the Elves—help to get the soldiers into position."

"I will." I nodded. "You be careful, too." I ran up the stairs. Mother and Sofia dashed after me.

Guards' footsteps boomed through the Citadel.

We formed a circle in the centre of the library.

"We need to shield the whole of Lake Delendil." Mother's fingers shook. "Not just the three of us."

"How can we be sure it'll work?" Sofia panted.

"Like I said, we have to try." I shook their hands to get their attention. "Think about it—we know every verse. Picture a large shield protecting the whole of Lake Delendil like a dome. That's what it looked like in the palm of my hands last night."

Mother and Sofia nodded, straightening their

backs.

We resumed the spell. As the words of the Noble Ones slipped from our mouths, the floor vibrated under our feet, paintings shook on their wall hooks, and books fell from the shelves.

A flash of silver light, a mighty gust of wind, and the scent of burned candles overwhelmed my senses.

"Come on!" I yelled over the loud currents whipping through the room like a storm.

The vibrations halted. The whipping wind stopped. Our connected hands broke.

"We must try again," Mother ordered as she clasped our hands once more, forming a perfect circle in the centre of the room.

The words of the spell tumbled from our mouths like a song, floating on the wind the magic created.

The Severance of Minds developed into an ethereal tornado around us, magic spiralling through it. The twister expanded, whipping around the building, as it grew outside the wall of the Citadel.

"It's working!" Sofia shouted over the surging sound of the spell.

My throat ached as I screamed the last verse. A loud buzz drowned out my yells.

The bookshelves shook. The library door slammed. A vase fell from the mantel and smashed on the floor. The table wobbled, knocking the goblets of water over, spilling their contents onto the carpet.

The spell snapped to an end. The hum disappeared.

I panted and clutched the sides of my pounding head. My vision tilted from side to side, and spots formed in front of my eyes.

Sofia stumbled into the table, her hair falling across her face. She scraped it back. "Did it work?"

"I'm not sure." I clutched the handle of the library door, eyesight still spinning. "There's only one way to find out."

I fled the library before either of them could question me, then flung open the door of my chamber. Every second counted, and I'd use each one of them to help my friends. I wouldn't be a victim again, and I wouldn't let them be either.

Rummaging in my wardrobe, I lifted mail and breast plate over my head and secured it to my chest.

Sofia and Mother hurried into the room.

"Evalyn." Mother gripped my arm. "We need to keep you safe. You can't go down there."

"Makdou *must* be stopped." I shook her off. "I *must* do this. She won't harm anyone else ever again."

"She won't even come here." Sofia rested her hand on mine. "She is using the Orcs to weaken us before she faces us head on."

"I know she won't be here." I didn't have time to deliberate her whereabouts with them—we'd already established she was in Sanctum City. "But I refuse to stand idly by while she uses her puppets to destroy my home and take more lives. I am a - queen—I will not cower behind my glass walls."

Mother raised her eyebrows. A smiled tugged at the corners of her lips.

I pushed past them and hurried down to the foyer—my gaze lingered on the stone statues upon their pedestals. I'd used them once before, and I needed them again.

Raising my hands, I chanted the spell. My voice rang against the high walls. The sculptures came to life, hoisted their swords into the air, leapt from their pedestals with a loud thud, then marched out of the Citadel and across the mosaic bridge. I followed them outside, watching as the defenders of this land took their positions.

"Evalyn!" Felix's voice caught my attention. I spun to him, donned in armour and his sword drawn. "Are you okay? The guards are in position, and we'll hold the line. The Orcs are on the way."

"I'm fine," I said. "Join the others. Don't worry about me." He opened his mouth to object, but I said, "I'll be fine. But the guards will benefit from another sword."

"My queen, the Elves, Dmitri, and Xurek are stationed on the other side of the lake until the Orcs get here," another guard informed me as he unsheathed his sword.

"Evalyn," Felix said, tearing my attention back to him. "I'm not leaving you. We'll do this together. I'll stand by your side, and we'll *fight* together."

Despite my direct order for him to join the guards, I couldn't fight the rising pride, the bursting of love within me. "Together."

A loud and low-pitched rumble shot through the ground.

I scanned the perimeter of Lake Delendil in search of enemies, but it was still clear of Orcs. A silvery hue rose from the ground, slowly stretching above the trees, over the Citadel, then formed a shimmery dome.

The ethereal shield glimmered in the late-afternoon sun. I gasped.

"Gods be good." Felix gazed at the gleaming Severance of Minds spell. His eyes brightened. "You are amazing. You've done it."

"*We* did it." I nodded to Mother and Sofia who jogged towards us.

Perhaps the gods were *finally* listening. I sent a quick thanks to Ebris, God of Conquest. Perhaps *he* at least hadn't turned his back on me.

"Oh my." Mother stared at the silvery dome encasing us like a snow globe. "What a magnificent spell. Goes to show how powerful the Noble Ones were."

"How powerful *we* are." I faced her and smiled.

"The Severance of Minds spell is a counter to the Crimson Kiss, meaning it will only protect our minds from its compulsion. It won't keep out our enemies. We will still need to fight." Mother pointed to the tree line where our friends and stone soldiers awaited the Orcs.

"At least we will have our freewill. How long will the spell last?" My gaze darted from the Orcs to my mother.

"I'm uncertain." She grimaced. "But as soon as we notice signs of it diminishing, we'll need to conjure it again."

"Let's get this over with." I manifested a bright red ball in my palms, the magic surging through my body. My hair glowed vibrantly. Strands had fallen free from my bun and flapped around my face.

Sofia created a white light of healing power, cupping it in her palms. "I'm right beside you."

"We can do this," Mother said. "Together."

The other guards took up position along the bridge behind the stone soldiers.

Sofia glanced across the bridge in Dmitri's direction, her eyes hollow.

"He'll be okay." I nudged her. "Trust in the training he received at the Temple of Peace. He's also not only fought against Orcs but trained with one, too."

I led the way across the bridge, to stand by Valneris' side. He frowned for a moment, then placed his hand on my shoulder.

"Although I hope you'd always stay away from battle, I know you'd never do that," he said. "You're not the type to sit back and do nothing in the middle of a war, but I promise you, we won't let them hurt you. I swear it in front of the gods."

"We fight together this time." A fire burned inside me as Felix came up beside me, and a fire burned in his eyes, too.

Flexing my hands, I encouraged the ball of magic to swell and swirl in my palms.

Other than the slight breeze rippling the water, Lake Delendil was silent.

The enemy breached the tree line, snapping the sapling trees in half. Orcs emerged from different points of the edge, with more behind them. Their snarling faces emerged, sharp teeth overlapping bulging lips and glassy, bewitched eyes. They formed long rows in front of the trees. How many more were behind them?

Valneris and the others kept their weapons pointed towards the Orcs, but not one of them stepped forward. The Orcs remained in line, also unmoving.

"The corruption of the lake's magic was healed during the time you were in Swynvale," Valneris said. "The Orcs won't be able to get through."

*'The Orcs wouldn't dream of setting foot on such sacred ground. The lake's magic repels all darkness and causes excruciating pain to those who pose a threat.'* Felix's words echoed in my mind. All those months ago, after we'd fled the Eyrie, he had uttered those words.

"Does anyone else think they look worse under the influence of Makdou?" Felix frowned. "We don't know what they'll do or when, especially if Makdou finds a way to override the lake's natural defences—it's the only thing keeping the Orcs out."

"The Crimson Kiss is performed with Blood Magic." I returned my gaze to an Orc's bared tusks. "Killing Makdou is the only way to free them of the spell."

"Wouldn't the Severance of Minds free the Orcs?" he asked.

"There's too many of them, and Makdou's hold on them is deep-rooted," Mother said. "She must be killed."

"I can't decide if that's what I want for the Orcs," he said quietly. "It sounds like mercy."

# Chapter Eighteen

Valneris brooded beside me, tightly gripping his sword. The Arogathean steel glinted in the sunlight. His eyebrows knitted into a frown as he fixed his gaze on the expressionless Orcs.

An Orc moved his heavy, round foot. The thud shook the bridge beneath me. He lifted the other foot and clomped one step closer to us. Snarling straight at Xurek, the Orc bared his tusks, curling back his thick lips.

"Never known an Orc to be so quiet," Xurek said. "One would consider this a positive thing if we weren't being threatened with an attack."

He puffed out his shoulders, raised his hammer,

then stomped towards the imposing rival. Another Orc counteracted his move and fell into line beside the first Orc. Xurek waited, under threat of checkmate.

I cupped my hands together and produced a spinning ball of red magic. It swelled to the size of a human head in my palms. The enemies did not move another muscle, their gazes unwavering. But one of the Orc's lips curved up into a smile, and the ground trembled. The sound of bubbling water had me peering over the bridge to the water below. Steam plumed from the lake's surface as it boiled.

"I think you were right about Makdou!" I called to Felix. "She must be doing something to the lake. Hold your ground. Prepare to strike. In case the protection falters, the Orcs will be able to pass through. And if they do, avoid the water, because it's reaching scalding temperatures."

"Evalyn, get back!" He hollered, and as I spun to face him, he threw his sword up to meet the impact of the Orc's hammer. Xurek swung his own hammer into the side of the Orc's head, spraying blood. My heart pounded, roaring in my ears as the Orcs drew nearer.

I sent a bolt of magic hurtling forward in warning, but the Orcs continued to close the space between us, until they were mere feet from the edge of the bridge. Yet the Orcs did not attack again.

"Makdou is trying to show us that she can have them do whatever she wants," I said. "And the lake can't help us. We must fight them. Hold them back from the Citadel."

The Orcs charged.

We struck.

I sent blast after blast of magic, tearing a line through the Orcs' tight formation. Felix feinted with his sword, as Valneris slammed his shield into an Orc's bulking body. Ducking beneath a swinging hammer, Felix slashed his sword through the Orc's knees, and as he hit the ground, Valneris drew his own weapon straight through its green skin.

With one enemy felled, they moved on to the next.

I focused on the swarm of enemies as my friends and soldiers fought to push them back, back to the treeline, and away from the Citadel. Within the dense forest, the Orcs wouldn't find it so easy to swing their crushing hammers. *We* were nimbler, and we could use it to our advantage.

"Keep pushing into the forest!" I ordered.

So we did.

With towering oaks around us, we swarmed the Orcs. I shot my magic through the spaces between trees, plummeting into a group of enemies. The magic exploded on impact, sending them hurtling, one became impaled on a sharp, protruding branch.

Then they froze.

"Stop!" I said, panting.

My men heeded the order.

Wiping the mixture of blood and sweat from my hairline, I surveyed the Orcs, frozen in line once more. I don't know how long we stood there for, staring into the faces of our frozen enemies. It could have been a second, a minute.

"We should retreat while we can. Evacuate the

Citadel—take the staff to safety." I shoved damp hair away from my face. "Have the stone soldiers guard the perimeter."

Spinning on my heel, I sprinted for the Citadel entrance, refusing to waste another second. Makdou wasn't going to get her Orcs to stand down—not for long—and I had to get my people out of there.

I bolted along the bridge, leaving Felix with the other fighting men, as stone soldiers formed a line on the shore, protecting the grounds in case the Orcs should push forward again.

"Gather all the staff immediately." I ordered the nearest guard.

"They're already underground for their safety, Majesty," he said.

"It won't be enough. We need to get them out of here. Bring them to me at once." I didn't wait for his response as I whirled towards the council room. I threw the doors open. The quickest option to get my people to safety was through a portal. Rubbing my hands together, I conjured a portal, its ethereal surface hissing and flickering until it became steady and strong. In my mind's eye, I focused on Swynvale, *willed* it to take place on the other side.

Shouts roared behind me, dragging my attention from the portal.

"Evalyn!" Mother sprinted around the corner, nearly colliding with the doorframe. "It's Dmitri."

"What?" I demanded.

"As soon as you left, Makdou ordered a strike. We fought against the Orcs, but they pushed us back to the shoreline. The stone soldiers held the line, and the Orcs can't get any farther, but Dmitri was injured."

"What happened to him? Where is he?" I fired off the questions. "I need to get the staff to safety. If the Orcs fight against the stone soldiers, they could fall, and if the Orcs breach the Citadel wall, the staff—*we*—will be killed. We don't have the numbers to hold them back for long."

The guard bounded around the corner, a cluster of handmaidens and servants hurrying after.

"Through that portal right now!" I ordered. "It will take you to Meridian, in Swynvale. You will be safe there. I will come to you as soon as I've dealt with this mess."

Swiftly, the guard motioned the servants through the portal.

I turned back to Mother. "Take me to him."

Together, we hurried outside. I came to an abrupt halt when my gaze landed on Xurek, holding a lifeless, limp Dmitri in his arms. If I thought too much of it, I might've thrown up right there, but I had to keep it together. Felix, grimacing, hurried to me.

"Are you all right?" He made a quick scan of my body.

"I'm fine." I waved it away. "I've got the staff going through a portal right now. We need to go. We can't hold the army of Orcs back forever—they outnumber us."

With a grim expression, he nodded.

Mother shoved loose hair out of her face. "I'm sorry, there's nothing I could've done to save him. And I've lost Sofia."

"What do you mean you lost Sofia?" My pulse thundered in my ears as I surveyed the treeline. There was no sign of her.

"I lost sight of her in the battle," Mother said.

"We'll find her later. Right now, we need to get everyone else out of here." I returned my attention to evacuating the grounds.

"Come with me. All of you." Setting a quick pace, I made way for the portal. "Go through."

As the last of the servants disappeared through the ethereal surface, the first of the guards stepped through.

Slowly, as if he were holding a flower, Xurek set Dmitri's body on the carpet. Sofia barrelled into the room, panting, her hair a mess. "Oh thank the gods, you're all okay. I got separated from you. What are you staring at?" She shoved past Felix and Xurek, then crumpled to the floor. Gripping Dmitri's hand, tears brimmed in her eyes.

"Sofia?" My voice broke. "I'm sorry, I know what you're going through. The loss. The pain. But we can't stay here—we must leave."

"We…we were supposed to marry." She wailed and threw her head back. I jolted back as vibrations shot through the floorboards, and the walls trembled. Another piercing shriek erupted from her mouth, and it felt as if the whole Citadel was buckling as Sofia unleashed her pain.

Stumbling, I pushed up against the window. The floor outside fractured, heading rapidly towards the bridge. The mosaic shattered, stone and glass tumbled, plummeting into the depths of the lake. Plumes of dust shot into the air. Waves splashed onto the bank, flooding the flowerbeds, and washing away the destroyed tulips.

Turning, I edged towards Sofia with an outstretched hand. While her wails had broken the bridge, blocking the Orcs' direct access to the Citadel, they could find another way around.

A silvery swirling magic formed around her. She looked through me as she began to fade.

"Please, don't go. I can help you. Wait!" I stumbled closer, then landed on the carpet.

Staring at the empty space where she'd been, I dug my fingers into the plush fibres. She'd done what I'd done—disappeared in the face of an all-consuming despair. My heart ached.

Felix crouched beside me. "Evalyn," he said, voice soft and gentle. "We need to go."

Running my hands through my hair, I tried to think of all the places Sofia would teleport to. She'd go somewhere quiet, where she could be alone. Lake Delendil was her home, and I couldn't imagine her anywhere else.

"We *need* to find her." I trembled, from fear or adrenaline, I couldn't tell. "The Severance of Minds spell won't hold forever, and we need her for when we conjure it again."

"Then we will do that," my mother said. "But first, we must heed your own order. Join the others in Swynvale. Devise a plan there."

"She's right. The bridge may be destroyed but the Orcs will walk around the lake. We can't sit here waiting to be slaughtered." Felix's hand was on my arm, steady and reassuring.

"Makdou is watching everything—perhaps

through her portals—we can't know for certain. Either way, she'll sense us leaving and order an attack," Mother said. "We must be quick."

I rose, flattening my trembling fingers against my thigh. "We'll call for aid once we're safe." I motioned to the portal. "Xurek, do not say a word to anyone in Meridian until I get there. Do not move a muscle. Stay with the guards, and I'll vouch for you."

Xurek rested his hammer on his shoulder, then stepped through the portal without argument. Mother followed him. The High Elves and my mother followed.

Felix glanced at me. "Together?"

"Together." I grabbed Felix's arm, then crossed through the portal.

It snapped closed behind us. Our bodies pulled apart into a million pieces, our hands separated, and my weightless consciousness drifted through the black mass known as the in between. Pure silence.

We reformed on the other side, then fell onto the grass in front of the Great Mother Tree at the back of Meridian. Felix fell to the ground beside me. I scanned my surroundings to find the staff, guards, and my friends.

"You're safe." Mother drew me into her arms. She cradled me against her chest. "Your magic. Truly magnificent. *You* are magnificent."

"I did what I could." I squeezed her arm. "If we'd stayed, my guards and staff would've died. We were all at risk."

"You've done all you can, my dear." She traced her fingers along my cheek. "Now you must find

Sofia. We can't return to Arogath until we have her. The Severance of Minds will have likely broken by the time we get back."

# Chapter Nineteen

Felix drew me from the mud and gave my hand a reassuring squeeze. I brushed myself down and focused on him. He smiled slightly.

"I've got you," he said.

"Mother's right. We need to find Sofia and make sure she's okay." I turned to Mother.

"She'll be anything but all right," she said, "but you're the only person she'll listen to."

Guards thundered across the cobblestones and through the tall grass towards us. Lucien and Xavier marched ahead of them, weaving through the gathering staff and guards from the Citadel.

"What is this beast doing here?" Xavier scowled at Xurek, looking him up and down. "Put down your weapon at once. And who are all these people?"

"He's an ally, rest assured. I promise in the sight of all gods he will harm no man, woman, or child of Meridian." I lifted my hand and slipped between them, although Xurek could defend himself. Knowing the people of Meridian had their own host of divine beings to worship, I appealed to their faith. "We had to flee our homeland. You know about my life from the scroll, so I wouldn't be surprised if you've heard of the natural, pure magic that lives within the Lake. The Orcs invaded it, and we were severely outnumbered. Our only option was to come here to give us enough time to call for aid."

Xurek snorted.

I shot him a glare to say *shut up*.

"Try convincing the men of Meridian who have spent their entire lives fighting at the hands of these creatures," Lucien said.

"You can't stay here." Xavier crossed his arms. "Not with *him*. You must leave."

"We've come to collect Sofia, and we'll leave, just as you ordered. You have my word." I looked him straight in the eyes. "All I ask is that you provide temporary accommodation to my staff and guards. When it is safe for us to return to Arogath, we'll do so."

Xavier scanned the crowd of people as if to determine whether any of them were a threat. "Fine, they can stay here, but why would Sofia be here?"

I touched his arm. My eyes welled with tears, but I fought them. Now wasn't the time for me to break.

He frowned. "What's happened?"

How was I supposed to tell this man his son had died? On my land?

"I-I thought Sofia was with Dierdre. Can…I…" The lump in my throat swelled.

"Dmitri died," Felix said, wrapping his arm around my waist. "I'm sorry."

Xavier stared at us with hollow eyes. "I don't believe you."

"We have no cause to lie," Felix said. "The Orcs invaded our home, and your son died of his injuries."

Xavier shook his head, grinding his teeth. Without another word, he spun on his heel, then left.

"I suggest you hurry and find Sofia. Xavier isn't one to deal well with emotion, let alone the grief for his only son." Lucien disappeared with his guards in tow.

"Thank you." I nodded in gratitude, then led the way over the bridge, down the cobble path, and between the row of cottages. The guards showed those I'd brought through the portal to their accommodations.

The smell of fresh, warm bread filled my nostrils, and my stomach rumbled. I pressed on towards Dierdre's house. Candlelight flickered in the windows. What would I say when I got there? There weren't any words. Nothing I could say would comfort her or Sofia. I knew as much.

I rapped on the door and waited.

Dierdre opened the door, her eyes bright red and puffy. "Evalyn."

"You know?" I squeezed her arm.

"My visions. Although they have been foggy as of late, this one was too potent for me to escape. Come in, dear." She stepped out of the way, allowing us inside.

Xurek ducked his head under the short doorframe, turned sideways through the narrow seating area, then stood awkwardly opposite the stairs. The rest of us entered.

"Although I worry for my husband, I couldn't bring myself to tell him. He one day hoped his son would return to step into his shoes but losing him altogether—I couldn't do that to him. I couldn't see exactly what happened to him, but I sensed it—something dark. But now he knows. You told him."

"I did," I whispered. "I'm sorry, I couldn't keep it from him, and I knew you'd see it. Dierdre, I promise, there was nothing we could do." I racked my brain for something comforting to say.

"My son was a good man. I sensed he did something honourable in his death." Her eyes glistened.

"He fought bravely to defend my homeland." I bowed my head in acknowledgement of his sacrifice.

"Then all I can do, as his mother, is hope he finds peace." Dierdre took a handkerchief from the pocket of her homespun dress, then dabbed her eyes.

"Is Sofia here?" The crackling fire warmed me.

"I'm afraid not." She sipped her tea, then set it

aside, staring out the window. "She's alone and cold. That's all I know."

"That's not much to go on." Felix frowned.

I held out my hand to stop him. "I'm sorry for intruding. We'll leave you now, but if there's anything I can do to help you, send me a word, communicate to me somehow even if I'm in Arogath. I'll come."

"I'll bear it in mind, dear." Dierdre nestled into a chair beside the fire, unfolded a blanket, then draped it over her shoulders. She moved her gaze to the dancing flames in the hearth. "I'd like to be alone to grieve for my son."

We left the house.

Xurek stretched outside. "Damn, that house is small."

I shot him a glare.

---

We gathered in the library in the main hall. Guards stood sentry outside the wooden door.

Mother collapsed into the armchair opposite me. Valneris stood by the window while Theodas and Kiirion nosed through the books on the shelves. Felix remained by my side while Xurek brooded by the fire.

Felix pressed his fingers to his chin, a frown creasing his brow.

I clasped his hand and squeezed. He offered a smile.

"Any wild guesses as to how Makdou managed

to successfully produce the Crimson Kiss spell through portals?" Mother asked. "Evalyn, she has your necklace, right?"

"Yes." Instinctively, my hand rose to my neck and clasped my new, enchanted locket. "It'll heighten her magic, but I can't say I'd know for certain just *how* she's doing it. Surely it can't be too difficult, though. I've made opaque portals, whereas hers must be transparent. Otherwise, how else would she see what's happening on the other side? She must have sight of the Orcs to produce the Crimson Kiss."

I traded glances with Felix. He shrugged. In times like these, I needed Sofia, yet I had no idea where she was.

*'She's alone and cold.'*

"Mother, could you help me do a location spell to find Sofia?" I reached across and touched her hand.

"Of course." She grasped my hands.

We chanted the foreign words, but unlike our previous attempts at the spell, no vision materialised. Sofia had blocked our spell.

"Damn it." I thumped the table. "She doesn't want to be found. What about the spell we used to reveal the Great Mother Tree?"

"It won't work. That spell is only good for revealing objects or things that don't really have a say in the matter. Sofia, on the other hand, will know you're trying to find her. She'll continue to block you."

Valneris paced the rug. "We can't stay here, but what choices do we have? The Severance of Minds spell won't hold forever. We need to take care of the rest of our people."

I rubbed my temples. "Mother, I'll need your help to produce this transparent portal. It's not something I've done before. Hopefully, we can use them to communicate to our allies in the Fertile Territories."

I rose, and with Felix's assistance, pushed the table towards the wall. "Time works differently here, so we can't stay for too long."

Mother and I linked again.

"Concentrate all of your magic on forming a portal." I looked her straight in the eyes. "I'll focus on getting it to show Bluefair Fort. We need to speak to Eric."

She bobbed her head.

I concentrated on the high sandstone walls, the tall towers, and the wrought iron gates.

The vision travelled through the centre of the fort towards the main hall. The stench of molten iron hung in the air from the blacksmith's burning forge.

Hovering towards the main hall, the spell passed through the closed wooden doors, along the corridors, and into the war room.

Eric hunched over the map stretched across the table. Wooden figures held the parchment corners down. He clasped a quill between his fingers, dipped the tip into an ink pot, then began writing on a piece of parchment. My dear friend.

"Eric." I cleared my throat, and that thread bonding me to the gods thrummed as if my faith in them renewed.

Despite my best efforts to condemn them for abandoning me, I couldn't fight the *hope* consuming me—the hope I placed in the gods that Eric could hear me.

He jolted his head at the sound of my voice, eyes widening when his gaze fell on the portal. He abandoned the letter and crossed the room in wide strides.

"Evalyn?" He raised his brows. "What's wrong? I was just writing to you."

I stretched to touch his arm, but my fingers fell through him.

"Hey, Eric." I couldn't fight the smile tugging at my lips. I missed him truly. "I need your help."

"Wait." He raised a hand. "Where are you? What's going on?"

"I'm in Swynvale again. We're all here." I grabbed Felix and drew him close so Eric could see. Mother peered into the portal and waved. "We need you and your men to go to Lake Delendil. The Orcs had the waters surrounded, and we were outnumbered. I evacuated all the staff, and they won't be able to return until it's safe. The bridge is destroyed, our guards are either all dead or injured. I'm not sure how many stone soldiers are left intact. I have no idea where Sofia is."

Eric, dressed in his armour with his shield over his back, dragged a hand over his eyes. "Damned Orcs. Just when we think we've got some peace. I'll rally my men and the Centaurs. I'll pass the word to the Elementals and call on any remaining knights from the Eyrie."

"Have people populated the Eyrie again?" I

missed my childhood home. Nobody had occupied the Eyrie since the Orcs butchered the king and queen.

"There's some knights down there restoring the lands." Eric waved the matter away. "Is there anything else I should be worried about?"

"The Orcs are bewitched," I warned, and he grimaced. "They're under Makdou's control. We've located her at Sanctum City, and I think she's trying to weaken us before coming for me directly."

"I'll sound the horns." He straightened his back. "Try not to let too much time pass, Evalyn, if you are to utilise your connection to Swynvale."

The portal snapped shut. I stared at the empty space on the floorboards.

Felix stroked my arm. "I'm here."

"I hated that—asking him to fight again. He's only recently returned home." I sighed. "Do you think this is all part of Makdou's plan? Lull us into a false sense of security, then hit us where it hurts? Dmitri, dead. Sofia, missing. Gods know what might happen to Eric or anyone else I care about." I beseeched Zahan, Goddess of Life, to protect Eric. I couldn't bear the loss of someone else I held dear.

Felix pressed his lips to my forehead. "We'll get through this. All of us."

―――――――⟋⟍――――――――

My head pounded from the constant stream of magic, yet I was nowhere near close to having a rest.

"We can leave now." My eyelids threatened to close, and a heaviness spread through my limbs. "Time moves faster there, so by the time we travel back to Lake Delendil, Eric and the army might already be there."

Valneris let out a sigh of relief. "That's one thing sorted. Evalyn, you look like you're going to pass out. The guards are here, too. Your staff will remain safe here until it's confirmed safe for them to return, but we'll need the Queen's Guard."

"I've conjured a lot of magic today, feels like my brain is going to explode." I rubbed my temples. "Time for another portal to get us the hell out of here."

My mother embraced me. Her warmth relaxed me. I leaned into her and squeezed, cherishing each moment with her.

"You are so brave," she whispered in my ear as she stroked my hair, rustling the loose strands from my bun. "I'm so proud. Now let's go kill these bastards."

Clasping hands with her, I envisioned the ethereal, translucent portal back to Lake Delendil. Through the centre of the gateway, I saw the shattered bridge, the wreckage in the lake, and the destroyed gardens. My heart ached.

"I'll lead the way." Xurek positioned his weighty hammer on his shoulder and entered the portal. The High Elves followed him.

Felix ran his hand up my arm. "I'll go through the portal now in case the Orcs attack as soon as we reach the other side."

"I'll be right behind you."

I watched him step through it and disappear. Keeping a hold of my mother's hand, we left the library.

I fell through the in between, surrounded by the all too familiar darkness of the void.

My feet hit the floorboards of the council room. Shards of glass from the smashed doors littered the floor amongst the remnants of vines. The staircase banister was splintered, the opposite doors ripped from their hinges.

I exited the Citadel. Bodies were strewn across the destroyed flower beds. A Centaur was impaled on his own spear. Gnomes lay face down in the mud. A burned Orc's body lay half in the lake. Shouts and cries of pain pierced the air.

On the other side of the lake, Eric's sword clashed against an Orc's heavy hammer. Centaurs, carrying spears and bows, flanked him. Undines and Nereids chanted their songs. Surviving Gnomes raised their mud creature, Golem, from the earth.

Based on my limited understanding of the time difference, one month in Swynvale equated to one year in Arogath. If my quick math was correct, the day we'd spent in Swynvale meant Eric had approximately two weeks in *his* time to rally our allies.

An Orc's roar boomed across the lake. They charged into the water. The Undines called upon the water element, lifting a tsunami-like wave, wiping out a row of Orcs, drowning them instantly. Ethereal hands pulled them into the depths where they would fall into the deeper layers of Elysium.

More Orcs continued to march forward, pouring in through different parts of the treeline.

Felix drew his sword and stood beside me. My mother formed a ball of magic—red like mine—within her palms, where it swelled and spun. The guards plundered ahead, breaking into the Orcs' formation.

Golem plucked an Orc from the ground, tore off his head, blood spurting, and threw his limbs across the tree line. Eric and the Centaurs fought the Orcs, their swords colliding with hammers. Arrows flew through the sky and pierced the enemies in the chest.

"I can't just stand here—I must help them." I cupped my hands together and a ball of bright red light expanded to the size of a melon.

I ran to the lakeside. Water lapped around my feet as I launched the ball of magic into the encroaching Orcs.

"Evalyn!" Felix shouted.

My magic was fuelled by the death of our loved ones and our allies who'd perished in our wars. The destruction of so many Arogathean villages. Losing Felix at the Badlands and finding him, spirit broken, at Southkeep. Finding my mother after her twenty years of imprisonment. The death of my child.

I shot the ball of magic towards a crowd of Orcs surrounding Eric and Human soldiers.

The magic hit the ground and exploded, shooting a crowd of Orcs through the air.

Several emerged from the water, now on our side of the lake. They growled, revealing their yellowing tusks. Leather armour covered only their shoulders, their broad chests exposed and decorated with war paint.

Felix stepped in front of me—he and the Elves formed a circle around Mother and I.

Five Orcs raced towards us. Felix and the Elves swung their swords against the heavy hammers.

Mother and I wove our magic together, and like a tendril, it streamed in the Orcs direction. The red and orange glow of our powers formed a sharp edge, and as if it had a mind of its own, it impaled an Orc. Blood spewed to the ground. The vine of magic tossed the corpse aside.

Water crashed around us as the Undines and Nereids continued to submerge the Orcs in the lake. Flames rose from the forest opposite the lake. I scanned the area.

Directly opposite me, Ignatius, the Salamander I'd met at the Vesuvius Caves, stared at me with his beady eyes. His tongue flicked out the corner of his mouth. He bowed to me, then raised his arms around him as the other Salamanders tore through the crowd, sending bolts of fire into the Orcs. The trees were ablaze.

"Watch out!" Felix sent me flying into the ground as he took the brunt of a swinging hammer against his own Arogathean blade.

I flung a ball of red magic towards the Orc. The magic set him alight, giving Kiirion the opportunity to plunge his sword through the Orc's thick skin.

Mother drew me to my feet. She rubbed her hands together, then held them out in front of her.

She chanted loudly—a spell I didn't

recognize—and the lake rumbled.

Stone shifted and reformed, stacking on top of each other, creating distorted soldiers out of the wreckage. Flecks of glass from the shattered mosaic acted as eyes, glistening a bright blue within the centre of the heads. Remnants of rock slithered into place to form brows. Stones loaded upon one another, forming tightly modelled spears. The soldiers yielded their weapons, ready to march on command.

I gaped. "How did you do that?"

"I've been a Mage a very long time." She grinned.

The Orcs froze in their spots, their bodies limp and weapons dropped.

Makdou must've seized her control of the Orcs—their eyes glassed over.

Mother traded glances with me. "What now?"

# Chapter Twenty

"It's time." I rested my hand on my mother's arm. "We need to go to Sanctum City."

"Makdou wants us to go to her," Kiirion said.

"How can you be sure?" Valneris kept his sword held high and snapped his gaze back and forth, scanning the area.

"It's the only reason to explain this." I gestured to our surroundings.

Xurek grunted. "I was looking forward to caving in some skulls."

Unable to ignore his snarky remark, I shot him a glare.

"I'll command the stone soldiers to hold off the

Orcs for as long as we can. We need to leave. Now," Mother said.

"What about Eric and the others?" I flicked my gaze to my friend who'd fought alongside our allies. "We can't leave them. Not again."

Mother gripped me and shook. "Evalyn, you don't have a choice. Listen to me, you *must* survive. No one else can kill Makdou except you. Create a portal and get out of here."

She shoved me away from her, and I stumbled backwards. I didn't want to leave her side—I couldn't afford to, but I didn't have a choice.

I steadied my shaking hands and envisioned a portal. My magic hummed as it coursed through my veins. Despite my efforts, the empty space on the ground in front of me remained empty. No portal. "It's not working. Damn it."

"Makdou must be blocking your magic. Take your horses and leave. I'll control the stone giant, and we'll find you after," Mother said.

Felix grabbed my hand and hurried me around the right side of the Citadel, through the destroyed gardens, past our son's headstone, and towards the stables. "They'll catch up with us. We need to get you out of here quickly."

"Felix, you're hurting me." I tried to tug free. "Let go."

"I'm sorry, my love, but your mother's right." He freed me, then placed his hands onto my shoulders. "I know you want to protect everyone, but you can't. You *need* to put a stop to this, you hear me?"

He hurried to prepare the horses—ushering them

out of the stables and throwing their saddles on. With urgency, he practically shoved me onto my mount. Using the stirrup, he flung his leg over his horse, then led the way past the haystacks outside the barn, down the trail alongside the empty blacksmiths, and onto a path past the Citadel grounds. Chickens clucked in their coops, loose feathers floating through the wire.

His eyes blazed. "Is there a spell you can use to conjure us some food for the journey or blankets for the night?"

"I could probably use a spell to help us *find* food. You can hunt game, and I'll build a fire." I shook the reins, encouraging my horse to keep up with his.

In the distance, the fighting resumed. The clang of metal and screams rang through the trees.

"Let's hurry. I can't bear to hear their pain, not when I have left them." I shook my head. "The others can track the horses' hoofprints until the find us."

When darkness fell over Arogath, I conjured a ball of light. It hovered above our heads, casting a warm glow over the trunks and canopy of leaves.

"Over there." Felix pointed towards a glade between the woods. "We'll set up camp for the night and wait for the others to join us."

I bobbed my head. My stomach rumbled and the thought of roasting wild rabbit over a warm fire made my mouth salivate.

"I'll collect some branches." Once we'd dismounted, I led our horses to a patch of grass, then scooped up a handful of dried twigs and sticks, slotted them under my arm, and held them tight to my chest.

In the centre of the glade, I stacked the sticks against each other. I struck two sharp rocks together until a spark lit the construction of branches and twigs.

"I'm going to find something for us to eat, water the horses, and fill our canteens." He rapped his knuckle against the canteen tied around his sword sheath.

"I'll keep the fire going." Using a long stick, I prodded the flames, encouraging them to grow. The fire popped and crackled, the burning smell of pine filling my nostrils.

Felix disappeared into the woods, leading the horses by the reins.

Producing more balls of magic, I set them at the four corners of the glade, providing enough light for the night. Shoving a small, fallen trunk towards the fire, I sucked in deep breaths. My muscles burned. The moss was soft and spongy beneath my fingers, and I hoped it would act as a cushion for us to rest our heads until our friends caught up with us.

A while later, Felix returned, a dead deer hauled over one of the horses' saddles. "Hunting can be tricky with only a sword. Luckily, I found this one already injured and put it out of its misery. There'll be plenty of meat for the others when they arrive."

He knelt beside the fire and began his work of skinning the game. He cut through the fur with his blade, slid it sideways, detached the skin from flesh, then hoisted the hide over his shoulder as it peeled away from the corpse.

I turned away as the stench of coppery blood

wafted towards me. "You know, I've been thinking…" I took a deep breath, gathering my confidence. "My coronation will happen as soon as Makdou is dealt with. We could be wed. You could become a king. Rule by my side."

He halted his work momentarily, then resumed. "I'm a knight. Fineries, titles—it's not me."

"That's a weak answer." I picked up a stick and prodded the fire to give my hands something to do.

"I don't want to have to live up to anyone's expectation," he said quietly.

"What do you mean?" I tossed the stick aside and fixed my gaze on him.

"If I become king, people will expect things of me, and if for whatever reason, I fail my missions, I don't want to let anyone down. Not you, not the High Elves, and especially not the good people of the Light Triads." He peeled the remaining strip of skin away from the deer and dumped it onto the mud.

"You protect me, my family, our friends, and the innocent civilians of this nation. You couldn't be anything more than what you are right now."

"Then I would gladly accept another role, one that allows me to protect. Make me the head of the Queen's Guard, if it pleases you, but we should be focused on finding Sofia, stopping Makdou, and making it safe for the Citadel staff to return." He sighed.

"You're right." My racing mind returned to my mother and friends. What was taking them so long?

I drew my cape tight around my shoulders, then rubbed my hands together in front of the fire.

He sliced pieces of meat, impaled them on sticks, then hung them above the flames to cook. "Shouldn't be too long. I found some berries that are safe to eat and some nettles for your tea."

"I don't think tea is appropriate right now." I stared into the flickering fire.

When the deer was cooked, he handed me a skewer. "Have your dinner and rest. I'll stay awake until they get here."

I bit into the slightly charred flesh as my stomach growled. When only bones remained, I tossed the stick aside and wilted against the trunk. I fixed my gaze on the evening sky. A single eagle flew overhead.

I wrapped my arms around my stomach. The balls of light dwindled.

"Get some sleep." He smiled slightly.

I closed my eyes, the fire warming me, and drifted out of consciousness.

---

"Evalyn, wake up." Someone shook me vigorously.

I stirred, eyes blurry from sleep, and stared at my mother who hovered above me.

Bolting upright, I gripped her arms. "Are you okay? Where are the others?"

"Right here." Eric's voice warmed me. "The guards have remained at the Citadel."

I scanned the glade. The High Elves sat opposite me, the fire separating us.

Sighing with relief, I sank back against the trunk. "Thank the gods."

And for the first time in a *long* time, I meant it. My faith thrummed as if it resembled a fire reignited.

"The battle continued until the Orcs froze. Makdou must've realised you'd fled. The Severance of Minds acts as a shield, which also blocks us from her view—she won't be able to track us anymore. Despite this, we shouldn't take our time reaching Sanctum City either." Mother lowered onto the ground beside me. "If two weeks have passed here in Arogath, then we know the Severance of Minds spell lasts for that long, at least. However, we still need Sofia—her healing abilities are second to none. While I know a few spells, healing is not my specialty. If we're to be set upon unexpectedly by Orcs, in this realm or in Arogath, we need to be prepared, and as of right now, we do not have sufficient healing knowledge between us. While it's my intention to not send the staff and guards home until it's completely safe to do so, I can't take the risk of not having a healer with us."

"I know what she's going through—she's overcome with grief and probably not thinking straight, otherwise she wouldn't flee, knowing people need her." I frowned. "And as for Makdou, she'll find a way. Call it doubt, or lack of confidence, if you will. She won't be blindsided by our arrival. She'll know we're coming."

"I bet you doubted the Crimson Kiss existed— no one had witnessed it since the Noble Ones. Why would you have believed the magnitude of its

power? At least, not until it was performed on you."
Mother's words stung, but they held truth. My baby
had paid the price.

She placed her hand on my arm. "I will be by
your side," she said, voice soft like the evening
breeze.

Departing from the area, we continued our
journey through grasslands, venturing further
north, leaving Lake Delendil and the rest of the
Fertile Territories far behind. The winds cooled,
harshened, nipping at my cheeks and neck.

Eric fell into position beside me, his horse
trotting smoothly. "May I speak with you, Evalyn?"

"Sure." I nodded.

"We failed you the last time," he said. "We
won't let it happen again."

Everybody had said the same. The High Elves.
Xurek and Felix. Now Eric too. The only person
who wasn't there was Aneirin, my father. He'd
returned to the Eyrie to help rebuild, but when we'd
called for the knights to help at Lake Delendil, he
hadn't come.

"My father didn't come." I verbalised my train
of thought. "How could he not come? After all we
have been through?"

"This is the man who hid underground for
twenty years because he feared what he may face
above," he said. "He is a coward."

"I am his daughter." I shook my head. "He is not
here. My own mother has come, and he hasn't.
Perhaps I'm naïve for thinking he might've. Two
years would've given him plenty of time to change
his mind, become the man worthy of his family.

277

Despite my mother telling me her time with him was unbearable, it's still difficult to accept that even now, he does not choose his family."

"Maybe your mother knows why he didn't." He shrugged.

I rode past him and Felix.

"Why haven't you mentioned Aneirin?" My voice held an accusatory tone as I eyed my mother. "Where is he?"

"It wasn't the right time to tell you, Evalyn. We were fighting the Orcs." She held out her hand. "He's gone. He's left me and you. Again."

"What?" Hadn't one disappearance twenty years ago been enough? He'd just found his wife and reunited with his daughter. Why would he want to leave?

"He's fled to the Newland," she said bitterly.

"Vrecrai," I corrected.

"Indeed." She kept her voice level.

When my father found her in Southkeep, he vowed to keep her safe. He'd even remained at her side when I was in Swynvale for two years. Could the slightest threat of war really send him across the Great Sea a second time?

"He's a faint-hearted man," I said through gritted teeth. "But you have me. I will be by your side."

She took my hand in hers and squeezed it.

"Calling him faint-hearted is a kindness." She grimaced. "He's far worse than that. I'm sorry."

"You don't owe me an apology; I shouldn't have left you with him." Anger boiled within me. I'd put my own pain and grief above the suffering she'd endured alone.

"Perhaps not," she said. "But it is what you needed, and you have learned so much."

The conversation dwindled. I'd learned so much from Swynvale and its natural magic. It'd given me strength when I was at my weakest. Now, marching into war once again, I was at my strongest.

"I love you, Mother." I stretched and patted her knee. "I'm so grateful to have you in my life, after thinking for so long you were far gone from this world."

Mother's eyes pricked with tears. She didn't say anything. Instead, she kept her tears at bay. We'd missed so much time together, so many memories unmade. I promised I would give her the time if we survived this.

---

When we stopped for the evening, an icy chill created goosebumps across my skin. I wrapped my cape around me as we settled in abandoned huts for the night. Who'd lived there and when? I didn't know of any Triads this far north.

Felix stirred in his sleep—his arm draped around my shoulders. His warm breath against my neck and his legs against mine was all I needed to feel safe in this unknown land.

We lay in a single cot in one of the small rooms. My mother slept soundlessly in the spare room with the High Elves, while Xurek patrolled the grounds.

"Felix." I turned in his arms to face him. As he

shifted against me, I stroked his soft stubble.

"Hmm…," he grumbled with his eyes still closed. Moments later, he pressed his lips to mine.

"I want to stay here with you," I muttered against his lips, longing for nothing more in the world than to be alone with him. I needed his touch, his skin against mine. A hungry desire inside me yearned for him.

"I will never leave you," he whispered against my neck before tucking a stray piece of hair behind my ear. The moonlight cascading through the window illuminated his face.

His dark hair flopped over his brows, and I pushed it away with a feathery touch.

We fell asleep in each other's arms and awoke to birdsong.

Felix squeezed me, then groaned as his eyes darkened. "We can't stay here long."

I climbed out of bed and headed into the other room. "Mother?"

"I'm right here, darling." She smiled, standing near a clay oven. The hearty scent of cooked meat wafted through the cabin. "I've prepared breakfast. Eric and the others went hunting this morning."

Felix entered the room and rubbed his eyes. "You should've awoken me. I could've accompanied them."

"I didn't want to disturb you. You needed rest. Both of you." Mother wrapped a piece of cloth around her hands, then took the pan out of the oven. The fire inside blasted a radiating warmth.

"Mother, you really didn't have to go to all this trouble." Once she set the pan aside, I drew her into my arms.

"Nonsense, dear, I've lost twenty years of preparing you food." She patted my back, then let go. "Now sit, eat. Both of you. We have a long day ahead of us."

We sat on a wooden bench beside a crooked table. Mother rooted around for some plates in the unfamiliar house. She wiped them down with her cloth, then placed them in front of us. Taking her fork, she impaled the meat, then dumped it in front of us.

"The Elves have also picked more berries for our journey." She set the pan down, then slid onto the bench opposite us. Stabbing a piece of meat, she popped it into her mouth.

Once we finished our meals, the three of us met our friends outside the hut.

"We have a very dangerous day ahead of us." There was no delicate way of putting it. "Makdou wanted to end the prophecy. She will do anything in her power to kill me. There is no underestimating how powerful she is."

"We'll be with you, my queen." Kiirion rested his hand on the pommel of his sword. "Until the very end."

"I'll put my hammer to good use." Xurek swung his weapon from side to side. He smiled, which looked out of place against his harsh Orc features. His yellowed tusks poked out around his thick, green lips.

"I'm sure it's this way." Mother pointed to the gravel path leading out of the settlement. "Without a map, we'll have to rely on what we saw in the location spell."

I nodded. "Head towards the snow-covered mountains."

# Chapter Twenty-One

"We're going to be okay this time." I glanced at Kiirion as we rode side by side. The crease between his brows had become a permanent fixture on our journey to Sanctum City. "We have to be. All of us."

"I trust you." He eyed the trail ahead.

Our friends rode in front—Felix beside my mother. In any other circumstance, it would've been a nice sight to see.

The travel dragged on in an eerie sense of uneventfulness. Silence enveloped us, aside from the breeze stirring the shrubs, and the horses thudding along the beaten path, crunching the frost. Not one Orc made an appearance. Was this Makdou's intention—lure us in with our uneasiness at its highest?

"I've been waiting for something—anything. A trap perhaps, if not an attack." I glanced up at the ethereal layer of magic hovering over us. "I'm glad we have this spell to protect us."

"Having more Orcs taunt us along the way would take the fun from her." Kiirion shrugged. "We know she likes in on the action."

The gravel path crumbled under the horses' hooves. It stretched across an open pasture littered with rabbit holes. A cool breeze nipped at my cheeks, whipped through the grasslands, and rustled the shrubs and nearby birch trees. I dug my hand into my pocket and pulled out a dozen whitebeam berries. Popping them into my mouth, their sweet taste spilled across my tongue.

We ventured through the fields and groves of trees until night fell over the north, and we sought shelter in a nearby barn. The roof sagged, and a dense blanket of vines scaled the walls. A breeze whistled through the windowless structure.

"Most of the cattle died during the plague two years ago," Kiirion said. "Breeding farms have been set up near Bluefair Fort. It's one of the things Eric looks after."

Eric smiled at the mention of his name. "The people are more than happy to step up and help."

"I'm glad to hear there's progress." I dismounted and stretched my legs, although it did little to soothe the cramp in my inner thighs.

"You'll be delighted to know we are breeding more horses too." He beamed as he and Kiirion hobbled the horses nearby.

Inside the barn, I knelt and scooped a handful of hay and propped it into a mound to use as a pillow. A plume of dust tickled my nose, and the dry, crisp straw stuck into my skin. I unhooked my cape and draped it over me, then glanced at the streams of evening light pouring in through the gaps between the wooden roof slats.

In desperate need of rest, I changed from one position to the next. My legs ached, and a heaviness in my eyes made it difficult to keep them open, yet the hard surface didn't encourage sleep.

Huffing, I sat up. Felix draped his arm around my shoulder and drew me against him. "Sleep."

"I wish I could." Unwilling to disturb the others, I kept my voice low. "My anxiety is sky-high. I have a knot in the pit of my stomach. I also wish Sofia was here—gods knows where she is, and I have no idea if she's safe." Tentatively, I prayed to Idon, God of Survival. With my faith reignited, I prayed with every ounce of my being that he would protect her.

"We'll find her at Sanctum City." Felix shifted around to face me—a seriousness emanated in his almond, brown eyes.

"I just want this to be over." This war was never-ending, following us everywhere we went, even into other worlds. "For good."

He kissed me lightly, then slid down onto the hay, pulling me with him. "One day at a time."

We rode at dawn the next day, stopping to graze

on berries and catch rabbits when we could. Late morning, we stopped to feed and water the horses before continuing north into Makdou's lair—Sanctum City.

The image of Makdou in the location spell flickered in my mind's eye. She'd been controlling the Orcs through the portals. If I killed her, her green magic would fade from Swynvale and perhaps the number of attacks would decrease. Although Dmitri was gone, knowing an armistice would be found in his home realm brought me peace, and his death wouldn't be in vain.

The chill of the north burned my cheeks. The mountains came into view across a lake. Far on the horizon, nestled in the mountains, was Sanctum City, signposted by old, weather-beaten trail markers.

"There it is." I pointed.

"If we weren't headed here for battle, I'd be very impressed." Felix glanced at me from the corner of his eyes. "I've always wanted to see this place."

"Remember when you said you wanted to go here when we fled the Eyrie? It seems like a lifetime ago."

"It used to be the safest place in these discovered territories, my queen," Kiirion added. "Before the Orcs gained so much control over the Dark Triads, taking sides didn't exist, not there, at least."

Even in my location spell, with Sanctum City crumbling and threatening to give way, it still looked beautiful. I couldn't help but imagine how mesmerising it might've looked before the touch of age battered its walls.

We followed the winding, frost-covered path as it grew further into the mountains, climbing higher into the clouds. The route was too steep for the horses.

"Watch your step." I stumbled as my feet slid across the ice.

We ascended the slippery steps up the side of the mountain. Sanctum City seemed further away.

Pausing, I frowned, fixing my gaze onto the jagged surface of rocks poking out of the cliff face.

"Evalyn?" Mother gripped my arm. "Are you okay?"

"Uh…yeah, I'm fine." I shook my head. "I could've sworn I heard something."

"There's not a lot to hear out in the middle of nowhere." Xurek huffed. "Other than the sound of our own footsteps. Jeez, how many stairs are there? You know, Zhah is built on flat ground—Orcs don't like stairs."

Through the stone archway at the top of the steps, began the winding path upwards through narrow gaps between the crags. The Citadel of Sanctum City towered into the clouds—its walls were damp and covered in a thick layer of moss. Vines climbed the towers and gripped on to windowless frames like claws.

A heavy mist hung in the air. My teeth chattered as I wrapped my trembling arms tight around my chest. Glancing up, I caught sight of an eagle flying overhead.

The roofs were caved in; broken tiles had fallen to the floor. Sanctum City was a ghost town.

The ground levelled out as we reached the centre

of the courtyard, the grand entrance of the Citadel in front of us.

"Tread carefully." I gestured to the debris scattered across the muddy, uneven floor.

Xurek grimaced as he clonked across the floorboards with his large feet.

"Stay here. We need someone to hold position outside while the rest of us scour the inside," I said at once. "Eric, stay with him, and don't get yourselves killed. The Severance of Minds will only go so far. Makdou is capable of anything, and the last thing we want is her infiltrating anyone's mind again. If you suspect she is doing so, bind and blindfold him."

Mother, Felix, and the High Elves came with me. I fixed my gaze on the faded copper knocker, then heaved the rotting, wooden door open. Despite my attempts to tread lightly, the staircase on the left side of the entrance creaked underfoot.

"I don't understand why she is here alone," Felix whispered. "She knows we are coming."

I grasped the dust covered banister as I reached the top of the staircase. "We're bound to run into her, or whatever else she has in store for us."

The Citadel was too quiet. There were no Orcs, no creaking floorboards to suggest where Makdou may be. Utter silence.

"I don't like this." Kiirion overtook me. "Something isn't right. If she's truly here, she wouldn't be hiding. She'd be ready for a fight."

"The vision showed us a room down there." Mother pointed to a chamber ahead of the Elves.

My hands sweated. The silence was deafening.

Valneris clasped his sword as he neared the room. He glanced quickly to Kiirion and Theodas before kicking in the door with his leather booted foot.

The three Elves flooded into the room. Felix stayed close to my side; his own weapon drawn. Within seconds, red magic swelled in my palms as I scanned the chamber. Wind whipped in through the broken window, stirring the dust-covered drapes of the broken four-poster bed.

A shrill scream and the clanging of swords came from outside the window. I hurried to the windowsill, Xurek and Eric fought against a strange animal, its form large and fierce.

"We need to help them!" I fled from the room, Felix hot on my heels. "Makdou could be down there."

He drew his sword in a swift motion. "What are they fighting?"

"I can't tell." I made my way down the creaking staircase. "They look like possessed dogs."

"Evalyn, slow down." Mother called from somewhere behind me. I spun around on the bunched-up, worn rug beneath my feet. "You need to stay with me and the High Elves."

"Makdou is likely behind this attack. Dierdre also said Sofia is somewhere cold and alone. Where else in Arogath is this chilly? She must be here. Plus, I have Felix *and* my magic—I'll be safe."

In the courtyard, Xurek and Eric slashed their weapons through the beasts.

"What are they?" I launched a fiery ball into the dog-like animal standing on its hind legs. It screeched as the magic set it alight. The High Elves launched into the fight, while Felix threw up his sword and blocked a launching creature.

"No idea, but I'll stay and fight. Go and find Sofia!" Mother shoved me away from the nearing beasts.

I tripped over dislodged stones scattered across the floor, then scrambled to my feet.

"I'm not leaving any of you again, Mother—duck!" I launched a ball of magic over her head into a crowd of growling beasts.

The Elves ripped their way through the charging dogs as more approached.

A dog had Felix pinned to the ground, snapping its sharp teeth at him, inches away from his face. His sword lay on the floor beside him, presumably knocked from his hand when he was knocked down.

"Felix!" I darted through the crowd, launching magic at the wild animals as they raced towards me.

One lunged, its large claws scraped down my armour, puncturing the metal. A searing pain shot through the wound in my upper arm.

The dog's mouth widened, growling in my face, bits of spit falling from its sharp canines. Valneris plunged his sword into the beast.

I rose, ignoring the burning sensation in my arm, then bolted towards Felix's sword. Grabbing it with both hands, I thrusted it into the side of the beast holding him. It screamed in pain and collapsed on top of him.

He threw the animal aside, then scrambled to his feet, panting. I shoved the sword into his hand.

Another wild beast pounced at us. He stabbed it with his sword, spilling a black, tar-like liquid onto the floor.

"Where are the others?" I spun in circles, firing balls of magic into the seemingly endless swarm of beasts.

He grasped my arm and pulled me hard, dragging me away from the battle in the courtyard.

"Makdou's not even here," Felix raged. Black blood, spattered across his face and armour, dried.

In a daze, I looked around, taking in the chaos. Dead creatures littered the floor. "How is this even possible? The location spell is never wrong!"

"Well, it's wrong now." He paced along the ground.

"Why did you pull me away from the fight? We can't leave our friends." I stopped him.

The shrieks of dying beasts dwindled.

"Evalyn?" Eric called. "Where are you?"

"I'm right here!" I spun to find Eric approaching me.

Trails of dried, sticky blood covered his cheeks and neck. Xurek's eyes were crazed—black blood dripped from his hammer. The Elves stood beside him, wide-eyed and gasping.

"Mother!" I dashed past the Elves, scanning the courtyard. Bodies littered the area.

A whimper was muffled by a pile of three dead dogs leaking blood into a pool beneath them.

"Someone, h-help me." My voice cracked as I tugged a beast's leg, but they were too heavy. "Xurek, quickly, they're crushing my mother."

He yanked the animal from the ground, then

291

hauled it into the stone wall where it collided with a loud thud. He threw aside the last two beasts, revealing my mother, beaten and bloodied beneath. Her red hair was fanned out around her head.

I dropped to my knees, scooping her into my arms. Tears sprung in my eyes as I clamped my palms onto one of her deep, gushing wounds.

"Oh, my dear mother. Hold on, you hear me? We'll get you out of here. Xurek, can you help her up, please? Quickly, she's losing a lot of blood." A strangled sob escaped my mouth.

"Evalyn." Mother held out her trembling hand. "It's okay."

"No, it's not okay, I'm not letting you die." Tears rolled down my cheeks, and a tightness formed in my chest. "Damn it. Where is Sofia? If we can just find her, she will heal you."

"I'm so glad…I found you…my daughter." Her eyelids drooped. "You need to…find the others."

"Xurek, didn't you hear me? Help her. Now. We need to get her help." I ignored my mother and blinked through blurry eyes, shaking her in a feeble attempt to keep her conscious.

"My dear…" Mother tugged my hand gently. I snapped my gaze back at her. "I don't have enough time. I've lost…too much blood."

"Shhh, don't say that." I choked on the lump in my throat and held her close to my chest, stroking her blood-soaked hair from her face.

Valneris knelt at my side. His eyes hollowed. "Your mother is right. I'm so sorry."

"What about the Tree? I could take her through a portal and…and I can heal her, right?" I gripped his arm and shook him hard.

"Evalyn…" Mother sputtered blood.

She lifted her trembling hand to my face. She cupped my cheek with her fingers. I clutched her hand and leaned into her embrace. Her face blurred through the fresh waves of tears streaming from my eyes. My heart shattered.

"My beautiful girl," she whispered as her eyes closed. "It's as if…I never truly…left you."

"I love you so much." I sobbed, weakness spreading through my limbs and settling heavily in my bones. "Please don't go."

"I will see you…again, my child." Her last breath escaped her pale lips, and her hand fell limp.

I pressed my shaking hand to my mouth, muffling my screaming from the all-consuming pain of losing her again. Sagging, my whole body went limp as if a part of me died with her.

*Oh, gods. You can't take her away from me. I can't do this without her.*

Felix drew me into his arms, and I clung to him, my body slumping against his. My energy was depleted. I had nothing left to give. Screwing my eyes shut, I willed the image of my mother's dead body away.

"I've got you," he whispered.

With a shaky breath, I opened my eyes as Xurek scooped my mother off the floor. "I'll carry her home." His face softened as he looked at me.

"Evalyn, you're injured." Felix tilted my chin to him, perhaps to tear my attention from my mother's lifeless body.

Either way, it didn't matter. The memory of her

would forever be etched in my mind and soul.

His fingers lightly touched the slit in the armour below my shoulder. "We need to go back to Lake Delendil. Sofia isn't here. We'll lay your mother to rest and tend to your wound."

"It's just a scratch. We can't turn back now," I growled.

"Evalyn," Kiirion said.

My gaze landed on the blood smeared across his chest. "You're bleeding."

"Those beasts have lethal claws," he said, words thin. "Eric needs tending too. We need to recuperate before we resume our hunt for Makdou."

Reluctantly, I nodded, then I hastened away, unable to look at my mother's still face. Instead, I cursed all the gods to hell, and that fire of faith blew out.

# Chapter Twenty-Two

Heavy rain pattered onto the barn roof. Droplets fell through the gaps between the wooden slats and dampened the hay beside me. I drew my knees to my chest and stared at the rain through the doorless entrance. The wind whipped, and my teeth chattered.

"Evalyn, I know this is a difficult time for you, but you must eat." Felix held a stick with rabbit meat skewered onto it. "While we may not be able to travel in these conditions, we can feast, gain our strength."

I took the stick and turned it over in my hands. "My mother's corpse decomposes every second and we cannot lay her to rest. I don't have time to sit around and wait for the rain to stop—we should be tracking Makdou and finding Sofia. Anything but this."

I kicked a stack of hay, sending tufts of straw into the air. A cloud of dust fogged the barn. A lump burned in my throat. While we'd cleaned our wounds and dressed them with bandages the moment we left Sanctum City, I hadn't been strong enough at the time to perform a location spell.

"I hate this." I launched the skewer. "There's absolutely nothing I can do about it until this damn rain stops. Arogath *never* rains—why now?"

"Why would you say there's nothing you can do?" He stroked my arm. "You're powerful and strong, not to mention everything you have been through…your mother's death is another one of the things you'll overcome. You've tended to your wound now. Why don't you try another location spell to find Sofia?"

I focused on his words. I'd never performed one alone, but I *had* to find her. Rubbing my head, I sighed. Rage bubbled through my veins, and my skin grew hot. Makdou took everything from me, and I promised *myself* I'd do the same to her.

"Concentrate," he said calmly. "You can do this. Let your anger—your grief—fuel the spell."

Relaxing my shoulders, I chanted the words. The soft syllables slid from my mouth with ease, the magic burning through my body, but my vision remained dark.

"She's blocking me." I gritted my teeth and balled my hands into fists. "I can try to remove it, but I'm uncertain it will work."

In my mind's eye, I envisioned Sofia's blocking spell as if it had a form—something encasing her away from me. From all of us.

Tilting my head from side to side, I let my magic course through me, filling every ounce of my body with power. I kept my focus on Sofia, encouraging her to let go, wherever she might be.

"I can feel her," I said. "She's resisting though."

"Keep trying." Felix stroked my back.

"I'm right here with you," I said aloud. "Sofia, it's me. I know you're hurting but let me help you."

For a moment, her resistance softened as if she was letting me in, but the beat passed quickly, and she raised her defences.

I rose, sending tufts of hay flying into the air. "She didn't want my help. I'm not staying here any longer. Sod the rain. Xurek, take my mother, we're leaving. The hex on the lake will have lifted by now. Makdou might be strong, but she can't pour her magic into *everything.* And even if she could, nothing is stopping me from laying my mother to rest."

Xurek scooped Mother into his arms.

The remaining journey back to Lake Delendil spanned two days. Xurek trailed us, clutching my mother's body wrapped in a worn blanket from the barn. I couldn't bear to see her lifeless, rigid form in his arms. Another person to part with at the lake.

On the second evening, twilight hung over Lake Delendil as we arrived. We gathered near the destroyed flowerbeds—the rubble still strewn through the water. Silence enveloped us.

Xurek settled Mother's body on a bed of straw

in a boat a few inches longer than her body. Servants lit torches and staked them in the ground, casting a golden glow across the ruined gardens. It was a small gathering—the Elementals had returned home after the defeat.

I plucked a handful of daisies from the garden behind the Citadel, then returned to Mother's resting place. Nestling the flowers around her, my eyes blurred with tears. My heart shattered again.

Felix embraced me as I trembled, lips quivering. Valneris stayed close to my side.

Xurek edged the boat into the water. It drifted through the lake, colliding with stones and rubble from the collapsed bridge. Kiirion lit an arrow with the torch, then handed it to me with my bow, which he'd fetched from the training ground.

I fired the arrow. When it collided with the boat, deep red and orange flames burst from the wood, its light harsh against the soft glow of sunset. The boat drifted into the centre and stopped above the connection to Elysium. The wood and my mother's bones would burn to ash and her soul would pass through. She would enter Elysium and join my son on the other side. I wished I could follow.

---

Half an hour later, I rolled a piece of boar around my plate with my fork. Candlelight illuminated the banquet hall. Felix scooted on to the chair beside me. A servant placed a goblet in front of him, filled it with wine, then topped up mine.

I gulped it down. "I couldn't save her." My eyes dried. Burned. "We've lost so many people. I cannot bear to burn any more dead."

"Makdou will pay for this," he said.

I slammed my fist on to the table. "I'm the Mage, right? I should have all the answers. I should know where Sofia is. Yet all I see is darkness."

He didn't say anything. No words could make it any less true. Instead, he rose and gathered me in his arms.

"I don't know where to go from here." I bunched the fabric of his shirt between my fingers. "Where does this road take us?"

"We have access to the one thing that can help defeat her—the Severance of Minds. If we can reach her, we can protect our minds from the Crimson Kiss. She will be rendered useless." He smoothed my hair. "Remember what we've said up to this point: together."

I took a moment to steady my ragged breathing, then let go of his shirt. "Stay with me tonight. I don't want to be alone."

"Always." His heart-warming smile eased the dull ache in my heart, and he led me upstairs. When we were sealed inside, he tended to the fire in the hearth. I sank onto one of the armchairs and brought my knees to my chest.

Felix grabbed a blanket from the foot of the bed, then draped it around me. "We *will* find Sofia."

I nodded, swallowing the lump in my throat, and we sat together in silence, watching the fire flickering in the hearth.

When the morning light broke through the glass

windows of my chamber, I knew what I needed to do. I stared at the ceiling and contemplated my decision. Sofia wouldn't like it. In fact, none of my friends would.

I needed to convince myself I'd made the right choice.

Sitting in bed, I flattened my hands on the cotton sheets and sucked in a deep breath. I'd already missed the morning meal, but I doubted anybody expected me to show myself the morning after sending my mother's soul to Elysium. Felix had already dressed and left, presumably to join Xurek in the barracks or assist the High Elves with court matters in my absence.

After dressing, I left the room. Quietly, I padded down the corridor towards the library. I clicked the door shut and locked it, leaving the key in the hole. What I was about to do required no distraction from servants or guards.

When I reached the first bookshelf, I rested my hands on the wooden surface. "There's only one way I can be sure to defeat Makdou. Blood Magic. You can do this, Evalyn."

I scanned each book spine. By the time I curled my fingers around a dusty leather-bound book, I'd convinced myself. My friends would never forgive me. The last time I used Blood Magic, it sent me to Elysium, and I wasn't sure I would be strong enough to withstand it another time.

I placed the book on the table and gripped the wooden surface. Sofia would've refused to let me do this alone. She'd find another way, so would Felix and my mother, but time was running out.

Blood Magic could be my undoing.

Hunched forward in my chair, I studied the book of detailed yet complex attack spells. Using these spells would strengthen our odds of defeating our enemies.

I heard Sofia's voice in my head. *"You don't have to do this. We'll think of something else. We're stronger when we put our minds and magic together."*

Yet my imagined words couldn't sway me. I remembered the fear in her eyes the first time I'd fallen into Elysium—after closing the portal at Southkeep. It hadn't been any smoother when we revealed the Great Mother Tree. What would Blood Magic do to me this time? It was unpredictable and dangerous.

The day raged on, and my patience thinned. I fidgeted in my chair, wanting to press forward and destroy my enemy.

A while later, someone heaved against the locked door.

I dashed across the room, buried the book in one of the shelves, then opened the door.

"Evalyn," Felix said, and his gaze softened as he approached me. "I hope you managed to sleep well or as well as can be expected in the circumstances. I thought you might like some company."

"I'm thinking," I brushed away his comment— if I acknowledged his sympathy, I would crumble, and I couldn't afford to, "I ought to perform the Severance of Minds again. The ethereal shimmer is dwindling, but I've not performed it alone. I'll need to prepare."

He eyed me with concern as I tapped my fingers against my side. I was on edge and maybe he could see it. "You are allowed to grieve for your mother, Evalyn."

"I've done enough grieving." I flipped my hand.

He furrowed his brows and fixed his gaze on the empty table. "Is there anything I can do to help? I know I have no magic, but maybe I can bring you something to eat or perhaps some water?"

"Sure…yes, I'd like that." I turned away, wanting to avoid suspicion.

I didn't want to betray him this way, but since he didn't know two spells apart, convincing him I'd be performing the Severance of Minds wouldn't be difficult. He wouldn't question it.

"Okay, well sit tight, and I'll be right back." He left the room.

When the sound of his footsteps dwindled, I relaxed, and my shoulders dropped.

Moments later, he returned with a tray in his hands. On top of it, was a plate with bread, meats and cheese, and a goblet of water. "Here, eat this."

He placed the tray on the table.

I sank into the chair and bit into the fresh, warm bread.

Sitting opposite me, he folded his arms.

"Stop frowning at me." I glanced at him. "I'm eating, aren't I?"

He held his hands in front of him. "Sorry. I'm worried about you, is all."

"I'm fine. Let's get this done." I pushed the plate aside, sipped a mouthful of water. Rising, I cleared my throat and rolled my neck.

"Can you do this alone?" he asked.

"We're about to find out." I focused on the spell. Every fibre of my being needed this to work—I couldn't let my mother's death, or anyone else's, be in vain.

I began the spell, chanting the words loud and clear. The ethereal cocoon of magic appeared, swirling high around me. It sheltered me before lifting and expanding.

It worked—a spell appeared like a shield, but a distraction to my friends. A mind trick, concealing any physical changes to my appearance caused by the use of Blood Magic. Such evil would destroy everything in my path, and it would be a perilous one.

His frown left his face, and he smiled. "Fantastic work, as always, my love."

"The shield will hold." My heart pounded.

"Let's find the others," he said. "We have lots to discuss."

---

The High Elves sat around the ruby encrusted table in the council room.

Xurek, with a feather light touch, shut the damaged doors behind him. "We ought to get these replaced."

Silence hung in the air. The Elves watched me as I slid into my seat.

"Don't give me that look. I'm fine." Although I said my words with confidence, the worry remained imprinted on their faces in the form of deep frowns.

Kiirion leaned across the table, stretched his hand out, then placed it on mine. "I'm sorry for your loss, truly."

"The loss of...my mother..." I cleared my throat, wincing at the sound of my words, "has only fuelled the fire. Makdou will pay with her life. Are there any suggestions on how to find her?"

"We could send guards to the different settlements," Valneris said.

"We don't have the time." Xurek clenched his large hands as he hunched forward and rested his elbows on the table. "We need to do something now."

The thought of Blood Magic played on my mind. It was the answer to all our problems. They would never accept it.

"She may have crossed the Badlands into Zhah. If she has the Orcs under the control of the Crimson Kiss, then there's no reason to expect she hasn't done the same to the other Dark Triads," I said. "Or, she may have sailed the Great Sea to Vrecrai."

"Vrecrai sounds like the most plausible suggestion," Valneris said. His face hardened with concentration. "The only known species to live there are the Krears aside from wildlife and the like. It would make sense for her to go somewhere barren where she can continue producing her portals and the Crimson Kiss undisturbed."

"We can always attempt another location spell." Theodas shrugged.

"The Elementals and the knights of the Eyrie have returned home," Eric said. He'd been silent up to this point, and I was curious to know what his thoughts were. "I'll rally the guards from Lake Delendil and prepare to march at your command once you have confirmation of where Makdou is."

"Thank you for your service once again, my friend." I nodded.

He offered a kind smile, which I returned.

"They should never have left," Xurek blurted, shunting his chair back from the table. He rose. "Their queen needs them. This is war, and they have marched back to protect their own lands. The war is here, and they should've stayed at their queen's side. At this rate, they'll have no homes to return to."

I admired his devotion, but what else did I detect in his voice? Frustration, anger. I understood why—he grew up in Zhah, surrounded by evil—he knew it better than any of us—and he turned his back on it.

When the High Elves and Eric filtered out of the room at my dismissal, Felix rose from his chair beside me and gathered me in his arms.

I relaxed against him. "We need to put an end to it." His chest muffled my words. "For good."

"What happened to your mother was awful, unspeakable." He stroked my hair. "But I've got you. We're together in this. I won't lose you again."

"You won't." I clung to him tightly, afraid to let go.

"I almost did before." He pressed his lips to my forehead.

"I'm here." I gripped his shirt between my fingers and relaxed my head against his chest. He was warm. Familiar. Safe.

I didn't tell him of my plans to use Blood Magic against Makdou. In killing my enemy, I would risk losing my own life. I couldn't burden him with my betrayal. Instead, I held him, desperately wanting the moment to last forever. For now, we were safe in each other's arms as if war couldn't touch us anymore.

# Chapter Twenty-Three

Later in the day, I attempted to find Makdou in Zhah, then the outer settlements of the Barren Territories. Despite my best efforts, the location spell came back blank.

Tapping my foot on the floorboards of the library, I fought to remain patient. I redirected the spell across the Great Sea to Vrecrai. If the spell didn't find her there, then we'd be back to square one. Even if it *did* work, I couldn't fully trust the vision.

The location charm directed me across open pastures and rolling hills. It guided me as far east as east goes, towards the coast. A small, buckling hut lay past a stand of trees. Its roof sagged and the wooden walls rotted. One window was built into the front of the building next to its wooden door.

The spell blurred for a second, then focused on the inside of the hut, transporting me through the walls. Two portals floated, ethereal but perfectly made.

Makdou was nowhere to be seen, but who else would've created those portals? Clanking metal echoed from the other room. I followed the sound through the doorway to see Sofia kneeling, hands bound with iron behind her back. Her icy white hair hung around her dirty face.

"Sofia!" As hard as I tried, no sound left my mouth. I couldn't communicate through the spell.

The magic disappeared, and I stood in the library.

"Makdou has Sofia captive somewhere in Vrecrai, past Aneirin's hideout." I shook my head, flustered. "I haven't seen this place before."

"Evalyn, are you sure you're okay?" Felix took my hand in his and squeezed.

"Most of my family are dead…it's overwhelming, and I can't stop. If I do, the grief will consume me, and I can't deal with it right now. I need to keep going." I looked away.

"I'll be by your side every step." He cupped my cheek and turned my head until my gaze locked with his. "You have my word."

"Come on, let's tell our friends." I tugged his hand, and we headed downstairs.

I met the Elves, Xurek, and Eric in the council room. Felix leaned against the wall next to the window.

Once everyone was aware of what I'd discovered, I rallied the guards in preparation for our travel to Vrecrai.

At midafternoon, we gathered outside the Citadel. The sun's heat beat down on the lake and the water glistened. A small blade I'd stuffed into my boot dug into my ankle. Guards gathered beside my friends.

Xurek wandered around the right side of the Citadel, through the destroyed gardens, with the horses in tow. "We can take our usual horses—the others aren't ready to be used yet. The guards will have to travel by foot."

"I am grateful you have all come to fight at my side once again." I looked at the faces shielded by silver helms. The guards' gold cloaks were removed, and their jewels stripped. There was no space for luxury at war. "I have great honour in calling you all the Queen's Guard. Let us bring home victory."

I held my shoulders back and stood tall and forced every ounce of confidence into my words. Felix placed his hand on my back and stroked lightly. With his other hand, he held on to his dented helmet from the Eyrie. He'd refused to swap it for a finer one from Lake Delendil. A piece of home stayed with him. With us.

The guards saluted, and Felix donned his helmet. Xurek commanded the guards to take the southern path around the lake to the Great Sea.

"He's found himself a favoured position." Felix nodded to Xurek.

"He makes for a perfect captain of the Queen's Guard." I rested my gaze on Xurek—his muscles flexed as he rested his hammer on his shoulder.

An icy wind whipped through the trees and rippled the water as I mounted my horse. We followed Xurek and the army away from Lake Delendil and towards the sea.

---

In the days passed since our departure, rain poured from the heavens. Large waves crashed and rocked the boats.

Night drowned the vessels in darkness, and everyone retired to their cabins except for Xurek and me. He held the wheel between his thick fingers and frowned at the churning sea ahead.

The sea crashed against the vessel, rocking it from side to side, and spraying water onto the deck.

"Whoa!" he hollered as he fought to gain control.

Heavy rain unleashed from the heavens. I shielded my eyes with my hands and squinted at the sky. A flash of light. The clouds twisted and turned until a face emerged. Sofia. Lighter clouds like soft paint strokes formed across the atmosphere—her silver, billowing hair. Sunlight burst through her eyes.

I stumbled, then crashed to the floor. "Xurek, look, quickly!"

"What? I'm a bit busy trying to keep this boat straight!" He yelled over the thunder ripping through the air.

"Sofia! I'm right here, oh, you clever girl. Send me another sign—I'll find you; I promise." I clambered to my feet and dashed along the slippery deck, keeping my gaze locked on her ethereal face.

"What did you say? I can't hear you over this damn storm," he shouted.

The vessel rattled in the churning sea.

Felix pounded from the cabin onto the deck, then straightened the sails.

I took this as an opportunity to disappear from their watchful gaze. Sofia had sent me a sign—a clue for her whereabouts. Who knew if she was safe?

I went for cover in one of the cabins and slammed the door shut. Rain pounded against the wooden shelter.

My ears rang as I clasped onto the table against the window beside the single bunk. A singular brass chamberstick stood in the centre of the table. If I wanted to perform Blood Magic, I needed to hurry. I locked the door then strode across the room. Waving my finger, a stream of magic lit the candle.

I rummaged in my boot for the small blade I'd hidden, then drew it across my palm and winced at the stinging sensation. Crimson blood pooled in the middle and trickled down the sides of my hand. I let my blood drip into the flickering flame and chanted the spell. A charm which would bind my blood to magic. Any spell I cast from then on would be fused with Blood Magic.

Sucking in a deep breath, I accepted I'd have no do-over. No turning back. My friends would soon realise my choices were for the greater good, despite my deception. I clung on to hope—my concealing spell would stop them from ever knowing the toll this evil would take on my body.

As the blood sizzled in the flame, a powerful energy surged through me. I sighed, my eyes rolled back, and I relished the strength it gave me.

---

We docked at the shores of Vrecrai two weeks later. Rain continued to hammer against the land, changing fields into bogs.

Lifting my sleeve, I stared at my scales, now glowing a vibrant red.

"What's wrong?" Xurek asked as he sauntered onto the dock.

"Nothing." I dropped the sleeve, then wandered along the path.

Producing a stream of red magic, I lit the torches along the trail.

"Wait a moment, I'm gathering the last of our food for the journey," Kiirion called from the deck.

A while later, he returned, along with Valneris and Theodas who guided the horses onto land.

The pounding rain made the journey long and harder to endure. My sodden cape weighed me down and my horse's mane clung to her. I stroked her side to soothe her, and she nickered in response. Most nights, we slept in any shelters we could find—barns, woods, abandoned huts.

Four days passed, and I grew restless. The island

seemed to stretch onwards for miles. My legs burned and my shoulders ached from uncomfortable sleep.

"This is getting ridiculous," Xurek moaned as he kicked a stone across the ground.

The rain hammered onto the land, and I trudged through sludgy mud and grass. Felix remained close to my side. His hand rested on the pommel of his sword.

"I think we're getting close." My body tingled. Why didn't I have this sensation when using the spell previously? Perhaps it was something to do with Sofia's spell.

We walked at the edge of an open field where the landscape tilted down into a shallow valley. An image of Southkeep flashed in my mind, and I flinched.

"Why do I get the impression we've underestimated what we're getting ourselves into?" Theodas looked over the valley—damp smoke shot up from pits, the rain drenching the flames.

In the distance, I spotted the forest of trees I'd seen in my vision. Green leaves seemingly too bright against a dull backdrop.

"Because this is a battleground." I waved to order everyone to drop to the ground. It may have been too late. Somebody may have spotted us. "What do you think happened here?"

Felix collapsed to the ground next to me, pointing at the corpses littered across the valley. "Whose bodies are those?"

"I don't know; it's hard to tell." I shook my head and buried my fingers in the dirt to stop them from

313

shaking.

"Krears," Kiirion said from behind me. He'd raised his head slightly to get a better look. "They're the only other Triad down here. Remember when their curse was lifted? They're in their natural state, although it is somewhat disfigured by fire and blood."

"They've been slaughtered." I gasped.

My ears rang, and my stomach knotted so tight I thought I might vomit.

"Who killed them?" Felix asked.

Although I'd seen portals in the location spell, there were no signs of dead beings from the other side. No Orcs on this side of the Great Sea. Just us and Makdou.

"Something's not right." I frowned. "The Crimson Kiss can't be strong enough for her to order all the Krears to kill each other."

"I don't know what she's doing, but she's not as strong as she thinks she is," Felix said. "My theory is this: she keeps moving because she knows we have the upper hand with the Severance of Minds, and her life is shortened. She's lured us to the place where *she* is stronger."

"We need to find out what is making her stronger." My fingers cut into the dirt. "It can't be my necklace alone."

"How will we know if the coast is clear?" Kiirion asked.

Valneris turned to face him over his shoulder. "We won't. Either we sit up here like idiots, or we make a move for it."

I climbed to my feet and bent forward to keep a

lowered position.

"Evalyn, wait," Felix whispered, then hurried to me. The others followed.

I ventured along the slope on the left side. Once on the flat ground, I stayed hidden in the trees. It was safer than running straight through the middle. The metallic stench of blood tingled my nose.

Over two years ago, we'd endured a battle in the deep gorges of Southkeep, but the Krears suffered this one for us. It seemed each time we found ourselves in battle, my friends and I faced the greatest odds. The only thing different this time was that we didn't know what we were up against. Makdou wouldn't have been able to do this on her own.

I stepped around and over the corpses and tried to keep my eyes on the tree line. If I looked at our fallen allies, I'd fall to my knees, and I wasn't sure I'd move again. I couldn't bear to see the lifeless faces we'd freed from the underground.

As I crept towards the trees, guilt twisted my gut. The Krears lived in their cursed goblin form underground to avoid the Dark Mages. As soon as they came above ground, they faced battle against a Dark Mage and whatever else she hid from us.

I lifted my chin, mustering all the courage and faith in myself as I could. I *would* survive whatever the Blood Magic would do to me. Felix crept behind me, with the others tailing behind.

"Keep your weapons ready." I glanced at my friends.

They drew their swords from their sheaths. Felix and Eric stayed close to me. The High Elves followed Xurek.

"Are you okay?" Felix asked. "Your face is as white as porcelain."

"I've no idea what we're getting into here." I slipped through the trees. "There are no portals, no Orcs."

"I'm sure we are about to find out." He clasped my hand. "Perhaps she is using this act of cruelty against the Krears as a threat. She wants us to think this will be us once she's done with us. More corpses on the floor to be burned."

"That's morbid." I tread over the twigs and brambles across the floor of the dense woods.

"It's true." He pressed his lips into a thin line.

We carried on through the forest until the hut came into view.

I raised my hand, and we held our position. "She'll know we are here."

# Chapter Twenty-Four

We remained as a unit as we slowly edged closer to the cabin. My ears rang. The tingling sensation coursed through my veins, and the red scales on my arms burned with evil magic.

I ignored the itchiness along my skin. Ahead of me stood a wooden hut, its door thick with moss, the hinged and ironwork knocker rusted. To the left was a small window covered in dust and cobwebs.

Felix took two steps ahead of me, twigs snapping underfoot. "Stay close."

I flexed my fingers, a stream of red magic swirling from my hand. "Get Sofia out of there."

Xurek brooded beside me, turning the hammer

around between his palms, ready to boulder towards the enemy within a second's notice. Eric and the High Elves pointed their Arogathean blades forward.

The door creaked open. Dust floated up from the ground. Makdou stepped onto the porch, the black hood of the sapphire-emblazoned robe covering half her face. She slowly raised her hands, drew back the hood, then sneered. Her eyes glowed a bright red.

Brutal images of my attack tortured my mind. Blood on the floorboards. My wails of pain and grief ringing against the high walls of the Citadel.

Magic burst from my hands in bright red tendrils. I fired it at her. She lunged out of the way. Her cape rippled behind as she sprinted across the mud. She fired icy sharp blades towards us. One zipped past me, skimming my cheek. Our formation shattered. Shards of ice punctured nearby trees.

I touched the wound on my face. Blood spilled onto my fingertips. "Free Sofia. Now!"

Makdou darted around the side of the hut, her white hair billowing behind her. I sprinted after her, pushing through the brambles scraping at my armor. Branches crunched underfoot. My lungs burned, and my muscles screamed.

"Evalyn!" Felix yelled after me.

Makdou's maniacal laughter filled the air. "You can't catch me."

I peered over my shoulder. Sofia joined the chase. Makdou launched a ball of red light, which flew past me, straight through the gaps between the trees.

"Oh my, Sofia, are you okay?" My words came out breathlessly.

"Stay focused! I'm okay, I promise," she said.

Makdou launched three balls of fire through the trees, but one collided with a trunk and set it ablaze. Flames danced beside us, and we continued our pursuit deeper into the woods.

She threw blades of magic over her shoulder. The shards impaled a nearby tree. It groaned, snapped in half, then plummeted to the ground, sending twigs and leaves into the air. Birds shot from the canopy of leaves, squawking as they fled the chaos. The tree combusted, and I skidded across the slippery mud.

"Get up." Felix yanked me to my feet, tugging me away from the spreading fire. Smoke filled my lungs, and I choked.

"We have to keep going." Sofia grabbed my hand. Her eyes widened, illuminated by the flames. "We can do this."

I nodded, although my heart threatened to leap from my chest. The pounding shot painful jolts against my ribcage.

I followed Sofia and Felix around the blazing trunk and towards the edge of the woods. Once we broke the tree line, Makdou stood at the edge of the cliff, overlooking the crashing waves of the eastern sea.

The High Elves, Xurek, and Eric held their weapons forward as they neared her. I lifted my hand, signaling them to stand back.

She raised her hands and chanted. A cocoon

formed around the Elves. Black claws sprouted from the magic, wrapping tightly around my friends. Vines weaved around their limbs and necks, causing them to choke.

"Let them go." I edged forward.

Xurek grabbed me and slammed me back into Felix's chest, who wrapped his arms tight around me.

"Don't be a fool," Xurek shouted—his eyes crazed, as wild as the other Orcs of Zhah.

"It's me she wants." I thrashed against Felix's arms.

"Stop fighting," he said. "I can't let her kill you."

"Do as Evalyn says," Xurek said to Makdou. "Or so help me, I will do more than crush your head with this hammer."

She bared her teeth at him. "By the time you cross the few feet to reach me, my vines will have suffocated them, and your efforts will be for nothing."

She stretched her arms, power pouring from her hands. It fed into the cocoon around the Elves and held them in suspension above the rocks.

"Let's make a trade," I shouted over the buzzing noise of the spell. "Me for them."

I bucked against Felix's grasp until I broke free.

"Evalyn," Sofia yelled. "Stop!"

"Maybe you should listen. Your friends speak wisely." Makdou grinned. "Perhaps not. You're all going to die at my feet."

"I know what you've done." I stared straight into her fiery red eyes. "You control the Orcs in this world and in Swynvale. You have them at your knees. You wanted to retaliate against them for using the Dark Mages. You know I will do *everything* to stop evil in the world. Orc or Mage."

"Do you really think you're stronger than me?" She sneered.

My rage for her bubbled into something all-consuming. I relished the buzz Blood Magic gave me—the need for dominion. I rolled my neck and licked my lips. Keeping my gaze locked on hers, I became a reflection of the person I hated. The power inside me strengthened into something I wouldn't be able to come back from.

I launched towards her—a red shield expanded instantly around me. Her eyes widened, and her concentration jolted for a second.

"Evalyn!" Sofia screamed. "What are you doing? Don't you dare!"

"What's happening?" Felix demanded.

"Why, shouldn't we let them in on your dirty little secret?" Makdou snapped her fingers. "Your darling queen is relishing in the ultimate high of Blood Magic. It's already taking its toll—"

I lunged at her and drove us over the cliff edge. The cocoon around the High Elves diminished and they fell to the floor. We plummeted hundreds of feet towards the icy water of unchartered seas. The wind rushed around us as we fell. My hands gripped her arms as we squirmed against each other. Her face blurred in the descent.

A few inches above the water, a portal swallowed us. We disappeared into darkness, and Arogath snapped away. The strange sensation of evaporating into nothing came in waves. We emerged, whole, on the other side.

My feet hit the ground. Stumbling, I scanned the area to get my bearings. Thousands of Orcs lined in formation across the flat ground. The steep, misty mountains in the background, where the Temple of Peace was situated... Swynvale.

"This isn't what you'd been expecting, right?" She nodded toward her army, all under the hypnosis of the Crimson Kiss. "You wanted the Blood Magic spell to take us somewhere of *your* choosing. It's about time you learned that *I* am the stronger Mage."

"You won't get away with this." I eyed the many rows of Orcs who stared back in a trance.

"I already have," she said. "The Severance of Minds may protect you from the Crimson Kiss, but I have other means of killing you."

"Why don't you do it then?" I looked her dead in the eyes. "Here I am. Alone. Isn't this what you wanted?"

"I wanted to show you what I am going to do to this world." She hissed like a serpent. "And to yours."

With a wave of her hand, an image appeared in front of us, hovering in the sky slightly above our heads. Meridian. Ablaze.

"That's impossible." I shook my head. "Their walls have never been breached."

Screams of innocent people rippled through the air. What of the Elders? Would the fire destroy the Great Mother Tree? I wondered how many died burning. How many survived.

Gasping, I covered my mouth.

"It is very real." She narrowed her eyes. "It's happening as we speak. My constant use of the Crimson Kiss has fused its power with my blood. It has become a part of me. Why do you think I was able to get the Krears to slaughter each other?"

Without delay, I conjured a ball of red light and threw it at her. It exploded in front of her, giving me a few seconds head start to dart across the field and into the forest below the mountains. If only I could reach the Temple of Peace.

A thunderous boom rippled through the air as she shot icy knives towards me. As I sprinted through the trees, I raised my hands, red vines stemming from my fingertips, and a shield of red mist encompassed me.

"Your shields won't save you," she yelled as she pursued me.

My body was on fire. My skin raged with the fusion of Blood Magic. Every inch of my body burned with its corrosion. A plague gnawed at my insides, destroying every ounce of good within me. I doubled over in agony, stumbling across the mud. I fought to keep moving. A purple feathered eagle squawked as it flew overhead.

Catching a quick glance over my shoulder, my vision of her blurred, mingling with the oak trunks. Her blast of magic skimmed my head and torched the trees.

My chest burned. I halted, clutching my abdomen. I wouldn't run any more. I wouldn't let her destroy any more land in this war. An eagle landed on Makdou's shoulder.

"Why don't you order your puppets to kill me?" I said. "You use the Crimson Kiss to get them to do your dirty work—why not now?"

"Perhaps," she said nonchalantly as her cape rippled in the breeze. "But not with you. At first, I thought I wanted to watch the life leave your eyes, but I can see the Blood Magic is doing my job for me."

She bared her teeth in a wild grin.

I grabbed a handful of my hair and pulled it over my shoulder to inspect. Its fiery colour turned an icy white. Soon, I'd be the double of her.

"Blood Magic isn't meant for Light Mages." She scowled. "Or for the *weak*. It will corrode your heart, your soul, until there is nothing left of you."

"You can't harm me." I glanced at the Severance of Minds ethereal shield around me, now glowing red with evil.

"The Crimson Kiss is done with you." She waved her hand. "You've seen what I can do. I can control thousands of Orcs in multiple realms. I'm unstoppable."

I wondered what would happen if I killed her then. Would the Crimson Kiss spell lift and the Orcs would return to normal? Or would it trigger them to kill me for murdering their leader? The Orcs never liked oppression or leadership from anyone other than themselves. I couldn't imagine them wanting me dead for killing her.

Facing Makdou at stalemate, I thought of the spell I'd memorised to kill her with. I remembered the inscription in the large book from the library. The price for her life meant the sacrifice of my

Light Magic.

A pang of guilt pulled at my heart. My friends would never forgive me. I wouldn't be able to be queen with a corroded soul. The Blood Magic would likely kill me before I got the chance.

I moved my hand diagonally in front of me. A black, ethereal javelin manifested in my hand. It burned my palm, sparks flew off the surface, and red waves of magic rippled through it.

Her eyes widened. She stood empty-handed.

"You murdered my son," I seethed. The words—the pain—flooded my body. The memory vivid as if I had relived it. "A life for a life."

Makdou grinned, raising her arms. "Kill me. The aftermath is far worse than anything I could do to you. Do it. Kill me!"

The javelin shot through the air and impaled her against the tree behind her. The Blood Magic erupted into swirls of black mass, expanding around her.

An unearthly scream escaped Makdou's mouth as the Blood Magic engulfed her. Her corpse blackened, then shrivelled.

The sharpest, jolting pain erupted from my heart, shooting me to the ground. I wailed in pain, bent over, clutching my body. The evil coursed through my body, rippling under the surface. My skin turned ice white and black fluid darkened my veins.

The piercing pain blurred my vision, the little I could see spiralled.

I collapsed against the spongy forest floor. The purple eagle hovered in the sky, then landed beside me to rest.

I awoke some several hours later, the eagle circling in the sky directly above. Darkness blanketed the forest, and my disoriented eyesight blurred the harsh outlines of the trees. The branches hazed into one.

Struggling to press weight onto my elbows, I tried to lift my heavy head as the pain transformed into an unbearable dull ache rippling through my entire body.

How was I going to conjure a portal back to Arogath if I was too weak to move? How long would it be before the Orcs, only a mile away, found me?

I looked at the disfigured arrangement of branches and leaves above me. Perhaps Elysium would take me one final time.

I fought to keep my eyes open, but my attempts were futile. There was no white light.

"Evalyn?" someone said.

The voice sounded distant. Moments later, hands shook my body, but I felt disconnected from them, far away from whoever found me amongst the foliage.

Smoke filled my nostrils. Even behind closed eyelids, I could not sense the flickering fiery light of handheld torches.

"Hey, it's me, Seth. What in the gods' names did you do to yourself?" He pulled me from the ground. My mind wandered elsewhere. "I'm going to carry you as you're too faint to walk. I'm going to take you somewhere safe."

I bobbed along as Seth carried me away. Other voices rang in the background, and I wasn't sure who they belonged to. And a female. Maybe Lilith. Why were they out there? Had they not spotted the Orcs in the distance?

"You there, take the body from the trunk," Seth ordered. "Bring her with us. She's finally dead, Evalyn. You did it."

The questions in my mind were near and far, but I couldn't formulate them into words. My tongue was limp and slack in my mouth. My head sagged over Seth's arm as he carried me. Where would they take me?

"Any idea why a peculiar looking eagle is flying low?" he asked. "One of Makdou's pets?"

In something dreamlike, I thought of Lake Delendil and the spot where souls passed through to Elysium.

I dropped in and out of consciousness, the endless layers of Elysium meeting me in my dreams. Lingering on the precipice of life, flashes of my mother and son's faces tormented me. They were so close, yet so far.

The fragrant aroma of burning wood stirred me. Someone dabbed my hairline with a cool, damp cloth.

I groaned as I came to—a fire flickered in the room, illuminating Lilith who held the compress against my forehead.

"Where…are we?" I managed.

"We're on our way back to Langhurst to make

sure my family are safe." Seth appeared at my side, blocking out the orange glow in the hearth.

His lips curled up into a gentle smile. He'd removed his armour, and several bandages were tied around his waist and biceps. Blood seeped through the cotton and stained it crimson.

I blinked several times, and after a few moments, my surroundings came into focus. "A…tavern?"

"Yes, we needed to stop to let you rest," he answered.

"What happened out there, Evalyn?" Lilith's voice trembled. "I changed you out of your armour…your veins."

My head throbbed. I clutched my temple with my hand, over the prominent pulsing in my skull.

"Blood…Magic." I rolled up the sleeves of my white cotton gown and followed the blackened veins with my fingers.

"This isn't normal." Lilith shook her head. "Makdou didn't look like this. Aside from the creepy white hair and red eyes."

"Signs of…transition…to Dark Mage." I cleared my throat. "I need to get out of here. We all do."

The image of the Orcs lined in formation reappeared in my mind's eye. Thousands of them. I remembered Meridian burning.

"You're too weak to leave." Seth patted my arm.

"The Orcs will now be free from the Crimson Kiss, which means they can go back to their holes and stay there." Lilith scowled.

"If you truly think they'll return to their holes," I lifted my gaze, "then you're a fool."

The following day, we left the tavern to return to Langhurst. Seth's parents darted along the cobbles, his mother dropping the basket of vegetables to the ground. Roots and tomatoes tumbled and rolled along the floor. They cocooned him with their arms and his mother cried.

"Thank the gods you're alive," she wailed.

The healers appeared at my side and took me to their hut. One of them began examining my blackened veins and colour-changing skin.

Another healer attended to the many bandaged wounds over Seth's body and applied fresh dressings.

"You'll probably feel concussed for a while." The healer poked and prodded at my icy skin, then took my chin between his fingers and turned my head side to side. "I advise you to come straight back here if you feel any worse than you do now."

"I can't stay here." I climbed off the bench, and my knees buckled.

"Stay here for the night." She caught my arm, then eased me back onto the bed. "Get some rest."

"I agree with her," Seth said. "Worry about getting back to Arogath tomorrow. You won't be able to open a portal by yourself. I have something for you."

He dug his hand into his pocket and drew out a necklace. The runes gleamed in the candlelight. "I found it on Makdou's corpse."

I grimaced. "She stole it from Lake Delendil to channel its ancient magic. It's the reason my son's dead. Get rid of it."

Raising his eyebrows, he glanced at the runes as

they slid along the leather cord. Keeping his gentle gaze on me, he placed the necklace on the bedside table. "I'll leave it right here…in case you change your mind."

As the words left his mouth, Sofia barged in through the door with Felix in tow. They rushed to my side. Felix's eyes widened. Sofia's lips contorted in disgust.

I dropped my gaze from them. I didn't want them to see me like this. I presumed my weakened state broke the spell I'd cast to stop them seeing my transition.

"Evalyn, what in the realm has happened to you?" He gripped me. I couldn't meet his gaze. Shame consumed me. "Look at me. Sofia got us here through a portal as quickly as she could."

I glanced at him, and I hoped he could see in my eyes how sorry I was. Yet no part of me regretted the choices I'd made.

"Why didn't you tell one of us what you planned to do?" His cheeks reddened. "We could have helped you find another way."

"There *was* no other way." I shook his hands off me. "It's done now."

"You put your life in danger." His outrage caught me off guard.

"My life was already in danger." The exhaustion had left my body feeling limp. I didn't have the energy to argue with him. "It was the means to an end."

"Did you stop to think about your own life?" He shoved his hair out of his face. Sofia watched, staying silent, which I took as her agreement. "You have no idea of the risks, the implications to your own wellbeing, your capability to rule."

"I did this for *our* son and *my* people." I coughed and clutched my throat. He knew more than anyone that I'd gone to the ends of my abilities to protect the realm from the Orcs and the Dark Mages.

"All right, all right, I think it's time you left Evalyn to rest." The healer stepped forward, raising her hand. Felix eyed her.

"I'm not leaving her," he said through gritted teeth.

The healer waved him over to a chair. "Fine, but she needs to sleep."

Felix slid onto his seat and propped his elbows on his knees, his gaze burning into me. I couldn't face the fear in his eyes, so I turned away.

---

When dawn broke the next day, I finally found my feet and left the healer's hut, Felix staying close and offering support if I needed it. Other than that, we didn't speak.

I grabbed my necklace—not that I needed it, but I couldn't ignore my attachment to it—shoved it deep into my pocket and avoided the mirror on the way out. I couldn't bear to look at myself. I didn't know when I would be ready to.

The purple eagle flew off the healers' roof and landed on a barrel placed against a stall. He fixed his beady eyes on me, then launched into the sky. I frowned.

After walking through the courtyard of Langhurst, I met my friends in the main banquet hall. Seth stood with Lilith, getting acquainted with Sofia.

As soon as I entered the room, Seth's gaze found me, and their conversation fell short. Nobody said a word. It didn't surprise me, and I couldn't blame them.

"The medics have given me the all-clear to go home and rest there." I couldn't look at Sofia, couldn't face her judgement.

"We were discussing the Orcs, Evalyn. We sent a party out last night to look, and they weren't anywhere to be seen," Seth said, filling the uncomfortable silence. "It looks like the Crimson Kiss has lost its control over them now that Makdou is dead."

A sigh of relief escaped my lips. "They've returned to their own settlements?"

"Yes, and the green magic is gone," he said. "We're free from Makdou's plague. May the Human-Orc wars continue…"

"Thank you for your hospitality once again, Seth," I managed a smile, "and thank you both for finding me. You've given me the medical attention I need for now."

"Evalyn," Felix interrupted our conversation. I caught his glance. Bags hung under his eyes.

My heart sank. He looked exhausted, having stayed beside my bed all night.

Whatever words he planned on saying never left his mouth. He wrapped me in his arms instead. He was stiff, but he held me close.

Sofia opened the portal.

"I hope Reuben, and the other soldiers make a quick recovery," I said to Seth.

"Me too." He smiled.

The ethereal shape of the portal stood in front of us, hovering a few inches above the ground. Would I ever return to Swynvale? I'd fulfilled my prophecy—I'd cleansed their world of poison. I'd got my revenge and paid the price for it.

We reformed outside the large Citadel entrance. I didn't know what to say to make it right. Neither did they. Would I rather this silence or their rage at my decision to handle Makdou alone?

Sofia stormed through the foyer, but Felix lingered close to my side in silence. I kept my head down.

A guard heaved in the council room door and the Elves hurried out.

Kiirion halted. "What the…"

"Are you all okay?" I scanned him and the other Elves in search of wounds from the spell used against them."

"Never mind us. What did you do?" Valneris grabbed my left arm, inspecting the blackened veins running under the silvered skin.

"She killed her," Sofia headed for the staircase, "and this is the price she has paid. She's transitioning into a Dark Mage, but it looks like her body is rejecting the Blood Magic. It's not reacting to her the same way it did to Makdou. It'll kill her."

She climbed the stairs and left us. My heart sank when she disappeared out of sight. Could I expect her to stay with someone who'd betrayed her? I'd done it alone. I hadn't asked for her help or advice. I'd made the call myself.

"Blood Magic?" Valneris recoiled. My arm dropped to my side. He stepped back. "How could you do this?"

"There was no other way," I whispered. Tears threatened to fall from my eyes.

"There's always another way," he yelled, and I winced. Valneris had never raised his voice at me before. The disappointment in his voice rang clear as day. "I'm not going to watch you die."

He returned to the council room, then slammed the door behind him.

I looked at Theodas and Kiirion, begging for them to stay. Kiirion shook his head.

"Please," I croaked. "I did what I had to do. I won't apologise for it. But I need you."

"We would've stuck by your side, Evalyn," he said in a small voice. "We always have, but you chose to risk your own life."

Kiirion followed Valneris into the council room.

"Give them time," Theodas said. "I understand what you did. I may not agree with it, but I understand."

He turned to leave, but I grasped his wrist. "I'm sorry she hurt you."

"We're fine. We sailed the boats back with Eric and Xurek as soon as you disappeared through the portal. I suppose the time difference comes in handy." He forced a smile, then joined the Elves.

"He's right." Felix clasped my hand. "They need time to process what you've done. The only reason why I'm still standing here is because I love you."

"She murdered my son, Felix." My eyes welled with tears, but I held them back. "*Our* son."

"I know." He enveloped me with his arms. "It breaks my heart every time I think about it. But she is gone now."

We stood in silence, holding each other. We listened only to the sounds of each other's breaths. I knew his love for me was unconditional. He may hate what I did, but he loved me with every fibre of his being.

"I'm sorry I didn't tell you." I wasn't ready to let him go. "I didn't know what else to do, Felix. I hope you can find a way to forgive me."

"There's nothing to forgive," he said, but I couldn't believe it to be true.

This wouldn't be something he'd forget. This Blood Magic would only weaken me, control me further. He'd watch me become a shell of my former self, controlled by its thirsty urge, until it ultimately killed me.

The only things keeping me together were Felix's arms around mine. His all-encompassing love—the forgiving kind—knew my mistakes, flaws, and chose to love me anyway.

"You should rest." He finally let go, then led me to my chamber.

Inside, he drew the curtains and lit the candles along the mantelpiece of the fireplace.

"I'll never get used to sleeping in here again." I stared at the stained floorboards, Makdou's ghost still lingering.

"You're more than welcome to stay in mine." He drew back the covers on the bed for me.

I shook my head. "No, this is my home, and I need to overcome it."

Felix helped me change from my clothes into a loose nightgown, the silk cool against my skin.

"I'll stay here with you tonight," he said. "I'm going to let Xurek and Eric know you're home, but I'll be right back. They've been out on a patrol."

"What patrol?" I glanced at him, halfway into the bed.

"To the Badlands," he shared. "They're making sure no Orcs pose a threat to us."

I nodded. "I expect Xurek and Eric will be wanting to speak to me. Tell them we'll converse in the morning."

He nodded. "Your handmaidens are just outside if you need them. I won't be long."

He left the room. Evening had fallen over Arogath, and the world seemed to slow with silence.

I sighed. The Orcs had returned to Zhah, and Makdou was dead. There was no threat we couldn't deal with.

As I sank onto the mattress, my silk nightgown shifted around me. I shuffled into a comfortable position and lifted my arms for a closer inspection—the blackness in my veins bubbled. I pretended, for a moment, the last couple of days hadn't happened.

# Chapter Twenty-Five

I jerked awake when Felix slipped into bed next to me. The slight orange hue of the candles illuminated his face as he placed his hand on my arm. His hazel eyes twinkled.

"Shh, it's just me," he soothed. "I'm sorry I scared you."

Jolting from his touch, I gasped. A layer of sweat formed on my hairline. I hadn't been this jumpy when Makdou was alive, why was I now?

I gripped his arm and dug my fingers into his flesh. He didn't grimace at the pressure. Laying on the bed, he pulled me onto his chest. I rested my head against him, waiting for his steady heartbeat to calm my nerves.

"What did they say?" I watched the candles flicker on the mantelpiece across the room. "Xurek and Eric?"

"They're devastated," he said, "but they're glad you made it home. I told them they can speak to you tomorrow. You won't be disturbed for the rest of the night."

"I don't know what I'm going to say to them." I traced circles along his sternum.

"Whatever happens to you," he moved to face me, then stroked the silver hair out of my face, "I will never leave your side."

His lips met mine. My mouth parted, and his tongue slid against mine. His love enveloped me. The rest of the world melted away, and we were alone beside the dancing flames.

The next morning, I eased into my seat at the council table, conscious of my shaking legs. A servant poured juice into my goblet. Silence festered between me and my friends.

Staring at the goblet's golden rim, I contemplated how I would begin.

Xurek barged through the door and took his seat.

"I think I'll be the one to start this little meeting," he said in a rough voice. His eyebrows were furrowed. "As much as the sound of Makdou's timely death is music to my ears, you cannot fathom my anger at the outcome."

I sat up straighter.

"What's done is done," Sofia said. I glanced at her with an arched eyebrow, surprised she came to my defence. "We need to turn our attention to how we can slow down the effects the Blood Magic will have on Evalyn."

The High Elves nodded in unison.

"The role will be delegated to you, Sofia, seeing as you have High Priestess abilities." Kiirion sat straight in his chair.

While his skin was grey from stress, his eyes twinkled. There was something profound about the end of a war—a heavy burden no longer shackled them.

Sofia didn't respond—she'd disliked my actions more than anyone.

"Now Makdou is gone, the Orcs can regain control in Zhah. While they won't forget we helped rid them of their enemy, they won't ask for a peace treaty," Valneris said.

"No." Sitting straight, I looked at Sofia.

She twisted her lips as she stared back. Grimacing, she shifted in her seat.

"They'll most likely want to regain control of the southern settlements. I wouldn't be surprised if the Eyrie is the first place to go, they've already got Orcs there." I eyed Eric.

He'd been sitting in silence with his arms across his chest, brooding. His gaze hadn't once lifted from the ruby encrusted table.

"Eric?" I touched his arm, but he jerked away.

"I won't be privy to this conversation." He rose. "I thought I could handle this, act like nothing happened. But I left my people, my home, for you, Evalyn. You are my queen, and I will do as you beckon. But you made the wrong choice. You are going to pay for Makdou's death with your own life, and I won't watch it happen."

"Please…" I croaked.

"Don't." He left the room, letting the door shut behind him.

"Give him time, Evalyn," Valneris said in his soothing tone. "He will understand. We all need our time to process what has happened and deal with it the best we can."

"He's right. I think *I* need some time." I left the council room and sought the peace of the garden.

The burning sensation returned. My blackened veins pulsed in my arms and my skin glowed a blinding silver. I recoiled, pulling my legs to my chest on the bench. I buried my head into them, rocking back and forth, longing for the pain to subside.

I rolled my head back, and my vision swayed. Searing pains shot up my spine. I jerked backwards against the bench and wailed.

*'It will corrode your heart, your soul, until there is nothing left of you.'* Makdou's words replayed in my mind. She'd meant it. Arching my back, I screamed and clutched onto the bench.

My heart pounded, unable to take the pain. My sight filled with black dots. With a tightening throat and an inability to see or steady myself, I collapsed.

A voice awakened me. "Evalyn, can you hear me?" a delicate voice asked. Someone shook me.

Through blurred vision, I glanced at Felix, but the sight of him swayed. He clutched my hand.

Sighing, he leaned in to kiss my head. "I'm glad you're okay."

"How did I get here?" I clutched my head as it throbbed.

"It wouldn't be wise for us to leave you alone. You're not well." He sat on the edge of the mattress and stroked my hand with his thumb.

"I need to get up." I groaned. "I can't stay here."

"Evalyn," Sofia said in a sterner voice. "This is worse than we thought. The healers gave you medicine to subside the effects for you to travel home, but nothing is working now—that's why you collapsed outside. The Blood Magic is literally eating away at your insides. I've used as many spells as I can think of to slow it down, like I did with Reuben, but I don't know what else we can do."

"Are you...okay?" I blinked heavily. "How did...Makdou get you?"

"I wanted to be alone after w-what happened." She cleared her throat. "Makdou intercepted the spell and brought me to her. I managed to conjure a spell to show you where I was."

"The clouds." I smiled weakly.

She flattened the blankets draped across me, then turned to the hearth and prodded it with an iron poker.

"Are you sure...this is what you...should be doing?" I blinked heavily. "You're grieving."

"I haven't the time for it." Continuing her distraction, she turned to tug the already drawn curtains. She smoothed the thick cream fabric with her hands and adjusted the ties. "I won't lose you too."

"Can't you take her to the Great Mother Tree?" Felix asked. "Or go alone and get some samples for her?"

"She's too weak to travel." Sofia shook her head. "But I'll enquire about samples. I'm not sure how many we'll need to keep the Blood Magic effects at bay."

"I c-can hear you," I sputtered, the words shaky in my mouth.

"I'm sorry, we'll have this conversation outside." Felix eyed Sofia to follow him outside.

"Any conversation you want…about me, can be said *in front* of me." I shot him a glare. "I am still…your queen."

"About that," Sofia clasped her hands in front of her. Her silk robes fell over them, concealing them within the sleeves. "Eric has decided to stay put in Lake Delendil while you are…ill. Your father has sent word from Vrecrai. He said he's going to visit."

"He runs away when there's any sign of danger and wants to return when something goes wrong, so he can act like a hero." Felix crossed his arms over his chest.

I patted his hand and smiled.

"He's not coming anywhere near Evalyn," he continued.

The afternoon sun streamed in through the window, casting shadows across the plains of his face and lighting the bridge of his nose.

"Felix." My voice was strained. "It's okay."

"We should let you rest." Sofia offered a bleak smile, then headed to the door.

"Wait." I turned to look at her. She lingered with her fingers wrapped around the handle and didn't face me.

"Please don't say it," she whispered.

"I'm sorry." I stretched my fingers towards her, longing to comfort her but the length of the room separated us. "I'm *so* sorry I couldn't save him."

She glanced over her shoulder. Her eyes brimmed with tears. "Xurek found a ring in Dmitri's possessions. It brings me comfort. We buried him in the fields nearby, underneath an oak tree."

Lifting her hand, she held it in the light, and caressed the metal band on her ring finger. She shook her head, then left.

I sighed. "There's nothing I can do or say to ease her pain. She's grieving and hating me for what I did."

"She doesn't hate you," Felix whispered as he stroked my cheek. "I think she's feeling guilty she couldn't do anything to help *you*. She's a Mage— just like you—and she couldn't do anything."

I hadn't given her the chance, more like.

My body ached, heavy against the mattress. I closed my eyes, longing for sleep. If the Blood Magic would be my undoing, then I would fade from this world holding the one I loved.

He lingered, eyes on me, soft and kind. He leaned in for a kiss and stroked my hair. Whatever we had, we shared an inexpressible past. A taste of war and passion. And I wanted more of it. More of him.

---

I stared at my reflection in the mirror of the bathing room. Silver skin, ice white hair. Black veins. I resembled next to nothing of my former self. My ribs and collarbones protruded, and dull circles formed under my eyes. The exhaustion from the Blood Magic was everlasting.

Sofia had created a portal, welcoming the staff back to the Citadel, while I remained close to my chambers. Over the last few days, I'd either spent my time in bed or bathing, my maidens always close by. There were moments like this when bursts of energy allowed me to have some privacy. I'd tried several times to conjure portals to Swynvale, but all had failed. Sofia reassured me she had it in hand.

I glanced away, scraped my hair into a bun on top of my head, then sank into the warm water of the bath. Letting out a deep sigh, I relaxed against the wall of the tub. Every now and again, the birds would sing from the trees—their tunes drifting through the ajar window.

Once I finished my soak, I climbed out, wrapped a robe around me, then fastened it at the waist.

Someone rapped the door. It creaked open, and Gwendolyn peered into the bathing room. "May I assist you, my queen?"

"Walk with me back to my chamber. My energy lasts only for a little while."

She nodded, tucked my hand in the crook of her elbow, and guided me to my room.

She drew the covers back, plumped the pillows, then turned to refill the hearth with kindling.

After climbing into bed, I yanked the duvet to

344

my chin as Sofia wandered in through the door.

"I've brought you some food." She held a circular tray with an assortment of breads and cheeses.

Next to it, sat a clay pot. I crinkled my nose. Another one of her concoctions of herbs and spices. She'd buried her head in research to keep her mind off Dmitri, and I couldn't blame her.

"Thank you." I smiled.

She placed the tray on my lap and took a seat in the chair beside my bed.

"I know you don't want to hear about it," she began. I avoided her eyes. She was right, I didn't. "But Felix is doing great at handling things for you, with the guidance of the High Elves."

Her words only made it seem real. I was dying, and the Elves prepared Felix for rule.

"I am not surprised," I said. "He should be our king, but he has requested a role in the Queen's Guard."

"Evalyn, I must warn you," she said quietly. "I have no idea if the samples from the Tree will be enough to heal you."

"I know." I gritted my teeth and clutched the tray until my knuckles whitened.

"I hate the fact you did this to yourself," she said, her voice soft and almost inaudible. "At first, I couldn't bear to look at you, but then it sank in. You're potentially on borrowed time, and we're still family."

"Just leave me be." I sipped my tea, the medicinal contents warming my throat as I swallowed.

She nodded, then headed to the door. With her hand on the handle, she turned to look at me once again. "I'll be heading back to Swynvale today, to request the samples. I'm not sure how much the Elders will agree to let me take, but some is better than none."

Two hours later, Felix appeared in the doorway of my chamber. Before I could tell him I didn't want to see anybody else, he'd crossed the room and pulled back the covers.

"Come on," he said. "We're going for a walk. You have been cooped up in here long enough."

"I went for a bath earlier." I rolled my eyes. "I'm fine *right* here."

I patted the plump blanket and made no effort to move.

"While you may order me to lead in your absence, you can't force me to turn a blind eye to your illness." He brushed my hair away from my face. "You don't want me to see you like this, but I haven't given up hope. None of us have."

"Sofia has already warned me that the Tree might not be enough." I glanced at the window, watching the dust particles float in the sunlight.

"Come on, I'll help you." He helped me out of bed, grabbed my cloak, then draped it around me.

I slid my feet into a pair of shoes and took his arm. "Then, you promise to let me sleep?"

Although I longed to stay in my chamber, I wanted to see the birds in the trees and the glistening lake.

He nodded, and while keeping hold of my arm, guided me down the staircase into the foyer.

The door to the council room was open, and the High Elves, Xurek, and Eric sat around the ruby-encrusted table.

"What are they talking about?" I somewhat envied them—as queen, it was my duty to make decisions on behalf of the realm, and I'd been detached from my duties.

"Restoration work for the bridge, you know...nothing big," he said. "When Sofia opened the portal for the staff to come through, Xurek and Eric went to help the people of Meridian rebuild where they can. They only went for a short time, so they didn't miss much here."

The guards hauled in the main door, and we went out into the sun. I shielded my eyes from the blinding light. Felix wrapped his arm tightly around me as we strolled through the gardens.

"Let's go to the bench." He led the way across the gravelled path to the bench among the rose bushes. Rubble no longer littered the lake, and fresh tulips budded in the beds.

I eased onto the bench and pressed my hands on my chest, finding it hard to catch my breath.

"Everybody is working very hard to keep the realm at peace. I thought you'd want to know," he said. "Guards patrol the perimeter of the Badlands frequently. The High Elves have been finalising plans to claim Sanctum City. We're finally at peace, Evalyn."

"You should send Eric home." I stared at my feet resting against the gravel.

"He won't leave until you're better." Felix kissed my cheek. His lips lingered, sending warmth through me.

He turned my chin with his finger until our gazes met. I wanted to look away, to hide my eyes plagued with Blood Magic, but he held me gently in place.

"I love you," he said, voice raspy. "I will keep doing everything I can to make sure you're okay and getting a moment or so of peace each day."

We stayed outside for a while as I relished the warmth of the afternoon sun.

As Felix escorted me back inside the Citadel, my friends gathered in the foyer. Kiirion drew me into an embrace.

"I *did* tell him to leave you be." Valneris sighed.

Kiirion let go of me and stepped aside. "I'm glad to see you moving about the Citadel, Evalyn." He smiled, his face softening. He'd tied his hair back, slick as usual.

Sofia strode down the corridor, halting in front of me. "I'm about to head to Meridian to speak with the Elders. Seeing as Xurek and Eric did what they could to help with their restorations, I can't see why they won't agree to me taking some samples. We also revealed the Tree to them in the first place. Without us, they'd be none the wiser. They owe us. And with the samples, I could create an elixir. We could give you several doses of the medicine to see if it works. If it can cure Reuben and the other soldiers, then it should cure you of Blood Magic too."

Despite the gleam of hope in her eyes, I couldn't bring myself to fully trust that the Tree would be enough. "I think…it's a lot to ask from a nation that are still rebuilding their entire home." I shook my head. "I'm going back to bed."

I tugged on Felix's arm who helped me up the stairs, through the corridor, and back to my chamber. "Although Sofia puts on this positive persona, I think it's a mask. I'm not sure she's convinced about the Tree."

He frowned as he shoved the door. He kept a hold of my arm until I was safely in bed. "I suspect she suggested it as a precaution." Lifting the covers up to my chin, he tucked me in.

A dull ache made its way up my limbs and into my eyes.

He strode across the room and unlatched the window to allow the sunlight to stream in through the crack. The crisp breeze circled in, caressing my cheek with its subtle chill.

"Fresh air will help." He tugged the already open curtains.

"Stop fretting. I'm fine. I've had fresh air all day. Sofia keeps me filled with her concoctions of teas. You should go train with Xurek and Eric—take your mind off me."

"I don't stand a chance against Xurek." He forced a laugh. "He holds more power in his left arm than we do in our whole bodies, but learning from him is invaluable. If we are to ever come face to face with the Orcs again, I want to be as prepared as I can."

"A good strategy." I leaned against the wooden headboard as my eyelids grew heavy.

"I promised you I wouldn't leave your side, and I don't want you to be alone." He crossed the room and planted a kiss on my brow.

I placed my hand on his chest where his heart would be, unable to find the words to comfort him. Kissing him deeply, I held his face to mine. "Let's hold out for these samples. Maybe they *will* help." I didn't know who I was trying to convince—it certainly wasn't me.

He groaned, but my body sagged against the bed, desperate for rest. Despite my suggestion for him to train with Xurek, Felix reclined into the armchair beside the bed and stayed by my side as I drifted to sleep.

The following day, Sofia barrelled into the room, clutching a tray with a mug and pot of steaming water beside it. She set it on the wooden counter, then withdrew a velvet pouch from her pocket. Glass clanked inside it, which I suspected was the samples, but from the size of the pouch, I was dubious to say the least. When Seth and Lilith took vials back to the soldiers, they had a whole basket filled with dozens upon dozens of vials.

I sat up in my bed and rubbed my eyes. "What time is it?"

"Late but don't worry, I wanted to let you know I've returned, and I've got the materials!" She beamed, thrusting the vials towards me.

"Are you sure this is going to work?" I eyed her as she poured the boiling water into the mug, followed by several drops of the medicine.

"I have faith, truly." She smiled sincerely, then handed me the drink. "I've never seen anything as wondrous as the Great Mother Tree. Doubting its magical abilities is like questioning the magic of

Lake Delendil. It's not done."

"How is everyone at Meridian?" I stirred the potion with a silver spoon. I wrinkled my nose at the sweet, yet earthy scent.

"As good as they can be. The fire destroyed a lot of the crops and market stalls, but they're managing. The Elders granted me access to the tree, providing Xurek and Eric continue to offer their support. They need as many hands as they can get."

"How many dosages will I need?" I sipped the drink.

Its peculiar flavour—something flowery and potent like lavender—coated my tongue and its taste reminded me of almonds.

"I'm honestly unsure." She sank into the chair and her eyes beamed with possibility. Hope.

"If you believe in this, then so will I." I gulped another mouthful. I needed to have faith.

A loud rap on the door caught my attention. I frowned—my friends would be eager to see the outcome of Sofia's handiwork.

They swarmed into the room as I held the mug to my lips.

Felix hurried in after them. "I tried to stop them, I swear."

Xurek came to my side. "Is it working, my queen?" He clasped one of the four posters of the bed in his large hand in anticipation.

I stifled a laugh—his tight grip may well snap the wood.

"It is too soon to tell," Sofia said, "but I have faith in the Great Mother Tree."

"All right, all right, enough of this. Leave her in

peace." Felix shooed them out of the room.

Kiirion lingered while the others left. "I have news for you, my queen. The Sylphs from the Highland Trees have been in touch. They, too, have conducted their own patrols. In small groups, they have flown over to Zhah and the other Barren Territories to infiltrate. There's been no sightings of planned uprisings."

"Well…that's great news." My voice came out several octaves too high.

How could I take away their happiness, knowing I'd been the one to bring them the most fear?

As Kiirion and Sofia left the room, Felix nestled on to the edge of the bed. A smile spread across his face. Was this false hope? Would I truly be healed?

"I know you may think me naïve for truly believing this." He took the mug from me as I finished its medicinal contents. He set it on the bedside table. "But we're finally at peace, Evalyn. Sure, it may not stay this way, we know what the Orcs are like, but we get to breathe. We finally get to…stop."

He clasped my hands and squeezed. We shared a deep-rooted love. The suffering, loss, and heartache. Out of war, we wove unbreakable ties. I couldn't imagine my life without him, yet my illness threatened to take me from him forever.

I focused on the gleam in his eyes and decided I would let him have his hope, for however long, or little, it may last.

# Epilogue

I traced my fingers along the skin of my wrists. My veins pulsed with blackness—the infection of Blood Magic that wasn't compatible with my body.

That, paired with the red eyes, I might as well be a living replica of my nemesis, Makdou. Even in her death, it seemed she'd found a way to haunt me. I'd anticipated happier feelings with the end of her torment, but the Blood Magic I'd used to finally free myself of her corroded my body from the inside out.

The samples Sofia has secured from the Great Mother Tree would only do so much. Keep the symptoms at bay, but it seemed, after several months of drinking the samples, the signs of my curse remained.

I scraped my hair into a bun and sank into the warm water of the bath. Letting out a deep sigh, I relaxed against the smooth slope and closed my eyes.

The room was silent. Every now and then, the faint songs of birds outside the Citadel drifted through the ajar window. And it would only be a matter of hours before a representative from each of the Fertile Territories' settlements arrived at the Citadel for a meeting to discuss trade routes and building a better regime in which the people of my realm would have a say in future policies that would affect their lives. Since I'd left them without a queen for two years, it was more important now than ever that I did the very best I could to provide them with a government they were proud of. Their voices had to be heard, and despite my ailments, I *would* hear them.

Once I'd finished bathing, Gwendolyn helped me dress into a golden gown and silk slippers, then pinned my hair away from my face. Thankfully, the gown's sleeves were long and hid most of the darkness pulsing beneath my skin, but there'd be no way to conceal the redness of my eyes or the unusual change of my hair colour from our visitors.

Downstairs, the maids darted about, polishing and cleaning, setting about vases of fresh cut flowers, and the scent of freshly baked bread and hearty stew wafted from the kitchens.

I met Felix in the council room. He was straightening an array of papers spread across the ruby-encrusted table. Then he flattened the lapels of his matching gold tunic and ran a hand through his hair.

Leaning against the door frame, I smiled at him. "You are nervous."

Jolting, he tore his gaze from the table, then casually took in the details of my gown. I ran my hands over the cinched waist, the intricate embroidery, and the jewels emblazoned along the fabric.

"You look beautiful," he said.

"You look quite handsome yourself." I closed the space between us and took his hands in mine. "Tell me, what has you worried?"

His jaw was set, and a deep frown creased his brows. "Today will be the first time I meet with the representatives of our settlements," he said, and his eyes searched mine, but I understood. I'd been in that position before. "The first time as the Crowned Prince."

I smirked. After days and days of asking, he finally accepted my offer to make him Crowned Prince. He'd refused at first, saying a position in the Queen's Guard would be suitable enough, but I wanted us to present a united front, and he'd still utilise his skills as a bodyguard. Instead of protecting just me, he'd be protecting the entire kingdom.

"You will be perfect." I squeezed his hand. "They have no reason to doubt you. Together, we will rebuild our kingdom *and* their trust in us. In me."

He pressed his lips to my forehead, and my skin tingled. Leaning into his touch, I closed my eyes, and for a moment, the ever-present concern of my health melted away.

"How are you feeling?" He lifted my chin up, so our gazes met once more.

"I'm doing fine. Truly. The samples obtained from the Great Mother Tree hold the side effects of Blood Magic at bay, but I go through bouts of energy. There are times where I feel weak, as if I might collapse, even." I cleared my throat when his eyes darkened. "But most of the time, I'm fine. There's no cause for concern yet. The samples will be enough until Sofia and I come up with a more permanent solution. We can't keep using portals to travel between realms—between timelines. We don't fully understand the consequences of time jumping, other than we *miss* time itself. I'm not sure if there are larger consequences that disrupt nature or fate." I grimaced. "And I don't think I want us to find out."

Felix nodded stiffly. "In the meantime, I will do what I can to support you—to support our kingdom."

"I know." I stood on my tiptoes and kissed him. "I'm grateful I have you by my side."

Someone knocked against the doorframe.

"Eric." I smiled, gesturing for him to come in. "What can I do for you?"

"Forgive me for interrupting, but our guests will be arriving any moment now," he said. "Shall I call for the High Elves?"

"Yes, please. Find Xurek and Sofia also." As he turned on his heel and left, I scanned the array of papers on the table. All signed documents from each settlement, electing a representative to attend quarterly meetings regarding policies and changes to the way the kingdom will be run. Together, piece by piece, we would rebuild. And this was just the start.

# Acknowledgements

Thank you to my family for their support throughout my writing journey—without you, I doubt I would have found this passion at such a young age.

Next up is my partner, Josh. Thank you for reading early drafts of the book and highlighting typos. He asked me questions, helped me build upon my ideas, and supported me through the publishing process and beyond.

I would love to thank Claire and Natalie from my Street Team for reading an early version of this manuscript, and for finding all those pesky typos. Thank you to Sophie Branford for your eye for detail, your thorough feedback, and your support. I really appreciated your help in making *Severance of Minds* what it is.

Charis, also from my Street Team, deserves a huge thank you for helping me perfect the cover design for *Severance of Minds*.

And finally, a huge thank you to everyone else in my Street Team, and the whole #bookish community on Instagram. Your support, loyalty, and kindness has kept me motivated and inspired. I'm thrilled to have found you all.

# Dear Reader

Thank you so much for sticking around for book 2 in *The Ancient Spells Trilogy!* I hope this part of Evalyn and Felix's story gave you some closure after the tumultuous cliffhanger I gave you in Crimson Kiss. *Severance of Minds* definitely explores some challenging themes—grief, acceptance, life after death, and healing. I hope I did them justice.

Evalyn's story has gone through *many* changes over the years, right from its first draft I penned about five years ago, to release. It's been such fun following her journey, and how she has changed and transformed in my mind—and on the page. I can't wait to see how her story is going to finish.

Jodie

I hope you enjoyed this as much as I did during the writing process. Please leave a review as a way to support me and ensure I can continue to bring readers books to love and enjoy.

Follow me on social media to stay up to date on my writing and #bookish content!

Instagram: @jodieangell_author
TikTok: @jodieangell_author
BookBub: @jodieangell_author

# By the Author

*The Ancient Spells Trilogy*
Crimson Kiss
Severance of Minds